TONGUE

RUTHLESS KINGS MC
BOOK EIGHT

K.L. SAVAGE

LIBRARY OF CONGRESS CONTROL: 2020922466

PHOTOGRAPHY BY WANDER AGUIAR PHOTOGRAPHY
COVER MODEL: JOHNNY JAMES
COVER DESIGN: WANDER AGUIAR
EDITING: MASQUE OF THE RED PEN
FORMATTING: CHAMPAGNE BOOK DESIGN
FIRST EDITION PRINT 2020

To Wander thanks for always being there and saving the day with Tongue's cover. Your Tongue is safe from our most Ruthless King.

And

For all the readers that have a shadow inside themselves that they don't know how to explain. It can be hard to deal with and how to comprehend the darkness. No one wants the void in their hearts. It's confusing, and sometimes maybe you'll wonder, "Maybe this is who I am."
And maybe it is.
Accept the differences that make you unique from everyone else. It's easier to be who you are than pretend to be someone else entirely.
Be a good person.
Fight for who you are.
And in no way are we saying to embrace the techniques Tongue uses in this book (No, no, please don't do that).
Accept yourself. Be with someone that accepts you.
And be happy.
Happiness is what we all want, even in our darkness, we crave light.

"The torture of a bad conscience is the hell on a living soul."
—John Calvin

PROLOGUE

Tongue

Twelve-years-old

I DON'T WANT TO TALK ABOUT IT.

I really dislike talking. It always seems to get me in trouble. I'm tired of being in trouble. When Jeremy says to go to the room for my punishment, it's always the same.

Close the door.

Undress.

Bend over.

But the number one, most important rule?

Don't. Make. A. Sound.

The worst part of it all is Jeremy always finds a way to make sure I'm in trouble. Jeremy isn't my dad, but he's all I have right now, and I don't know where else to go. My parents died when I was four, leaving me with Uncle Jeremy.

I don't think they would have if they knew what kind of person he is. They never touched me, and Jeremy touches me every chance he gets. It's usually after a night of working the corner. I might be twelve, but I'm not an idiot.

I mean, I *am* an idiot, but I know things.

Every night he snatches his wig off, digs into his bra, and pulls out a wad of dollar bills that are always crinkled and stained. He kicks his high heels off, puts his feet on the coffee table, and lights a cigarette.

I glance at the clock and tears brim my eyes when I see the time. The night is young before the routine starts. It's only six at night, which means he's going to make me come to his room and help him get dressed. I hate it when he makes me help him. At least he will be gone for a few hours. It's the only peace I get before he comes back and ruins the rest of my day and says I'm in trouble.

Run away.

My inner voice tells me to get out, go far away and never look back, but where would I go? I have a roof over my head here, food, and it sucks when he touches me, but he isn't all that bad sometimes. I can deal with him until I turn eighteen.

I don't want to deal with it.

It hurts.

No, I have to man up. I have to be a man. That's what Jeremy always says to me when I'm crying into the pillow.

"Wayne Hendrix! You get your ass out here and help Mama get dressed, damn it. You know what time it is." He pounds his fist against the bedroom door, and the silver knob jiggles from the force. No locked doors are allowed, but when my door is shut, he respects my privacy.

He must be in a good mood.

"Two minutes before you're in trouble!"

I gasp. "O-okay, I'll be ri-ri-right out, Uncle Jeremy," I raise my voice so he can hear me and put my journal down. I know it's a lame thing to do, but it's the only way I can get my thoughts down without getting... Well, I don't want to talk about it anymore.

It's in my journal. That's what matters. I don't write since I don't know how, but I draw. I draw all my thoughts and feelings onto the page, and it helps me deal.

I roll out of bed and stare at myself in the mirror, wincing when I reach down to pick my shirt up off the floor. My butt is killing me from the last time I was in trouble. I haven't been able to sit on it in three days.

Be appreciative you have a home.

It's something I say to myself every day. I have a bed, it's small, but it allows me to sleep. I don't have a dresser, but I have plastic bins with my clothes in them, which is better than on the floor. Other than that, the room is bare. The floors are carpet, stained, old, and torn in a few places. The walls have a yellow tint to them from cigarette smoke because sometimes Uncle Jeremy likes to kick back and relax after he punishes me.

Don't go out the door.

I have to.

Don't.

The hard threads of the carpet dig into the pads of my toes, pricking them like needles from the build-up of grime over the years. No amount of vacuuming can help at this point. This house is filthy for life.

Just like me.

Not by choice.

It is. I choose to stay.

The door groans as it swings open, and Uncle Jeremy is leaned against the wall. He has pink and blue rollers in his light brown hair, an extra-long cigarette hanging between his red-painted lips, and his pink silk robe is open and untied, showing the thick hair on his chest. The cigarette bobs in his mouth as he blows out the cloud of smoke. He hollows his cheeks as he takes another inhale, then grabs the orange butt between his fingers and drops his arm to his side.

A wild stampede thumps in my heart as he stares at me. I stay silent, like I usually do, and tilt my head down in submission. I peer up, staring through my lashes, and his brown eyes, so familiar to mine, narrow.

"What took you so damn long?" he asks as he readjusts the sparkling blue bra he is wearing over his flat pecs. His fake nails rake across his stomach and dip into his belly button, and that's when I notice the matching panties. His legs are covered in fishnet stockings, and his feet are bare, toes polished red to match his nails.

"Sorry, Uncle—"

He backhands me, and the flow of blood drips over my tongue, making its way to the back of my throat. Uncle Jeremy wraps a hand around my throat and slams me against the wall. My ears ring, and my skull explodes with sharp pain.

"What did I tell you? When I'm getting ready, you call me Justine. God, you're stupid. So, fucking dumb. Nothing can get through that head, can it? Is it just air in there?" He knocks his knuckles against my temple. "Hello? Is someone there besides a fucking idiot?" Uncle Jer—Justine places his cigarette in his mouth, sucks in, then blows the rotten fog in my face. "You remember what happened last time you called me by the wrong name, right?"

I nod, remembering very vividly. It took my tongue weeks to heal from the cigarette burns. The cigarettes would sizzle until the ember was out, and he'd light another and start the process all over again.

"Speak!" he yells.

"I'm ... I'm ... sorry, Justine. I'll ... I'll try hard ... hard ... er," I struggle to say.

"Well, try harder!" He slams a fist against the wall to the right side of my head, adding another dent. Applying pressure to his grip, he keeps his hand tight around my neck and slings me into his bedroom.

I gasp and lose my footing, hitting the edge of the bed. I bounce off and hit the new hardwood floors Jeremy had installed. He has all the upgrades. His bedroom is another world, another type of house. It's hard to believe something so fancy is in this home. There is a chandelier in the middle of the ceiling, a round bed that vibrates, a closet bigger than my room, and he has a walk-in master bathroom. Everything is marble.

And everything reeks of smoke.

"Now, sit on the bed. I have some new outfits I bought, and I want to wear one of them tonight."

I scurry onto the bed and grab one of the purple shag pillows. It's soft. It's comforting, and it gives me something to focus on and hold onto while I'm being forced to watch him change.

He shucks off his robe and tosses the silk onto the floor, then he struts into his closet. I turn my head when I notice he's wearing a thong. My stomach turns in discomfort. Sometimes he makes me wear that exact same one.

"Okay, so I bought this beautiful Chanel dress. It's black with a red neckline that dips down. I need an opinion. What do you think?" His voice is distant for a second, lost in the darkest depth of the closet before he steps out and holds the dress against his body. "So? Yes, no?"

I shake my head. "I... I don't like it. I don't th-think it does anything for your ... your ... fig-figure." Something I've learned Justine appreciates. Uncle Jer ... Justine doesn't talk about his body, but when he's in Justine mode, the figure is all that matters.

He holds the dress out in front of him and analyzes it, pursing his lips. If I'm wrong, I'm in trouble.

If I'm not...

I can go to bed without having to cry myself to sleep.

"You're right. I knew you were good for something." He tosses the dress down hatefully and spins around on his foot to disappear into the closet.

I rub my cheek against the pillow and sigh, wishing I had the comforting touch from someone. Not a hateful touch, not one that hurts, just one that is warm, like a mother's touch.

I miss my mom. I wonder what she was like. Was she pretty? Kind? Did she sing lullabies to get me to sleep? Did my dad try to teach me anything? Did he have a beard? I know it's silly to question, but I've always wondered. I don't have any pictures of them because Uncle Jeremy says I don't deserve to see them.

My eyes burn as I stare at the floral wallpaper.

"Hey! Eyes on me, you stupid bastard. What about this one? It's Gucci." Next in the expensive line of skimpy silk gowns is a purple dress. It seems too small for his body, but at the end of the night, he isn't looking for class and fine wine.

He's looking for cash, and the skimpier his clothes, the more money he makes.

"I think it lo-lo-looks ni-nice. I like th-that one. The purple looks goo-good against your ha-hair," I stutter like the complete fool Uncle Jeremy thinks I am. I only have trouble speaking because of the scars from the cigarette burns. My tongue hasn't been the same, and I don't think it ever will be.

"Look at the back," he says excitedly. He takes another hit off the cigarette, and a grin that reminds me of the Cheshire Cat stretches across his lips. "Sexy, right?"

It has ribbons down the back, crisscrossing so low it becomes inappropriate. I don't care about what he thinks is sexy. I just want to play outside or make friends. I want to go to school, but that's something I've never been allowed to do.

"I think it's a winner," I say, laying the pillow on the bed. I swing my legs over the edge and stand. "I'm … I'm … I'm … going to go get a snack if that's okay, Just-Justine." I hate stuttering, but after all the burns on my tongue, I'm not able to say things as quickly as I used to.

"No, it isn't okay. Did I say you could leave, Wayne? Have you learned nothing? You're such a disrespectful little shit. I hate that I got stuck with you."

His words are a kick in the gut, but I've heard them so many times, it almost doesn't cause pain.

Almost.

"I-I-I…"

"I-I-I…" he mocks me, pretending to stutter, and then he spits in my face. He reaches into my mouth with his fingers and pinches my tongue. "Can you ever string together a sentence? Are you dumb?" The growl that leaves his throat sounds like an animal about to attack.

He releases his grip on my tongue and flings me backward, and my tongue throbs as blood rushes through it. "No, Justine. I—"

"No? Are you disagreeing with me, Wayne?" He pushes the cigarette against my shoulder, and I scream when the ashes burn through the material of my shirt, sizzling my skin. "You know that you're always wrong. Don't forget the roof you live under, Wayne."

I hold a hand over my shoulder and whimper, doing my best to hold the tears in. I hate it here. Would I be better off dead? No one would miss me. No one knows of me. If I die, it's as simple as being put into the ground, but I doubt Uncle Jeremy would do that. He'd probably give my body to science so he wouldn't have to deal with me.

"Now, lay on the bed, pull down your pants, and bend over. Mama needs a warm-up before she goes to work."

Immediately, sweat breaks out over my nervous, heated skin. A bead of liquid salt drips down my neck, and I take a step back. "N-no. P-please."

"You mumbling, stumbling, stupid fucking retard. Do what you're told, goddamn it!" he shouts, slapping me across the face so hard my ears ring. "Lay on the bed, bend the fuck over, and spread your cheeks!" he roars so loud his voice cracks, his face turns red, and spit flies from his mouth, landing on my lips.

I can't handle doing that again. No more. Every time it happens, another piece of me dies. I can't. "I-I-I don't ... wa-wa-want to."

He grips me by the roots of my hair and yanks me to the front of his body. "You don't know how to listen, do you?" He stares at me, puffing his cigarette breath onto my face, and a curl of his lips promises something bad.

"Uncle... Un..." I catch myself before I call him Jeremy, but I didn't catch myself soon enough.

I want to die.

Why couldn't I have died in the car accident with my parents? Why did I have to live? Why, out of all the people, did I get stuck here?

I'm useless to society. I can barely talk. I haven't ever gone to school.

And I don't know how to read or write.

I try. I try so hard to read, but I can't figure it out. It's too late to learn for me. I'm going to be a dumbass forever just like Uncle Jeremy says.

Maybe I should just do what he wants.

He smacks me on the side of the head with his palm. "What? What? Cat cut your tongue?" He slaps me again, this time across my ear, and the burning flush takes over the left side of my face. He chuckles when I stand there, unmoving, waiting for what's next.

I don't know what to do.

I should've run when I had the chance.

"Sit. Down," he growls, reaching into his pink robe pocket to pull out the packet of cigarettes. He places them on top of the dresser, sliding one into his mouth and lighting the brown tobacco until it's glowing orange.

It's hotter than it looks; believe me, I know.

I do as he says and sit on the edge of the bed, folding my hands in my lap. I keep my head down, and my hair falls in my face. I'm breathing faster because I know what's about to happen. It isn't fair.

Or maybe it is. Maybe life is supposed to be like this and involve nothing but a series of challenges until it kills me.

I'm only twelve. I'm not supposed to know so much about the cruelty the world offers yet. That's what the neighbor said to her son when I overheard her talking about me. I wonder if it's true. Is life not like this for everyone?

"Get undressed."

I gasp, tilting my head up. Uncle Jeremy stares at me with so much hate that if it were possible, I'd die from the daggers he's shooting at me. "Ple-ple-please," I beg him as my emotions well up in my throat. "Please, don't ma-ma-make me do it. I'll do any … anything." Water fills my eyes, and I tremble all over as I stutter over my words. I hope in time the way I speak gets better.

I don't want to live the rest of my life sounding dumb. Being stupid is one thing, but sounding it? It lets people know, and I don't want anyone to know.

"I said—" He shapes his lips to a small O shape, and fog breezes from his mouth again. "Get undressed. Don't make me repeat myself, boy. I'm going to the restroom. When I come out, you better be ready, or I swear, Wayne, you won't be able to sit for a month." Justine sashays away from me, a word he taught me a few years ago. I remember him saying, *"You have to own your walk, your strut, or no one will respect you, and you better believe no one will give you a fucking dime."*

I don't want to learn how to strut.

I want to learn how to *run*.

With wet cheeks and unsure hands, I grip the hem of my shirt and pull it over my head, tossing it on the floor. There, in front of me, is a full-length mirror. It's wide, tall, and has a thick silver frame around it. I have cigarette burns all over my body, small craters pimpled all over my chest, shoulders, and back. The new one that burned through the shirt a few minutes ago turned my skin pink, swollen, and a bit bloody.

Holding back puke in my throat, I stand and drop my pants to the floor. I'm never allowed to wear underwear.

The boy in the mirror is someone meant to be forgotten.

I wasn't born to live. I wasn't born to make something out of myself. I was a mistake.

I was only born to die; I'm starting to realize that. I didn't die with my parents, so I can realize how I'm not meant to be a part of this world. I'm too weak for it. I'm nothing.

Justine.

Uncle Jeremy.

Whatever he wants to call himself, he's right.

I'm useless; well not yet, just until I'm used up enough *to be* useless.

I sit in the middle of the bed and pull my knees to my chest. I'm his living breathing ashtray, and every scar hurts when I remember this is the man who's supposed to be my family. The silk sheets rub against my bare bottom, and a drip of spit leaves my bottom lip, falling onto my thigh. It's then I realize how hard I'm crying because the silk sheets remind me of what is to come.

Peering around the room, it appears like a wealthy man lives in this house when we barely make rent every month because of his extra lifestyle. It's the kind of room that makes it appear like someone has their life together.

It's cruel how appearances can lead someone to trust, but I have the truth stamped all over my body.

"Get into position, Wayne," Justine orders, and the sound of his voice has me tilting my head up and wiping the water from my eyes to see him leaned against the wall. His robe is off, the rollers are out of his hair, and big curls tumble down his shoulder. The slight chub he has around his stomach hangs over the tight panties he wears. I can ignore all of that, but I can't ignore the cigarette in his mouth. I know what he's about to do, and I'm sick to my stomach.

What if I fight him? What chance do I have? I've never thought about it before because, for the longest time, I thought it didn't matter.

But what if it does? What if I can find a home better than this? Is it possible? Will someone want me? Am I worthy of something other than pain?

Justine's smile is anything but nice. He steps into the light, his large feet stuffed in pink high heels, and he stops at the end of the bed. "You really don't know how to listen, do you? Your parents, my sister, God rest her clueless soul, died probably to get away from you. Who would want a kid like you, Wayne? Hell…" He takes a long drag of the smoke, and the ashes tumble free when the cigarette can't support how heavy the burnt tobacco is. "You can't talk to save your life."

That's not my fault. No one has taken their time to teach me. My tongue is damaged because of him too. Everything has been against me. It gets too tiring when I'm the only person in my corner.

Swaying like snow as it falls, Justine wraps his long skinny fingers around my ankle to make me stay still. I try to get away, but he digs his nails into my skin, and I arch my back, crying out when the ashes land. The smell of burnt leg hair is quick, instant, and as quick as the scent is there, it's gone.

"You're that kid their mother should've aborted." He laughs, and smoke tendrils out of the spaces between his teeth. "I tried to tell her. I tried to tell her that your father had bad seed, but she didn't listen, and she had you anyway," he raises his voice as he lectures me and stabs my thigh with the cigarette.

I cry, shouting how much it hurts into the walls. I gag, and my stomach turns when the scent of burnt flesh fills the room. I don't bother begging for mercy because I know he won't give it to me. I bury my face into the pillow, but he grabs ahold of my hair and snaps my head to the right until the muscles are stretched to the point I'm afraid they're going to tear.

"Don't get your tears on my pillow. You'll ruin the silk," Justine seethes as his palm settles against my airway.

I cough and try to slap his hand away, but he's bigger, stronger, and filled with more fight. I struggle to speak, but the pressure is too much. I gasp, blood rushing to my face. The heat in the back of my eyes water, and a tear falls to my cheek.

Justine reaches toward the headboard and pulls one of his scarves from the post. I know what these scarves are used for. He likes to tie up his partners. It's one of the things they pay him to do, strutting around in leather as they lay helplessly, playing the victim.

I bet none of them have ever been victims.

Not like me.

"So weak," Justine mumbles, trying to tie the scarf around my left wrist to pin me to the bed. I pull against him, yanking my arm so he can't control me, but he growls, tightening his grip. "Stop fighting me!" He rears his arm back and punches me across the cheek. "Stop!"

"Un-uncle Jer … emy, please," I sob.

He tugs the ends of the material around my wrist so tight, pinpricks tingle the end of my fingers. "What did I tell you about calling me that? Huh? You're like talking to a fucking wall." He takes another scarf and ties it around my other wrist. His fingers trace my jaw, and I jerk out of his hand, but it doesn't do any good.

Hovering over my face, his cold fingers dig into my cheeks, forcing me to turn my head. "You might be an idiot, but you're a pretty idiot. I'll give my sister that much." He trails the pads of his fingers down the side of my neck, then down my chest, and around my nipple. "So pretty, Wayne," he purrs, closing his eyes as he maps the scars along my chest. "Shame. All these times that you didn't listen. Just like you aren't listening now." He pauses his touch and struts toward the dresser where the packet of cigarettes is half hanging off the corner. Justine pats the package against the palm of his hand and stares at me.

I'm shivering. My body is cold. I'm scared. Warm liquid drips down my legs, and that's when I realize I've peed myself.

"You goddamn incompetent boy! Look what you did! Fucking look! That's the second time you've ruined my mattress. Why are you so weak? Why can't you be normal?" Justine pours the cigarettes out, and all of them land on the bed next to me. He sighs in frustration, rubbing his tongue over his teeth, then fluffs his hair. A bead of sweat drips down the beak of his nose, and his red lipstick is smeared from how many times he has rubbed his lips together. His foundation is starting to crack within the wrinkles in his face, right along the edges of his mouth and forehead.

"You make me do this; you know that? You make me be this person," he says, grabbing a cigarette and lighting it. "You make me hurt you. Why? Why do you make me do it?"

"I..."

"Oh, I know. Poor Wayne. The wittle baby. So hopeless." He pats my cheek and digs the burning cigarette against my thigh.

I scream, something I'm not allowed to do, but I can't help it. It hurts so much.

He lights the cigarette again, even though the stem is wrinkled, and makes the tobacco glow again.

I'm still screaming, but it isn't for the pain in my thigh.

It's for everything. I hope someone can hear me. I can't do this anymore.

"God, you never shut up, do you?" he reaches into my mouth and pinches my tongue between his fingers, yanking it from my mouth. I shout the best I can through muted, panicked sounds. I kick my legs and bounce on the bed to try to get away, but he throws his leg over my naked waist and straddles me to stop my legs from kicking. "Always so stubborn, never wanting to listen. How many times does this need to happen before you understand?"

I nod, wanting to do anything and everything to make him stop and get off me. I'll be good. I swear. I'll be good. Tears fall from my eyes, and I can see him clearly now. The hate in his eyes has me laying completely still.

We lock eyes.

I'm too afraid to move, to breathe, to make a sound.

"I hate you," he says, emotion curling his lip. "You look just like her. That bitch of a sister always thought she was better, prettier. Look at me now! I'm fucking beautiful. Me! I make money off my looks, not her, and I'm going to make sure you never can. You hear me?" He doesn't give me time to react before pressing the cigarette against my tongue.

I arch my back and clutch my hands into fists. I can taste the smoke working its way down my throat. The ashes dissolve against the saliva pooling and mixing with blood. The pain is unbearable. He tosses the ruined cigarette aside and picks up another. I watch in horror as he lights it. It could be a still-image with how many times I've seen him light the same cigarette, with the same disinterest on his face, and evil promises in his eyes.

The orange glow sets his face in a sunset hue. I only know

of the sunset because he allows me outside once a week to get fresh air, always at night, so fewer people see that he has a kid.

I might be a kid, but I feel like I've lived a hundred lives, and I'm ready to be laid to rest. I lay there entranced by the delicate way the smoke string leaving the cigarette billows up toward the ceiling; it tunnels in an invisible chimney, searching for a way out. Justine's face disappears as he leans into the cloud, and another gut-wrenching burn crackles along my tongue, adding to the circular scars. Justine is smart.

He knows exactly where to put the scars so if we do come across someone, no one can see how ugly my body is.

"Hmm," he hums, tossing the butt onto the ground and grabbing another, lighting it. He presses it on the underside of my tongue instead.

I know I'm making some sort of noise, but between the spit and blood clogging my throat, and the sobs, I don't know if I'm screaming. I think I am.

Justine finally releases my tongue and rubs his hands down my bare body, kissing the middle of my chest. "I wish you'd just behave, little nephew. It would be better for the both of us." He reaches around and grabs my ass, and the touch is all I need to wake up. There's a single moment of the pain lifting. Through the blood dripping down my chin, the swollen tongue, and the burn marks all over, I realize what he's about to do.

He's about to turn me on my side, spread my cheeks, and ruin me in another way. He does that. He's always done that. Justine has done that for as long as I can remember.

Maybe it doesn't have to be this way.

Something inside of me wakes up, and I lift my foot and smash it between his legs. I'm not sure how effective it is since

I hit him from the back, but it has to hurt because he falls to his side, cupping himself in the front with one hand and in the back with the other.

Scooting my legs up until I'm in a better position, I sit up. The tip of my tongue is sticking out of my mouth since it's so swollen. Through tears, hate, and disappointment, I roar my agony and kick his face.

And I keep kicking.

All the years of being silent, being in the corner, in the darkness, and being forgotten slam against me. All the years of his abuse, the burns, the unwanted touch, the lessons in his fashion, everything has always been unwanted from him.

His cheekbones crunch, his nose breaks and snaps to the left, and he wheezes a ragged breath. Justine sputters and spits out a pool of blood with a few teeth I knocked free.

I stretch my neck up and push through the pain, then bite down on the end of the scarf. I yank back, untying one knot around my wrist, then wiggle my hand free. It doesn't take long before I'm untying my other wrist, and I'm free.

I'm … free.

What do I do? I never thought I'd be in this situation.

I push Uncle Jeremy onto his back and see what I've done.

Something inside me changes when he licks his lips and groans. At that moment, I'm numb. I scurry off the bed and open the bedside drawer where he keeps all of his toys, including a knife.

Some of his clients like to be cut.

He moans again, and I turn to see him rolling to his stomach. He's too weak to get up. The blade gleams against the light, twinkling like a star, hypnotizing me. My reflection is mirrored back at me. My face is swollen, wet, the tip of my tongue pushes between my lips. When I open my mouth, I see the black dots from the cigarettes.

Something cold settles in my chest. Something dark.

I grip him by the hair, then turn him on his back. I straddle *his* waist. I reach into *his* mouth. I pinch *his* tongue with my fingers.

I don't make a sound as I dig the knife down the smokey hole of his throat and cut. This time, it's his screams that fill the air. It's his cries that are telling me to stop.

Never.

The knife finishes cutting, and I hold up my prize. It's dripping with blood, thicker than what I thought it would be, and so satisfying.

Oddly satisfying.

Who's the one who can't make a noise now?

Next, I cut his throat without blinking and wonder for a brief second what kind of monster he's turned me into as he gurgles, drowning in his own blood.

I've only done what I needed to survive. I didn't want him touching me *there* again. I wipe my knife on the bed, then walk away. I'm in no hurry, but I need to get dressed. I know better than to dig through his dresser. All I'll find are women's clothes.

I expect to feel different. Lighter, happier, better, something other than nothing, but I don't.

In my bedroom, I dig through the plastic bins and pull out some shorts, slide them on, then right as I'm about to head toward the kitchen to get the phone, a loud pounding on the door stops me in the middle of the hallway. I lean against the wall and peek around the corner. Through the crack of the green curtains in the living room, there are red and blue lights.

That's impossible.

No cops are ever out this way.

I don't have time to answer the door because someone kicks it in. I cover myself, the courage gone, replaced by the boy who pissed himself in the bed.

"Houston Police Department!" a cop yells, followed by a stampede of footsteps. The steps come closer until I see a pair of boots in my line of sight. "Hey, I got a kid here!" the police officer shouts over his shoulder to his partners. He squats, and his knees pop. "You okay, kid? Does Jeremy Cooper live here? Can you tell us anything?"

Don't make a sound.

"I know you must be scared. You're safe now. Look at me. Let us help you."

"There's a dead body back here!" another voice booms from Uncle Jeremy's room.

I whimper, shake my head, and start to rock.

"Do you have something to do with that?" he asks. "Your uncle was involved in some pretty shady things, kid. You aren't in trouble here. I just need you to talk to me."

I can't.

I lift my head and meet his eyes.

"Holy shit," he hisses and clicks the button on his radio that's attached to his shoulder. "We need an ambulance to…"

I tune him out when I see an officer coming out of my room holding my journals. I run toward him and try to yank them from his hold, but the cop that called the ambulance holds me back. All I do is grunt and shake my head, pleading with them not to open the journals.

They hold all of my secrets.

"Did Jeremy Cooper do this to you?" the man opens my

19

journal to the middle and flips through page after page, show-ing images that I drew.

Pictures of what Jeremy did to me.

"Did he do this?" the same man asks, waving his hand over my body.

I nod.

"Jesus Christ, we knew the guy was fucked up, but we never knew he had a kid." He seems guilty, like he should have known better.

Maybe he should have. I don't know.

"You're safe now. We're going to get you to the hospital. We're going to find you a good home." The officer that called the ambulance stands in front of me, taking the place of the cop holding the journals. His name tag says Lionel. I reach for his arm and squeeze it tight, trying to tell him that I don't want to stay with strange people.

But I can't get the message across because I can't make a sound.

CHAPTER ONE

Daphne

Present day

THERE IS NOTHING LIKE THE SMELL OF OLD BOOKS. FLIPPING the worn, discolored pages sets my soul on fire. I love the ink embedded in the paper. Someone's mind came up with an idea, and letter by letter was written until the story was complete. It's fascinating.

We have a book by Emily Bronte, but it was published under Ellis Bell, and it's titled 'Wuthering Heights.' It's from 1847, the original publication date. It's a freaking classic. Everyone needs to read it.

I'm not allowed to touch the book. No one is. It's on display, safely guarded in a glass box, flipped to the title page.

It's unfair. It's like my boss enjoys tormenting me. Imagine a kid going through a toy store and their mom says, "Don't touch that. Keep your hands to yourself." It's like that, but much worse.

One page.

That's all I want. I only want to flip one page, and my life will be made.

And only the manager's key can open the gosh darn box. I'm *only* an Assistant Manager.

"Daphne, step away from the glass box," Andrew, my boss says from the front desk. He isn't even looking at me. He's indexing a new arrival of books.

"I'm not even near it." I stretch my leg behind me and take a big step back, nearly running into the bookshelf where all of the non-fiction reads are.

Blah. Non-fiction is my least favorite. Who in the world wants to read something real? Real life surrounds us every day. If I want to read a book, I want to get lost in magical romance, fantasies, paranormal, realms, shifters; whatever it is, I want to read it.

"Liar," Andrew teases, smirking.

Yeah, he knows how much I want to hold this copy of 'Wuthering Heights' in my hands, and he loves to watch me squirm for it.

"Can I just—"

"No."

"Just one time—"

"No." He chuckles at our conversation that happens at least twice every day.

One day I'll break him. One day.

Until then, I have to keep my hands to myself. I sigh dramatically and fall onto the black velvet chair nestled in the nook next to the window. I glance outside the window and place my chin in my hand, watching the empty street. It's early morning and no stores are open yet, including ours. Well, the exception is the coffee cart at the corner, but everyone needs to start their day off right.

Coffee is the nectar of life, and anyone who disagrees with me must only drink tea.

Yuck.

Tea is good when you need something warm to drink before going to bed.

But the thought of a hot caramel latte with whip cream and a dash of cinnamon has my taste buds coming to life. The watch on my wrist reads 7:30 in the morning. I have another half hour before the store opens, and I've done all the work needed before we unlock the door to start the day.

"Hey, Andrew? Do you want coffee? I'm going to run down to the coffee cart."

"Sure, I'll take it black."

Black? Who would want to miss out on the yummy number of flavors that creamers offer? I'll never understand.

As I push off from the couch, the soft material rubbing against my fingers causes me to sigh. I want to curl up on my own couch with a blanket and a spicy romance novel that reminds me that love is possible. Then, I want to fall asleep and dream of my one true love.

Yeah, like that will ever happen.

Maybe I read too many books…

Now, that's just crazy talk.

I skip down the aisle between mystery and suspense and head toward the back room to grab my purse and cardigan. Vegas might be hot, but when cooler weather starts to come around, the mornings are chilly. I slide my arms through the dark blue cardigan and wrap the strap of my purse over my shoulder, then peek inside where I see the cash folded up in one of the side pockets.

I haven't seen the man who tossed forty dollars at me in a few weeks. He overpaid for the book he grabbed by twelve dollars. He never came back for his change. He was interesting and handsome.

He had long hair, which isn't my type of thing on a man usually, but he made it work. He was mysterious, tall, broad, and wore a leather cut. I only know what they are because of all of the romance books I read. He was astonishingly quiet for a man who was so good-looking, and there was no reason why he couldn't have all the confidence in the world.

I have no way of figuring out how to get his change to him, but I don't have it in me to spend it. It isn't right.

"Okay, I'll be right back. Don't open the store without me!" I say, skipping down the aisle toward the door. I run my fingers over the spines of the books as I go.

"Like I'd want to!" he shouts after me.

I give him a parting smile and unlock the golden knob, then turn the handle. The door chimes when I push against the antique wood with my hip. I lock it behind me, so a customer doesn't come in before we're open and shiver when the cold air smacks me in the face.

"And this is why I live in the freaking desert because I can't stand the cold weather," I mumble to myself, tightening my cardigan around my waist before I brave the first step onto the sidewalk. I'd hate living in the snow. I hate being cold. It's why I always have a cardigan on or a blanket draped around my waist.

The loud rumble of motorcycles fills the air and that has

me stepping out onto the sidewalk. The bottoms of my feet tingle from the reverberations traveling through the ground. I hold my breath when I see three bikes pulling up next to the coffee cart I'm about to walk toward. They are wearing the same cuts as the man I met in the bookstore a few weeks ago. Maybe they would give him his change if I gave it to them?

Everyone at the coffee cart line starts to disperse, running away scared from the big bad bikers, but not me. I'm intrigued, and maybe they can lead me to the man who's been invading my thoughts lately more than books have.

Which never happens.

I'm pretty one-track minded. Books. Books. Books. That's me. I don't have boyfriends. I don't date. I don't go out. I don't party. I'm a homebody.

And I've been wishing he would walk through the door again. I want to hear his voice. It was different, unlike anything I've ever heard. I want to listen to him read me a book until I fall asleep. His voice was deep and raspy, like speaking isn't something he likes to do.

With a smile on my face, I scurry toward the coffee cart. I look both ways before crossing the street and run to the other side. There's a candy store called Paula's, and the old woman is cleaning the windows, keeping her eyes on the bikers at the coffee cart. So many people judge a book by its cover without trying to see what it's about.

I bet they aren't that bad. Everyone is so dramatic.

I pass a hardware store and wave to Jerry through the window. He gives me a toothless grin, then scowls when he realizes what he just did. He's grumpy, but I think he tries to be. On the inside, he's a teddy bear.

A wall of fresh coffee hits my nose, and I straighten my

back and perk up. I get in line behind the bikers, and now that I'm closer and see how big they are, my courage dissipates.

I swallow, suddenly wondering if the coffee was a good idea. Why am I so impulsive sometimes? I don't think. I push my glasses up the bridge of my nose and look at the massive back in front of me again.

Holy Moly.

I'm way out of my comfort zone here.

There's a skull wearing a crown with hollow eyes and smirking at me like it's about to eat me. 'Ruthless Kings MC Las Vegas' is written around the skull. The only thing I can think about is the 'Vegas' part. That means there is more than one.

Oh man, that means all the big bad bikers could come after me and kill me if I don't give this money back.

I'm screwed.

I jump when my cell phone rings and leather creaks. I feel eyes on me, and when I look up, the bikers are staring at me.

"You going to answer that, blue-eyes?" the one in the middle asks. He's good-looking, but he isn't like the other guy who came into the bookstore.

"Leave her alone, Slingshot." The one in front slaps the man named Slingshot in the chest. It's an interesting name, maybe a road name? Isn't that what bikers have? I need to re-read my books if I'm forgetting. It's their fault. I can't think straight with all of their eyes on me.

"What? She has blue eyes, and what if it's an important call? I'm trying to help, Prez."

"Yer being a pain in the ass. If she wants to ignore it, she can. Don't ye worry. I got ye back," a redheaded man wearing a kilt says, giving me a wink.

Oh, wow.

He really knows how to wink.

My cheeks heat, and I take that moment to look down and open my purse. Getting coffee wasn't a good idea. I had no idea they would all be so good looking. It really isn't fair for us women. We don't stand a chance when men like this are walking around, all tattooed and in leather.

My palm wraps around my phone, and honestly, I'm thankful I changed my ringtone from my favorite 90's song. How is that the only thing I can think about right now?

"Hello?" my voice cracks, and I lay my hand against my throat, clearing it. "Hello?" I try again, and Slingshot gives me a flirtatious grin.

"Hey, sweetie." Aunt Tina's voice is louder than usual, and that's when I realize I've put her on speaker by clicking the button with my cheek.

The guys chuckle, and I close my eyes in humiliation. "Hi, Aunt Tina. What's up?"

"I was wondering on your way home if you could stop by the grocery store? We need a few things."

I give the bikers my back and lower my voice. "Aunt Tina, now isn't the best time. I'm … I'm getting coffee."

"I miss you, blue-eyes! Come back to me!" Slingshot yells from behind. Great. Bikers are picking on me.

"What is that? Where are you?"

I turn around and narrow my eyes at the untamed biker in the middle. "I thought I was in the line to get coffee, but apparently, I'm at the zoo."

Slingshot's smile vanishes in an instant, and the other two men roar in laughter.

"Aye, she got ye, lad. Oh, she's funny. This trip for coffee was worth it." The redhead slaps his stomach and then his demeanor changes when he sees a bagel. "Oh, I need breakfast. I'll take three of those bagels, please, and vanilla bean Frappuccino," he gives his orders to Walter, the coffee cart guy.

"I'll call you back, Aunt Tina. Love you." I hang up the phone and slide it into my purse. "I actually have a question for you guys." I want to forget the annoyance of being called blue eyes and remember the man who gave me forty bucks. I step up and tuck my hair behind my ear. "Walter, I'll take my regular, and then plain black for Andrew."

"Andrew your boyfriend?" Slingshot asks.

"He's my boss. I work at the bookstore." I roll my eyes, then catch myself, hoping he didn't see me. What if they plan a hit on me and shoot me in my sleep?

"Wait—" The man who seems to be in charge crosses his arms, and my eyes fall to his chest. He has a patch that says Prez, which is what Slingshot called him. He must be the man in charge of the entire club.

He's the one who will give the order to kill me.

I sip my coffee and really enjoy it, letting the caramel melt over my tongue like it's the last time.

"You work at the bookstore? Right there on the corner?" he asks.

I nod. "Yeah, 'Page by Page.' It's right across the street." I point to it and then wonder if I should have shown them where I work. I need to stop being paranoid.

"That makes a lot of sense as to why he's been carrying that book around," he says, trying to rub a smile off his face, but it isn't working.

"Actually, that's what I wanted to talk to you about. I think one of your ... uh ... friends gave me too much money. He came into the bookstore, and he didn't say much, just tossed money at me and ran away. I want to give him his change." I dig through my purse, and my glasses slide down the tip of my nose. I take the cash between my fingers and hand it to them. Slingshot pushes my glasses up my nose, then taps the tip of it.

"You're too cute," he states.

"Puppies are cute," I mumble, waiting for the Prez to take the cash, but he stares at it instead.

"The man you're talking about. Is he about this tall—" The Prez holds his hand above his head a little bit. "Kind of creepy looking, silent, brown eyes."

I smile when the man's face flashes in my hand. "Yeah!"

Then I frown. "I wouldn't say he is creepy. I hope his package was okay. It leaked all over the floor. Red stuff. It stains too. I'm not sure what items he was trying to send, but I doubt it got there in one piece. I hope it wasn't pie."

"Pie?" Slingshot bursts out laughing. "Oh my god, she's so cute. She thought it was pie. I can't breathe. I can't ... oh God. My side hurts."

I pull the money away from them and scowl. I don't like to be laughed at. I know there are a lot of things I don't know about, but he doesn't have to be rude about it. "Well, I'm sorry for wasting your time. I didn't know that he was such a joke to you. Apparently, everything is." I probably shouldn't have said that, but I want to defend a man I don't even know. Sure, he looked rough around the edges, but his eyes told me a different story.

And I want to know it.

I spin on my heel and start to walk away when the man who calls himself Prez cuts me off, standing in front of me. "Woah now, hold on a second. We're sorry. We don't talk to people who have interactions with Tongue. He isn't exactly the social type of guy. You want me to give him the cash back, I will. I swear it."

"Yeah, that would be great. Tell him there are other books in the store. If he likes 'The Great Gatsby' that much, he should come back." I want to see him again. "Wait, his name is Tongue? Why?"

"I'll be sure to tell him that. Honestly? Ever since I've known him, that's what he wanted to be called. We all have road names. I'm Reaper."

"But do you know his name?" I prod.

"Cash and I'll make sure he gets your message." The way he says it tells me that this conversation is over.

But it isn't.

"I want his name."

Reaper's jaw ticks, and he steps forward, leaning his face a few inches from mine. "Let me tell you something, blue-eyes. We only go by our road names. Our given names are only shared with the people we truly care about. The people we love. If Tongue wants you to know his name, he'll tell you."

Holy moly. This man is intimidating and scary. I can't back down. "Do you even know it?" I ask.

An annoyed glint flashes in his eyes. "I know everything about my members, and I don't do well with people constantly questioning me."

I do my best not to tremble in fear and hand him the money I have in my hand.

He gently tugs the cash from my palm, and I have to break the intense eye contact. It isn't sexual; his eyes are full of rage, but something else too.

Concern.

"What's your name, blue-eyes?" he asks.

"Daphne," I whisper.

"That's a nice name. Look at me, Daphne."

I glance up and meet those hard eyes again, but the corners have softened. "You seem like a sweet girl. You have a good life, a good job, it looks like. You're cute. I mean this with the best intentions. You need to stay away from Tongue, okay?"

"Prez—" Slingshot starts to step forward, but Reaper holds his hand out to stop him. "Tongue is a good guy. He deserves—"

"Don't talk to me about him, Slingshot." Reaper points to him in a warning.

I try to move around Reaper to head back to the bookstore, but he stops me again. "Please, let me go." I keep my voice low. "I'm sorry I interrupted your morning, but I'm not looking for trouble."

"You are when you're asking about Tongue. Stay away from him; got it, Daphne?"

"I got it." I hate how submissive I sound, but Reaper scares me. I just want to go to work.

"Look at me."

I do as he says, tears in my eyes from the fear engulfing me, and he looks guilty. "I'm sorry for scaring you. I am. I only have your best interest, Daphne. If you really knew Tongue, you wouldn't ask about him. The fact that you piqued his interest worries me enough. Stay out of his way, and don't ask about him. You understand me? He is dangerous. We all are. We aren't knights, but when I need dirty work done, Tongue is my go-to guy. Remember that the next time you get all doe-eyed when you think about him or want to come up to us and ask about him, pretending you want to give his cash back."

"I did want to give his cash back. It isn't mine to keep. I'm not a thief." On that note, I successfully sidestep the badass

31

biker and successfully make my way toward the bookstore. All I can think about is this guy named Tongue and the warning Reaper gave me. Tongue didn't seem like he wanted to hurt me, but what do I know? I've never been with a guy before. I'm probably reading into this too much.

Even knowing the warning, all I can think about are the light brown eyes of Tongue staring at me. He didn't seem like he wanted to harm me; in fact, he almost seemed scared of me as I tried to talk to him.

He was flustered. He didn't know what to say to me. I'm sure Reaper is right about the kind of man Tongue is, but I'm interested. I can't lie and say I'm not.

When I get to the door of 'Page by Page,' I peer behind me to get one last look at the bikers, and they are still staring at me.

All three of them.

What have I gotten myself into?

I slide the skeleton key out of my cardigan pocket and unlock the door. A cool breeze ruffles my hair, but something has me giving my attention to the opposite direction. Nothing is there. It's just an empty road, but I feel ... something.

Holy moly. I'm a crazy person now. I'm paranoid. These damn bikers made me all jumpy.

I let out a deep breath once I walk through the door, then sag my back against it. I'm sweating. I need to take this cardigan off. I have ten minutes before the store opens, and I'm too flustered to focus.

Work.

Coffee.

Books.

"Right. You're okay." I blow out a raspberry, vibrating my lips as I try to relax.

"Hey, where's mine?" Andrew asks, and I can hear the pout in his voice.

"Sorry, I … uh … forgot. You know me."

"Yeah, and you don't forget. What happened?" He crosses his arms over his chest, and I turn around to get a look at the coffee cart again. The bikers are gone.

"I ran into a few people that made me nervous, that's all." I take a gulp of air and lean my forehead against the cold glass of the door.

"That's all? Where are they?" He moves to get around me, grabs my shoulders, and pushes me against the wall. He opens the door and runs outside, then stops on the sidewalk, looking left and right. I can't help creeping forward to peek around him and look for them too.

He's a good man. A bit older than me, but that doesn't matter. I wish I were attracted to him. He's smart, we enjoy the same things, and he is good looking, but he is too polished and perfect. Nothing is ever out of place, and I feel like I'm a constant wreck.

"No one is out here. Are you okay?" His hands fall to my shoulders again and squeezes. "Maybe you should go home. Get some rest. You look pale." Andrew brushes a piece of hair out of my eye, and a thud smacks against the door.

"What the fuck?" Andrew tilts his head and that's when I see a long knife, the metal gleaming against the sun.

"Oh my god! Are you okay?" I can't believe that just happened. That was so close to his face.

He pushes me away, and another knife lands in the door with another hard knock.

I scream as Andrew tackles me to the ground, pushing me inside the store. My head hits the floor causing my ears to ring, but other than that, I'm okay. Andrew cups my face and whispers harshly, "Stay back, Daphne. Stay away from the door. I'm going to go call 911." He kicks the door shut from where we're laying, and he pushes himself to his feet. He locks the door, then grabs a chair and pushes it under the knob. "No wonder you hurried back here. What if that would have hit you? Oh my God, you could have been killed, Daphne."

Yeah, but it wasn't my head the knife landed by.

I don't think I was the target. But do I know that for sure? No.

I creep toward the bay windows and sit on the bench and stare outside, trying to find the source of where the knives were coming from. The familiar feeling of someone watching me takes over again, and something moves across the street in the alley between the candy store and the laundry shop. The alley is dark. I can't see anything, but I look straight ahead.

I feel the moment we lock eyes because my breath gets taken away, and my heart stutters. I get to my knees, the cushions providing support against my legs, and lay my hands against the window.

Someone is there.

The shadow moves and when he steps forward, the light glistens off his dark hair, but I can't see his face.

"What are you doing?" Andrew yanks me from the window and drags me between the bookshelves until I'm behind the front desk, safe.

Is it odd that I felt safer locked in a stranger's eyes than I do right now?

CHAPTER TWO

Tongue

I'M GOING TO KILL HIM.

I don't like that guy being all over Daphne like that. I intentionally missed his head. I didn't want to scare Daphne, but I wanted to scare him.

She's *mine*.

I don't know how I can make her mine. I've never been interested in a woman before, so I don't know what goes into convincing a woman to date. No, not date. I don't want to date.

I want to be submerged, and I'm already obsessed.

And when I set my eyes on a target, I never change direction. I hunt until I get what I came for. The problem with Daphne is I'm not sure what I'm hunting for. I don't want to hurt her. I want… I want…

Damn it, I don't know how to put it into words. All I know is when I stare at my hands, then look across the street from the alley into the bookstore window, I don't want to hold a blade. I don't have the urge to kill when I look at her. I don't have the need to cut out tongues.

I think—no, I know—when I see my murderous hands, all I can see them doing is holding her now.

I ache for the solitude I know she can give me.

I'm not sure what to make of that. I love my blade. I love cutting out tongues. It's something I need to do in order to survive. No one knows my story. No one knows what I've been through, not even Reaper. I'm fucked in the head after what my uncle did to me. I'm as good as I'm going to get, and people either need to take me or leave me.

I want Daphne to take me.

No one knows what to do with me, so I'm ignored. I know I'm different and misunderstood, but part of me wants to come out of the dark. I live in the corners, in the shadows, and it's where I feel most comfortable and safe. But Daphne is all light, a bright sun rising on my nighttime soul.

She makes me crawl out of my hole because her light feels good. It's warm. I'm always so damn cold, and I've never met someone who thaws the frozen blood pumping through my veins in the matter of an instant. Part of me is brought back to life from the quick moment we shared those few weeks ago.

It scares me.

I've only been this type of man.

A killer. A fucked in the head murderer. A sadist.

I'm not the kind of man a woman like Daphne wants. She's supposed to be with men like the guy in the bookstore. All pretty and normal.

Yeah, but I don't want her to be.

So she *won't* be.

If I knew what is good for her, I'd let her go. Lucky me, I don't know the definition of 'good' too well.

I step into the darkness of the alley again, and my heart pounds from our eye contact. She knows I'm here. She felt me until that fucking guy pulled her away from the window.

I sneer, curling my lip when I think of his face and perfectly parted hair. Is that what she likes? Does she like short hair? I reach up and grab the ends of my straggly mane and grunt. It's just hair.

But would she like it?

I run my palm over my head, debating if I need to cut it for her. Maybe Sarah can cut it for me. She's my friend. She'll understand.

Sarah is great. She's Reaper's ol' lady. We've connected in ways I haven't ever connected with anyone before. I think it's because she's kind of like a mother hen to me. She cares about me, and I soak it up because I've never been cared for. It's nice to feel love.

I flatten my hand on the brick wall, letting the rough stone rub against my callouses. Feels good. I need to leave before the cops get here, but I can't seem to move. I need to watch her to make she's okay.

Police sirens whirl in the distance and quickly come closer. Red and blue lights reflect in the window of the bookstore, bringing back a memory I wish would stay gone forever. The night I killed my uncle. I don't regret it. If I had to turn back time, the only thing I would change is killing him sooner.

Two cop cars park right in front of the store. A big guy steps out of one, and he has a huge round stomach and a turkey neck. My fingers itch to cut all the extra fat off and send it to my swamp kitties, but I think it will be frowned upon if I killed a cop. Reaper can only be tolerant about so much, and becoming a cop killer is stretching it.

Maybe.

Maybe no one needs to know about it.

It's something to keep in mind.

The other cop is in shape with tattoos down his arms. His uniform is a bit too tight, and he puffs out his chest when he sees Daphne through the window.

I growl under my breath. I want her eyes only on me.

The guy who works at the bookstore opens the door and steps outside to talk to the cops. My eyes land on Daphne, who stands in the doorway, and her shoulder leans against the wall. Her cardigan is pulled tight around her, emphasizing the small swells of her tits. I wish I were her sweater, right up against her skin, cloaking her.

I bet she's so soft and smells so good. I want to get close enough where I can find out. Something tells me she smells as warm as she makes me feel.

Her eyes search in the alleyway again, and they fall on me. I know she can't see me, but she can feel me. Daphne takes a step outside, and the muscular cop stands in front of her, blocking my view of the only object in the universe that's found a way to ground me.

Sneering, I almost launch myself across the street and slit all their throats and throw her over my shoulder to take her away. I dig my nails into the brick to stop myself, and my breathing becomes harsh and ragged. Sweat beads across my brows and rage fills my veins. I knew I shouldn't have used both of the knives that I had on me to throw against the door.

Damn it.

I wait for him to move out of my way, but he doesn't. I

can't leave because I parked my bike in the alley, and if I speed out of here, I'll look guilty, even though I am. So I have to wait and watch as he gets closer and closer to her.

I slide down the wall and sit on the filthy ground, tangling my hands in my hair. I start to rock. The urge to kill is humming through my body. I'm coming unhinged. I need to see Daphne. She soothes the killer beneath my skin.

Turning my head, I see her again as she steps to the side, away from him, and I hold back the beast I know she wouldn't love. I want to kill those cops. I want to kill the man who touched her. I want her to only be mine.

Her eyes search the darkness for me again, and when those big blues land on me, I let out a huge breath, sagging against the brick wall.

I can breathe again.

I'm obsessed with her.

It's dangerous.

I know what it means when I'm obsessed with someone, and usually they end up dead.

Not this time.

I want to possess her. I want her to be dependent on me. I can protect her. I know that is something I will be able to do. Anyone who dares come close to her, I'll slice out their tongues.

If she accepts that part of me.

Part.

Who am I kidding? Cutting is who I am.

My cock starts to come to life when I notice her push her glasses up the bridge of her nose. Fuck, she's pretty. I rub the growing erection in my jeans and groan. I don't ever get hard unless I'm spilling blood.

Sexually, I haven't gotten hard. I've never been interested in sex after what my uncle did, but Daphne makes me interested.

Very interested.

And that scares me. I'm not a man to be scared of anything, but having sex with a woman is something I don't know how to do.

Need someone tortured? I'm the guy to do it.

Need someone's tongue cut out? Fucking pick me. I love that shit.

Love?

I don't know how to do that, but after meeting Daphne, I know I want to learn how.

If I can even be taught. I might be a lost cause, a hopeless case, a stupid person for the rest of my life. I'm incapable.

I'm trained to shed blood.

I was born to inflict hate.

That's who I am.

I am hate.

But I don't hate her, and that's a new feeling for me to process.

The tattooed cop hands Daphne a small business card, and I'll bet anything it has his number on it. I watch her narrow face for any sort of reaction, but she seems disinterested, sliding it into her cardigan pocket.

Good girl.

The cops get into their car, turn off their blue lights, and drive down the road.

Fucking finally.

Now I can kill the man in the bookstore. There's one thing I always carry, just in case I don't have my knives on me.

I pull out my nine-millimeter and aim directly at his head. My finger rubs against the trigger. His hands drop to his hips, and he says something out of the side of his mouth to Daphne, which has me lowering the gun and hesitating to shoot.

I do not hesitate.

I lift the gun again, but I can't seem to make myself pull the trigger. Daphne might be upset if I kill her friend.

She can always make new friends, right?

Trying again, I hold the weapon between my hands and lay my finger on the trigger. Come on, why can't I do it? This isn't like me. I need to get this guy out of my way. He wants Daphne. Daphne will want him. He is better than me. Everyone is. If that means I need to take out everyone, then that is what it means. I will kill everyone on this goddamn planet making us the last two people on earth if I have to.

Damn, that actually sounds kind of nice.

It's a long list. It will take me a while, but it can be done. My swamp kitties will be nice and well-fed too. The idea is something to consider. It's on my list.

She nods at him after he speaks to her. I wish I could read lips. Hell, I wish I could read, but I can't, so I'm stuck wondering what the hell he's saying to her. Is he admitting his love? That thought has my finger twitching on the trigger. I need to be smart about this. I could stage his death.

He could die in a horrible car accident, and then I can finally have Daphne all to myself.

It sounds selfish because it is.

I want to be selfish when it comes to Daphne.

The fucking walking dead man gives her a hug, but she doesn't seem to reciprocate it in the same enthusiasm. She turns her head toward me and lays her cheek on his chest, arms to her side, and her eyes are staring down this dark alley again.

All I can hear is my breathing. My heartbeat. It's deafening, and after spending a few hours in a box in the ground because of some killer on the loose, my heartbeat sounds pretty fucking good right about now.

Shit.

That reminds me, I'm supposed to be at the clubhouse helping the club clean up Skirt's old house so they can break ground on a new property.

I can't leave Daphne just yet.

He finally releases her, and she vanishes inside the bookstore, then comes outside a second later when she has her purse. It's a nice green color. I can see why she likes it. It can go with all the clothes she wears and still look fashionable and bright. She gives him a wave and walks down the street.

By herself.

Fuck no.

She's not ever going anywhere by herself ever again.

I wait for the shitbag who works with her to disappear. I watch as he locks up the shop, then trots over to his fucking Prius. What a pussy.

What man drives a car like that?

No man does, which means he's a bitch. Daphne doesn't need a man like that. She needs someone who is strong, a protector, someone who isn't worried about needing to charge his car before they go out on a date.

I should have brought my silencer. This mess could have been dealt with already and one less Prius loving, plant-fucking guy would be off the map. Damn it.

He rolls down the windows and—oh dear, all the blades in the world—is that a saxophone? He's listening to jazz! I'm too baffled to shoot him as his car hums like a honeybee before driving down the road in the opposite direction.

Inching out from the alleyway, the sun is high in the sky, and the cool morning is now a thing of the past. I run across the street and then throw the hood I have attached to my cut over my head, staying close to the quaint brick buildings. They look old, like they have been here awhile.

Keeping my head down, I count the cracks in the sidewalk, smiling when I remember when Sarah taught me how to count over ten. Sometimes, I count for the hell of it just because I know how. People don't know how good they have it. Life is easy for others because counting, writing, and reading is something people learn so early, and they really can't remember when it started to flow so easily that it has been embedded in their minds.

Sarah says she's going to teach me how to read soon, right after I perfect writing my name. I'm close. My handwriting is sloppy, but it's better than not writing at all. A man my age, I should know how to do all those things, I know that. I know I'm not smart, not like the rest of my friends. I guess I have my own strengths, but I haven't figured them out yet. My insecurities are too strong.

I'm cruel when I need to be, but that's all I am, and discovering Daphne makes me want to figure out if there is more of me. There has to be, right? I can't be an empty vessel, and if it's all I am, then I guess I'll be living a life away from Daphne. I'll have to settle for watching her from a distance for the rest of my life.

I won't be happy about it, but I'm starting to think happiness is something learned, and if my history has proven anything to me, it's I'm incapable of being taught.

Passing freshly black-painted parking meters, I round the corner of a local barbershop. Hey, maybe they can cut my hair if that's what Daphne is into. I'll become whoever she needs me to be, but will she do the same for me?

I tilt my head up and turn my body at the last second to miss running into a guy around my age smoking a joint. "Hey, fucking watching it, guy," he dares to snap at me.

Right as I'm about to place my gun against his temple and blow his brains out, I catch Daphne up ahead, turning around, and I dip into the alley to hide.

"Fucking freak," the guy sniffles, scratching his nose with his fingers. His hollow orbs don't give me another glance, but he has no idea how close I am to shooting him in the chest for disrespecting and challenging me like he did. And he had done it in front of Daphne?

This fucker just made my kill list.

I count to thirty and peek around the edge of the alley and see the fashionable green purse bouncing on her hip as she walks down the sidewalk. Pushing off the wall, I slide my hands in my pockets and follow.

I'm far enough away where I'm not suspicious. I stare at her back, watching her hips sway, and she's wearing those leggings again. I like them. They hug her ass just right, and all I want to do is watch my fingers sink into the flesh, then my teeth, and then—

"Ow." I rub my forehead and scowl at the fucking pole I just ran into. "You have no idea who you're messing with." I point my finger at it just as an old lady dressed in a purple dress walks by, her chihuahua prancing in a matching sweater. She gasps, placing her laced-gloved hand against her chest and giving me a wide berth. "No, not you, ma'am. The pole." I chuckle, rubbing the spot on my head.

She hurries away, her little yapper of a dog barking at me. I sneer at the tiny rat, and he whimpers, prancing away on his paws.

Stupid fucking dog. Stupid fucking pole.

Damn it, Daphne!

Panic has me running down the sidewalk when I don't see her. She's gone. All I see are trees lining the sidewalk. The roads are clean, unlike the Vegas strip, and there is a blue mailbox on the corner without posters of naked women taped to it. Something out of the corner of my eye has me turning in the other direction.

There she is.

Daphne is climbing the concrete steps to a duplex across the street. I dodge behind a red car when she tenses. Her brown hair blows as the desert wind kicks up a bit of sand, and the grains hiss against the buildings. A circle of sand swirls along the road before laying still as the breeze comes to a halt.

She feels me.

Oh, I feel you too, Daphne.

I watch her through the windows of the car I'm using as a shield, and she disappears inside, closing the door behind her. I'm nowhere near done following her. I can't rest until I know she's safe in her bed.

And maybe a little after too. I want to watch her for a little bit. I know how it sounds, but I want to watch her breathe. Knowing someone so beautiful exists is a rarity. She's like seeing a comet for the first time or a double rainbow, and I have to stare for as long as possible because seeing something so extraordinary only comes around once in a lifetime.

Taking a quick breath, I run across the street and climb up the steps of her duplex. I jiggle the knob in hopes, by some chance, it is unlocked, but it isn't. That's fine. I triple check my surroundings to make sure no one can see me and give the door a shove with my shoulder.

Oopsie.

There's a staircase to my right that leads to the other half of the duplex. It's nice. This place looks like somewhere Daphne would live. It's clean, pretty, and I bet there is a story behind the building. The light flickers above me, casting a yellow glow along the scratched hardwood floors. There are black and white photos along the floral wallpaper of a married couple with a soccer team of kids.

I'm not sure how I feel about kids. I never thought about having one.

I'm not interested in pictures. I'm interested in my comet, my once-upon-a-lifetime, my Daphne. The gold-plated mailbox slots shine beside the staircase.

Her name is written above one slot on a white sticker in black ink. The writing is flawless, pretty, and serene. It's cursive. I remember Sarah showing me the two different types of writing. Print and cursive.

At least, I think it is her name. Since her name is Daphne, I know her name starts with a D and the name below hers does not. "Number two," I say when I see the number at the end of her signature.

Something I've yet to perfect.

My hand lands on the wooden rail, and it's cold to the touch. Daphne has touched this rail. My eyes roll to the back of my head at that thought. I creep up the stairs, and the heavy weight of my body has the stairs creaking. I freeze, hoping she doesn't hear me.

TONGUE

I know what I'm doing isn't right, but I don't want to hurt her. I promise.

I'll be a ghost in the darkness, and she won't even know I'm there. My phone vibrates in my pocket, and I know it's Reaper calling me wondering where the hell I'm at. All the guys always text me, but since I can't read, I ignore them. They think I don't care, but they don't know how long I've glared at those messages and tried to sound them out with my stupid voice and broken tongue.

I reach the top of the stairs and find the door with a two on it. I step forward and blow out a breath. I put my hand on the knob and quiet the rush of thoughts jarring in my mind. Is this right or wrong? It's a chance to open her door. She could be right there, and she could see me, but am I willing to blow my cover for one last look of her? With a shaky hand, I twist the knob, and fire brews in my body when it's unlocked.

Anyone could come inside and not just me. Someone who intends to hurt her. Oh no, that needs to be changed. I'll have to install automatic locks when she isn't around and a security system. I have to make sure my comet is safe.

As quietly as I can, I open the beautiful cherry red door and see I'm in an empty living room. There's an oversized green couch near the windows, and books are everywhere.

I mean everywhere.

They are in piles on the floor, the coffee table, on top of the TV, the arms of the couch, windowsill, and I bet every other surface she can find. The walls are painted a light blue, and there is a red rug on the floor, almost covering the entire space of the living room. I can't see all of it since there are books stacked in rows on top of it.

My little bookworm.

Maybe she can read to me sometime.

My brows shoot to my hairline when I see the kitchen. Well, what used to be a kitchen. The countertops are littered with books and takeout containers, and the table is lost under more books.

I smirk. She's cuter by the second. I'll make her a big bookshelf. I bet she'll like that. I'll give her a damn library if she wants.

The hiss of the shower has me turning my head in the direction it's coming from, and I hold my breath. She's naked, wet, and alone.

I'm here, yes, but I don't count. I'll lurk in the shadows to keep my eye on her. Being this close, in her presence without her knowing, it sends a thrill of excitement through me, something akin to slicing tongues. I move quickly; she'll never know I'm here. Lurking. Watching from the shadows.

Shadows can't be seen in other shadows, and that's where I plan to stay when it comes to my comet.

CHAPTER THREE

Daphne

I WAKE UP WITH A GASP, MY SKIN PRICKLING WITH AWARENESS. MY BODY is hot, my nipples are hard, and the space between my legs is throbbing. I'm not afraid. I'm not sure if what I'm feeling is real or if my brain is still sleep-induced and imaging brown eyes staring at me.

My body is on fire from a ghost of a man I don't know. I swear, I feel his intensity surrounding me. I feel watched, but I know that's impossible. I haven't seen him in weeks, but I could never forget him.

Running my hand down my chest, my body buzzes with the thought of him watching me. I can feel him here. I must be out of my mind, but it's okay. It's only me here, but I wished I weren't alone. I wish he were here. I don't understand my reaction to him, but I'm allowed to want someone I'm not allowed to have. It's natural to dream about a guy that is handsome, dangerous, and forbidden.

Yeah, I'll keep telling myself that.

I moan when I think about the tattoos surrounding his neck, disappearing down his shirt, and traveling down his arms. I'd like to get a better look at them, up close and personal, just once. One time I want to experience what it's like to be with a man like Tongue.

Tongue.

What kind of name is that?

I want to know why it exists. Is he good with his mouth? Is that it?

"Oh!" I arch into my hand, circling the bundle of nerves at the thought of his lips between my legs. I bury my hands into his long, shaggy hair, pulling him harder against me for more friction against the scruff on his face. His eyes slide up my body, and the intensity glaring from them match the grip of his fingers along my flesh.

A growl from the corner has my fingers pausing their rapid movements. I sit up, elbows against the bed, my breathing ragged. I search the room, but I can't see much since it's dark. I reach toward the nightstand and pat around until I find my glasses. I slide them on, and now the darkness is clear instead of blurry.

"Is someone there?" I ask the shadows like a crazy person. I probably just heard a noise from outside, a dog at the dumpster in the alley.

All it will take is for me to turn on the lamp, but I stop myself from pulling the switch. The promise the darkness holds is better than the truth that waits in the light. Maybe I'm imagining him there in the corner, and it's only adding to the fantasy; seeing the space empty will only disappoint me.

What the hell is wrong with me? If someone is in my

house, I need to snap the hell out of it. I try to summon an inch of panic, but the hairs on the back of my neck aren't standing up in alarm. I feel safe.

And as long as I have that comfort, I'm not going to ruin the only fantasy I've ever had. My hand falls to the top of the nightstand, then rubs down the lip of the top, migrating toward the silver knob. I slowly open the drawer and grab my vibrator, swallowing spit to try to coat the dryness scratching my throat.

Am I really going to do this?

I must've had too many glasses of wine before I went to bed.

"If you're there, you don't have to say anything or do anything. If you're not, I guess I'm not losing out, but I hope you are," I say, hoping I don't sound ridiculous if I'm speaking to a wall. "I can feel you," I whisper, spreading my legs wide. "Or I'm losing my mind, but I swear I can." My room always has an empty feeling to it, but right now, there is this energy I can't explain. It's intense and completely overpowers my body.

I don't feel the urge to run; I only feel the urge to give in.

The devil is knocking on my door, and my sin is turning the knob to allow him in.

I lay back, the memory foam pillow cupping my head gently. I wonder if Tongue has a gentle touch. His appearance is rugged, tough, but I bet there is a side that appreciates a careful caress.

The straps of my nightgown fall down my shoulders, almost exposing my breasts, and I swear I hear an inhale from the corner.

Or it's me since I'm breathing so hard.

With a free hand, I wiggle free of the gown, pushing it down to my waist, freeing my body. I hope he likes what he sees. The cold air circulating from the fan causes my nipples to bead. I imagine it's his hands, his calloused fingers brushing over them, and it tugs a moan from the middle of my throat.

"Oh god," I gasp, bringing his mysterious face in the front of my mind, remembering every defined line when I met him. Strong jaws, high cheekbones, eyes the color of honey mixed in cinnamon, and there's this uncertainty I saw when I stared at him. He has an innocence about him I can't put my finger on.

I'm not saying he isn't the kind of man I need to stay away from; I know he is.

But I don't think I can help it.

My thumb presses the button on the vibrator in my hand, and I rub it over my tight nipples, gasping from the sensations. I've always been sensitive. I can bring myself to climax just by tugging on them. I need more than that tonight. I need to see if this relieves the pressure in my head, and maybe the need for Mr. Mysterious will fade.

I turn my head to the right and stare into the corner, hoping to see an outline of him, but it's only darkness with the hint of the moon peeking between the curtains. I bite my lip as I glide the silicone shaft down my body and insert it between legs. "Yes," I hiss, letting my eyes roll to the back of my head.

Another grunt coming from the corner has me rocking my hips back and forth, needing more friction. I want the vibrator deeper, filling me, stretching me, but it isn't big enough. I can't stop moaning. I'm drowning out any sounds that are coming from the corner, if there are any, and I turn up the vibration level.

"Oh god!" I cry out, spreading my arm to grip the edge of the bed. My thighs tremble, and there is a molten hot swirl in my lower belly. "I'm going to come," I announce to the fantasy and snatch the pillow from the left side of me and smash it against my face to mutter my sounds.

Liquid drips down my thighs as I orgasm, shaking uncontrollably. I think of Tongue, the stranger in my dreams, the haunting I hope is in the shadows, and my muscles spasm again.

The vibrations become too much against my sensitive pussy, so I reach between my legs and turn it off. I throw the pillow off my face and a flash of his face hovers over me in my drunken, orgasmic state. I freeze, staring into the eyes that have been embedded into the marrow of my bones in such a short amount of time.

He's beautiful.

I gasp, holding my breath as I hurry to turn on the light to see if it's really him. I stretch and pull the string of the lamp. With a click, the bulb flashes on, and I smile to myself when I realize I'm finally going to get to see him.

Forgetting that he's in my house watching me without being allowed in. Semantics. We can work those issues out later.

"I've been thinking about you so much—" But when I turn around to talk to him, he's gone. "Lately," I finish my thought. I slide my arms through the string of the nightgown and tug the hem to my knees, then frantically straighten my hair and tuck it behind my ears. "Hello?" I call out to my dark apartment, but all I hear is the echo of my voice.

There is no way I imagined all of that, is there? I throw my legs over the edge of the bed, forgetting the vibrator between my legs. It falls on the floor, leaving me empty and feeling a bit awkward when it thuds loudly, shining wet against the hardwood.

"Thank God I live alone so no one can witness this," I mumble, grabbing a tissue from the purple container and then pick up the vibrator off the floor and carry it to the bathroom. I'll clean it later. I swear, he was here. I'm not losing my damn mind.

I take the robe from the hook on the back of the door and wrap it around my shoulders, gliding my arms through the holes before securing it around my waist. "Are you still here?" I call out, staring at the faint glow of the streetlights from the windows in the living room. I step around the stacks of books and flip the lights on, but I'm alone. There isn't anyone here.

And I have no idea why that upsets me so much.

Maybe I am losing it.

With a sigh, I make my way toward the kitchen to make myself a cup of tea when I notice something off about the room. I study every stack of books, trying to figure out what looks different, but I can't put my finger on it.

The takeout containers are gone.

I rush to the corner of the table and rub the empty spot with my bare hand. "There was a book here," I say to myself, knowing that I'm not losing it because I was creating a new stack. My apartment isn't big enough for all the books I have, so I have to use all the space. I tap the secondhand wood with fingers and grin. "There was a book here." I squeal. "I knew I wasn't crazy. He was here! He was here. The man from the bookstore was here. He took my book. Why?" I ask, thoughts drilling my mind a million miles an hour.

And why did he clean my kitchen?

I check the fridge for a note, for something to tell me that it was him who came to see me, but there is nothing. All I have are tingles from my orgasm, a possible flash of his face, and a missing book.

Disappointment crashes through me. What if this is all we

will have? What if we don't even have this and I'm imagining it? What if he listens to Reaper, or if I listen to Reaper, and we never get to know each other because of the rules stamped on us?

"I need to go to bed. I'm obviously losing my mind." I press my hand against my forehead and forgo the tea. Opening the white cabinet, I reach for another bottle but find my wine gone. "What the fuck?" I curse. "Okay, I know for a damn fact I had another bottle in here." It's gone. I slam the cabinet door and reach into the Lazy Susan to grab the whiskey instead. I hate whiskey, but I use it for emergencies, and this seems like an emergency because I'm fucking losing it.

The seal breaks as I twist off the cap. The burning scent has my eyes watering, and I'll bet my nose hair is singed because holy moly that is strong. I take a swig and immediately spit it out, spewing it all over the books across the table. "Oh my god, who drinks this stuff?" It's literally burning a hole in my stomach.

Note to self: stick to wine.

I weave my way through the books on the floor and take another swig when I remember I'm alone. I'm always alone. Lonely Daphne in the big sin city all by her little self. It's what my dad said when I left home, but not in reassurance. He doesn't think I can make it out here, but he is wrong. Aunt Tina lives around the corner, and while she's MIA half the time, she loves me and means well.

And that's more than I have ever had from my father.

I check the lock on the door to make sure that I stay alone for the remainder of the night.

Another thought hits me while I take another awful swig of whiskey, a thought I haven't considered until this moment.

What if it wasn't Tongue in my apartment?

CHAPTER FOUR

Tongue

"**W**HERE THE FUCK HAVE YOU BEEN, TONGUE?" REAPER asks as soon as I walk through the front door. I'm holding a bottle of wine I stole from Daphne's apartment and a book in the other hand.

I had the best night of my life. What I shared with Daphne, I've never had with anyone else before. I don't want Reaper to ruin it for me, but it's Reaper. He's our Prez. I have to listen to him, but I have a feeling if he says anything to me about Daphne, listening is the last thing I will do.

"I was out," I state, simply, eyeing the guys who are sitting around on the couch at nine in the morning. I might have left Daphne's apartment, but I stayed outside until she went to work. I hate that I have to take my eyes off her for one minute, but the club is my family. They are my home.

"You were ___ out?" Reaper asks, nearly red in the face

"Out? Are you fucking kidding me? After what happened on Halloween, I really thought you would be more responsible, Tongue. We need to stay together right now. We need you here at home. Skirt needs his home rebuilt. The walls are going up around the compound. I can't have you doing whatever the fuck you want, when you want because you fucking feel like it right now." His eyes drop to the book in my hand and the wine bottle in the other. "The bookstore girl, that's who you've been with?"

I forgot he knows about her now. I saw him at the coffee stand while I watched her from the alley. I was hoping she'd be my secret for a little while, but Reaper always figures everything out. "No." It isn't a lie. Technically, she had no idea I was there, so she can't say she was with me.

"So you stopped at the store and grabbed a book and a bottle of wine?"

"What's the harm in that?" I say. I remember the times when I could barely say a word without stumbling over myself. I've learned how to speak without sounding like a complete fool since my tongue has healed.

"You're not to leave the compound until further notice. Do I make myself clear?"

Like I give a flying fuck what he has to say. Nothing is going to keep me away from Daphne.

"We have more important things going on than you chasing some ass."

"I don't chase ass," I say darkly, itching to grab my knife. I crack my neck, twisting it right and left until it pops. "You know damn well that's not what I do."

"I know, but you being around that sweet, innocent girl will bring her nothing but pain, and you know it. Stay away from her. If you want what is best for her, leave her alone."

What feels like a sharp knife pierces my heart, then twists. I can't leave her alone. Now that I finally have her, she always needs to be by my side. A baby cries in the kitchen, and Skirt gets up from the couch and gives me a nod, exiting the room silently to go care for his newborn daughter, Joanna, named after Doc's ol' lady who tried to run into a burning building to save him. They nicknamed their daughter Joey, so it's less confusing.

Slingshot digs into a bag next to him and unwraps the foil around his food. It's a breakfast burrito. I've come to learn he eats when he's nervous.

And he's constantly nervous.

Usually what I do when I'm nervous is cut tongues, but things haven't exactly been a revolving door of people who deserve to die, so I need to do something with my time. It's better than being here, in that damn Church room, or even near it, reminding me that I was buried alive. I only lived because Sarah heard me punching through the floor.

And then there was another attack on the compound. Doc was a busy guy that day. A lot of people were injured, and we lost two cut-sluts. I don't give a fuck about the club whores, but some do, and I guess it's sad. If you can find it in yourself to care.

Because of all the action lately, Reaper has been running a tight ship. Walls are going up around the property line since people keep getting in and fucking with what's ours. We haven't had time to rebuild Skirt's house after it burned down in the attack that Joanna's ex-whatever he was hired college kids to take us out.

I know people expect me to be afraid of the dark now, but it isn't the case. I'm not afraid. Someone got the upper hand on me and somehow buried me. Every time I enter Church, I get angry, and I'm barely able to contain myself from blowing the fuck up and cutting out the person's tongue who is sitting next to me when I'm triggered.

It's usually Slingshot, and considering how much he loves tacos, I don't think he'd appreciate that very much.

"Now, since everyone is here, we have cleanup to do from the attack that we still haven't gotten around to—" Reaper pinches the bridge of his nose, and I slam the front door shut, hoping what he said to me is forgotten. I don't care what I have to do to see her. I'll do it. "Things have been hectic. Between the attack, Doc's mom's funeral, and what happened on Halloween, there hasn't been a lot of time to think about anything else, but now is the time. We need to regroup. We need to prepare. We need plans in place. The Groundskeeper has not revealed himself; he's been silent. I don't know if he's still in the area, but if he is, I doubt he's going to leave us alone. I don't want anyone leaving the compound unless it is for work purposes. I don't give a fuck how inconvenient it is. If you disobey an order, I'll carve my signature heart in your chest. Don't fucking test me on this. We have women and children here. We have kids here that we still have no idea what to do with. No one has come forward about them. We need to focus." Reaper gives me the evil eye, and I scoff, then make my way to my damn room.

I don't need this shit.

Are you fucking kidding me? I always stay in line. I do what's needed. I'm the one who inflicts the twisted, sick pain our enemies need to feel, and I'm the bad guy right now?

I guess that's the thing with guys like me.

I'm always the bad guy; I'm never the knight.

I'm always focused. I'm always here. Half the time, they don't even notice me. They forget about me in the corner, saying I lurk, but they don't go out of their way to get to know me, do they? They don't know why I'm the way I am. They don't question it because what I am is good enough for them, but it isn't good enough for me, not anymore.

I have a dangerous void inside me, and it's growing by the day. I'm afraid I'll lose myself to it and get lost in a darkness that I can't find my way out of.

Now that scares me.

I've always known when to pull back, to stop my mind from getting too far gone.

Maybe that's my problem.

I need to realize that I'm already too far gone, and there is no hope for me. I'm a killer. I am death. I'm who Reaper calls to entice fear and pain. I cut.

And I'm the guy who gets the job done when no one else can stomach it.

Reaper is right. I have no business going after a woman like Daphne, but a mess like me needs a mental break too. Even with all the crazy going on in my dumb head, I still need peace.

"Where are you going?" Reaper barks at me, but I keep my back to him, anger rushing through my veins.

I've never felt more like a child than I do right now. I stop in the middle of the hallway, and the heaviness in my tongue tells me if I speak, nothing I say will come out right. They treat me like I'm incompetent, and it's starting to grind my damn patience.

There's a difference between being uneducated and incompetent. I'm perfectly capable of understanding conversations and what is being said to me. Just because I don't know how to read or write doesn't mean I'm fucking stupid.

"I'm not fucking stupid!" I roar, almost throwing the bottle of wine across the room at Reaper. "I've done everything that has ever been asked of me. I'm allowed to have some goddamn privacy. Stop acting like I'm … I'm incapable of being able to do things that don't involve you or the club. Stop treating me like … like…." I feel my stutter coming back, and in the back of my mind, I can hear my uncle's voice.

You goddamn idiot. You can't listen, can you? Like talking to a wall. You'll always be stupid.

"Woah, Tongue, no. That isn't what it's about," Reaper tries to argue with me, and his expression is bunched up as if I've slapped him in the face.

Maizey walks out of the hallway and rubs her sleepy eyes and gives me a wave. "Hi, Tongue. How are you?" she asks.

She's the only one to ever ask how I'm doing, and this time, I'm going to be honest. I stare at Reaper for a long moment before I look at her again. "I-I'm … I'm not do-doing too go-good." Fuck, there I go again, sounding stupid. It isn't good; it is *well.* I'm not doing well. Sarah taught me that.

I need to get out of here. I can't breathe.

"Tongue, you need to calm down." Tool inches his way forward, and Skirt is right next to him, ready to take me down if he needs to.

Please, what a joke.

It would take four Ruthless Kings to take me down.

I spin on my heel and hurry to my bedroom, then slam the door behind me. I lock the door and sit on my bed. My heart is pounding. I lay my hand against my chest and feel it flutter against my palm, racing. Sweat drips down my back, and the material of my shirt sticks to me. The walls are closing in, and my head swims.

Everyone thinks I'm this emotionless monster, but I feel

just as deep, if not more, than others. It takes its toll on my mind, my soul, and not being able to understand them only fucks with my head further.

It's why I am the way I am.

Madness created me.

Abuse broke me.

And then madness stitched me back together again.

I'm insane with moments of being lucid, and I was created from something hopeless, which means there isn't much room for improvement.

I'm starting to wonder if my soul is lost, or if I'm soulless and chasing a life that's never meant to be mine.

The book falls from my hand, and I set the bottle on the ground, then let out a heavy exhale. Pressing the palms of my hands against my eyes, I breathe. I've never been like this before. I've always known my place in the club. I'm the crazy one, the one who's obsessed with knives and loves getting bloody. I don't think there's something wrong with that, but one glimpse of Daphne and I want something else for the first time since I killed my uncle.

I always do for others, but what about me?

I want something for *me*.

I want something that's *mine*.

I want Daphne, my comet. Seeing her, she ignites hope in that meaningless void in my chest, and the feeling is addicting.

Standing, I open the closet and reach into my pocket for the key to the filing cabinet that holds all the journals I've drawn in since I was a kid. I grab a new one, close it, and lock it back up. The charcoal pencils are in a cup next to my bed already. I kick off my boots and whip off my shirt, getting more comfortable. Opening my journal to the first page, I take a pencil in hand.

TONGUE

Black dust transfers to my fingers instantly, and besides blood, it's the only thing that ever coats my skin.

I glance down to draw, but the scars across my chest get my attention. No one knows that I'm covered in cigarette burns. No one knows I was constantly raped as a child by my uncle. No one knows that I've never had sex before because the idea of sex scares the hell out of me. If people knew what made me tic, they wouldn't respect me like they do now.

Everyone is scared of me, and I'd rather them fear me than pity me.

I stick out my tongue and rub my clean hand across it, the bumps reminding me of the pain and torture. They're everywhere, and no matter how many people I kill or mute, I'll never be able to get them off me. I'm a disease. I infect.

The first thing I did when I turned eighteen was cover eighty percent of my body in beautiful tattoos so no one would have to see how hideous I look. It was awful being stared at like I'm some sort of freak. On top of not being able to speak properly, I was the person that everyone stopped and pointed at, laughing. I was always the joke.

And I guess in a way, I still am.

I'm the one-stop-shop for a circus.

It would have been better if my uncle had found a way to kill me because the person I've turned into is the horror story people tell their kids they will become if they don't do their homework.

My stomach rises as I inhale, and then I place the pencil against the paper and draw my favorite moment from tonight. Of course, I draw Daphne lying in bed, asleep. She tossed and turned for a few minutes, groaning in her sleep. She felt me. My presence. Not once has she been afraid of me. Is that because she doesn't know me? What if she got to know me and, like everyone else, looked at me like I don't belong?

There's more to me than people see, and it's my fault I don't let them in. The truth is too ugly; the realization that I'm not who people thought I was would confuse them.

A soft line appears as I draw the outline of her body. A grumble of pleasure vibrates my chest as I swoop the pencil to create the curves of her small tits. Fuck, she's perfect. I let the nightgown pool around her waist, shadowing the necessary angles and curves. When she said she felt me, I thought I was going to combust and tackle her on the bed. I wanted to ravish her, but I stopped myself.

I'm not good enough to touch her, not when my hands have seen more blood than a butcher.

My cock grows hard in my jeans when I draw her wet pussy. She has a small tuft of hair between her legs, and I sketch her hand over the spot that made her body jerk. When she came, I came in my jeans, and when she shoved the pillow over her face, I had to get close for a second. I had to smell her body. I wanted her scent tattooed on my lungs.

I want her branded on me.

And then she removed the pillow, and I ran.

I draw the entire scene, taking up a few pages of the journal by detailing my day. On another page, I decide to draw a close-up of her gorgeous face. So innocent. So pure. Daphne looks like darkness hasn't touched her, and I want to keep it that way. If my shadows get anywhere near Daphne, I'm afraid the horrors that hide in the darkness surrounding me will cast around her, damning her light to my hell.

My brows pinch together when a smudge appears on the paper, right where I start to draw her eyes. Another one appears, then another, and I reach out to see what the hell it is, and it's wet. I look up to see if the ceiling is leaking and then I look out my bedroom window to see if it's raining, but it isn't. We are in a drought.

I stare down at the paper again, knowing I'll never be the man she'll need. She'll grow old with someone else, love them, make love to him, and have his kids. She'll forget all about the freak in the bookstore holding a box of tongues to priority mail to his swamp kitties. Daphne will make a future because that's what happens when you deserve greatness.

A man like me, I don't have a future. I'll die a biker, probably someday soon, and I'll die alone. My future was carved in stone the moment my uncle touched me.

I'm a machine. I'm programmed to be heartless.

Bad omens fill my blood.

I'm doomed.

Another droplet smears the charcoal on the paper, and I get frustrated because I have no idea where the water is coming from. I snap the pencil in half and throw it across the room. I'm angry that my drawing of Daphne is ruined. I need to find where the water is coming from. I refuse to have her face anything less than perfect because it would be an injustice to her true beauty.

A knock at the door stops me from standing on my bed and inspecting the ceiling for any weak spots. "What?" I grunt, annoyed to hell. I'm mad at Reaper. I'm mad at this stupid water that only seems to drip whenever the fuck it wants. I'm mad at who I am as a man. I won't ever be able to change.

Blood, death, and killing are too much a part of what makes me, me. I'll always need violence as an escape. My uncle needed it too. Maybe it's my blood that's wrong. I'll need to make sure I don't have kids, so I don't risk infecting the innocence in them. What if they come out like me? I can't do that. I can't make their lives a living hell because I decided to be selfish.

"Tongue, it's me." Sarah's voice is muted behind the door, but hearing it makes me smile. I jump off the bed and run to the door, unlocking it to see my favorite person. Well, one of my favorite people. Daphne is number one now.

Reaper is behind her, and immediately I feel betrayed.

His eyes soften when he sees me, and Sarah gasps, covering her mouth in shock. "Tongue, what's wrong? Are you okay?"

"I'm fine," I drawl. "I'm just…" I almost give away my secret. Sarah doesn't know about my journals. She knows about everything else, but the journals are mine. "I'm trying to figure out where a leak is in the ceiling. It's ruining what I'm working on. It's pissing me off, and I can't kill it, so it's frustrating," I huff, scratching the back of my head as Reaper stares at me in concern. "What?" I ask as my fingers get tangled in my hair, which reminds me that I need to cut it. Daphne likes short hair.

Sarah lays her hand in the middle of my chest, and her eyes well as she pushes me further into the bedroom. Reaper follows behind her and shuts the doors.

"Sa-Sarah," I stutter, then hit the side of my head with my fist when I hear it. I'm becoming weaker by the second. I'm useless. I'm worthless. I'm a fucking idiot.

"Stop it. Don't." She takes my hands, knowing what I'm thinking about myself. "You aren't any of those things, Tongue."

I'm nervous with Reaper here. He doesn't see me as weak like Sarah does. I'm his enforcer. A droplet of water drips on my hand, and I point to it. "See, look. It's coming from somewhere."

"Tongue, look at me," Sarah says, cupping my face in her hands. She wipes her thumbs across my cheeks and pulls her hands away, showing me water. "It isn't a leak. The water is coming from you. You're crying." A single tear drips down her cheek. "Tongue, what's wrong? You never cry. I've never seen you cry."

"I'm not crying," I say. "I don't cry. I haven't cried since…" Since the night I killed Uncle Jeremy.

"Tongue, you are." Reaper slaps a hand on my shoulder, and I yank away from him.

"I'm not. I don't cry. I'm an enforcer. I kill." I lift my fingers to my face and stumble away from Sarah when I feel the droplets. The back of my knees hit the bed, and I sit down, staring at my hands as if they belong to someone else.

I don't understand why I'm crying. I don't feel any different. Maybe it's a mistake. A fluke.

"You're human," Reaper says. "Tongue, you're human. I think it's time to talk about what's going on. You haven't been yourself."

"You don't know anything about me," I say darkly. "The only person who gives a real damn about me is Sarah."

"That isn't true. How can you say that?" Reaper asks, hooking his fingers through his belt loops as he stands like a stranger near the bedroom door. He's in a place that's out of his comfort zone. He's in my space, and that leaves people more uncomfortable than not.

"Please, leave." I rub my temples when my head starts to hurt. "The both of you."

"Tongue, I'm here for you. Reaper came to find me when he said you came in and seemed upset."

"I'm getting treated like a child. Everyone thinks less of me. Just please … get out."

"Tongue—"

"I said get out!" I roar, standing to my feet. I'm tired. My insides are shredded apart, and even the best of killers need a damn break. "Get me when you need me like you usually do." I open the door to show them the way out, and Sarah's bottom lip trembles. I hate that I hurt her. Sarah means the world to me, but I have so much going on in my mind that I need time by myself.

"I always need you," she whispers, her voice broken and weak. "You're my best friend. I don't know why Reaper is here, but he isn't here with me. I came to check on you; he followed."

"Then you can leave," I tell Prez, not caring if it earns me a scar. I have plenty of them. I can add his to the collection.

Reaper glances away and crosses his arm before rubbing a hand over his mouth.

I shake my head and stare at him in disbelief. "You came in here because you do need me." An ironic laugh leaves my chest. "Fucking knew it."

"Mercy is here. We have problems. I need my best enforcer. I'm sorry I'm asking at a bad time."

No one ever needs me for anything else.

What if I say no?

"He can go after he talks to me. Even the best, even the strongest, most savage men need to talk. Can't you see he needs me, Reaper? I can't believe you right now. You have plenty of other members you can use," Sarah argues in my defense.

"None like Tongue."

Yeah, there never is.

"You're sleeping on the couch, Jesse," Sarah hisses as she stomps out of my room, vanishing down the hall where Maizey is.

TONGUE

"You're worth it," Reaper chuckles, slapping me on the shoulder.

I wouldn't be too sure about that.

The rotten core inside me always boils over to purge, but right now, it's barely simmering.

CHAPTER FIVE

Daphne

I'M PLACING A NEW BOOK ON THE SHELF WHEN I FEEL THE PRESENCE again. I inhale, letting the rush roll over my body and energize my heart. The dusty shelf is in the way of my sight, and my breathing picks up when I feel the tension rise. I see specks of leather on the opposite row in front of me, and I can't help but wonder if I'm caught in a daydream.

Blood rushes to my cheeks when the hint of his cologne hits me in the face. It's light, like he sprayed it on his cut a few days ago, and it's lingering and is now influencing my brain. I can't breathe. I can't speak. I can't think.

His face is blocked by the fan of his shaggy brown hair. His arms are up, gripping the top bookshelf, and the tattoos on his arms swirl around the thick muscle. I can't see his face, but I remember what he looks like. The shelves are in the way from me having the perfect view of the man who's been waking me up in the middle of the night.

TONGUE

Without saying a word, I slide a book in its rightful place, and he grabs it from the other side, holding it against his chest. He brings the spine of the book to his nose and sniffs.

"Do you like the smell of books too?" I whisper over the dust and grab another book from the cart, then glide it across the shelf too.

He takes the 'Moby Dick' novel from my hands, and our fingers graze together. My mouth drops open when a spark travels into my veins and up my arm. What is it about this man?

"I like the way *you* smell." His voice is tinted with a Southern drawl and another unique quality I can't put my finger on. I close my eyes for a moment as the baritone crawls through my senses and weakens them.

I smile, then nibble on my lip as I double-check to make sure no one is around to overhear our conversation. It's an odd one, and I don't want anyone to get alarmed. "Why won't you let me see you?" I ask him, placing another book on the shelf.

He takes that one too and remains silent.

"Do you like to read?" I question him and pull the cart closer to me to set another book on the case.

"No."

My brows pinch together in confusion, and I lean in, my fingers wrapping around the wooden edge of the shelf. I stand on my tiptoes to try to get a better view of the biker giant, but his hair is in his face. "Why take the books?" Oh my god, what if he burns them? I can't let a catastrophe happen like that, even if he's hotter than any fictional character I've ever read about.

"You," he answers shortly, snagging another copy from my hand.

At this rate, I'm never going to stock the shelf.

"Me? I don't understand."

My head falls to the side as I watch him bring another book to his nose. He inhales again, smelling the leatherbound books so hard his shoulders rise from the expansion of his lungs. The leather of his cut stretches across his shoulders as he rolls them.

"What's your name?" I ask, then step toward the end of the aisle to face him, but he backtracks, moving further away from me, staying in the dark where I can't see him. "Who are you? Are you going to hurt me?" I whisper, needing to know if everything I'm feeling is something I've made up and if he is someone I need to call the cops about.

"Never. I'd-I'd never hu-hurt my co-comet." Do I make him nervous? He sounds like he can barely speak to me.

"Your comet? Is that what I am? Is that why you're following me? You are, aren't you? What's it mean to be your comet?" I bombard him with a bunch of questions, hoping he will answer one of them.

He falls quiet again. I can't take it anymore. I run around the bookcase, but he runs behind another one. The one further encased in the dark.

"Please, talk to me. Tell me your name."

Nothing.

I can hear him breathing. The sounds are harsh, like he's unable to control himself.

"Tongue."

"That isn't your name," I say, dragging my finger across the wood of the shelf. "Your real name. Reaper told me the people you guys care about only know your real names. Is that true?" I whisper, making sure no one can hear us.

Silence.

"Please…" I feel him everywhere, all the time, and it's

getting to the point where I need more than him watching me. "Please, tell me something."

"I'll always be watching you," he says just as quickly as the space on the other side of the aisle is empty.

The doorbell chimes, and I spin around to get one last glimpse of him, but no one is there. It's only the melody of the bell swaying back and forth as the door slowly closes. I walk down the aisle, giving a customer a polite grin, and speed up my strides as I pass the middle-aged woman. She's in the romance section, reading the back of a book to see what it's about.

I open the door and run down the three steps until I'm outside in the sun, standing in the middle of the sidewalk. There are a few dozen people on either side of the street. Some are entering Paula's Candy Shop, and some are entering the hardware store. I push my glasses up my nose and examine each side of the street, looking for any sign of leather or the sound of a bike.

He's a phantom, appearing out of nowhere and vanishing without a trace. He makes me wonder if he's real or if I need to seek medical attention. Tongue is messing with my head and my heart.

"Are you okay?" Andrew asks from the doorway of Page by Page. "What's wrong?"

"Nothing ... I—" I spin around again, hoping I can see him because I can feel him. He's here. Where? Where is he? It's like he's bathing me in his vision, memorizing me. I know it should freak me out, but my gut tells me he won't let anything happen to me. "I thought I saw someone I knew. I'm sorry. I guess I didn't."

"You look like you've seen a ghost. You sure you're okay?"

"Actually, I don't think I'm feeling well. I'm going to go home for the day. Is that alright? Do you need me here?"

"No, you go ahead. It's fine. Get some rest."

I run up the steps and give him a hug. "Thank you. I'm just going to run in and get my purse. I'll be on my way."

"Call me if you need anything," Andrew says, giving me a kiss on the cheek.

I don't question it, but the kiss was a little too close to my mouth for comfort. Andrew has always been an affectionate guy, so I'm not going to read into it. "Hi, how are you?" I ask a customer as I pass them, giving them a quick nod as I make my way to the employee room. I pass the bookcases where I spoke to Tongue, and I wait to see if he appears out of thin air, but it's only books.

Only. Books.

I never thought I'd ever think of books in such generality, yet here I am, disappointed to be staring at a bookcase because I'd rather see his face. I've been forbidden to see him, warned away, and was bluntly told the guy is dangerous.

I don't care.

There's a force pulling me toward him. Tongue has made roots somehow, latching himself onto the inside of my heart and soul. The longer I'm away from him, the tighter the roots constrict around my bones. When I'm near him… When I'm finally able to breathe again, I'm exhilarated.

It isn't normal, but it all makes sense as to why I've never dated before. Normal isn't something I want out of someone. I need more. I need a story.

I want to write a book from beginning to end with someone, chapter by chapter, ache by ache, until we get our happy ending.

"Excuse me?"

I close the door behind me after grabbing my purse and smile at a customer. "Yes?"

"Where is your porn?"

I blink at the woman. She has to be in her nineties. She's hunched over with a long wooden cane in her hand and a scowl that would make that guy Reaper flinch.

"Well?" she asks me impatiently, huffing when I take too long to answer.

"Ma'am, we aren't that kind of store. We sell books."

"No shit. I'm old, not blind. I'm looking for books."

"You must want the romance novel section. Two aisles over on your right," I say, showing her the way by pointing to the rows.

"Thank you," she huffs, hobbling as she walks away.

I glance down to get my keys out of my purse when I notice it is unzipped. I remember closing it, but maybe I didn't. The last few days have been odd. If my mind is screwing with me about Tongue, then small things like remembering to zip my purse are going to happen too.

"I'll see you later," Andrew says, opening the door for me as I leave. "You should relax. You can take a few vacation days. I don't mind. You never take time off."

"I wouldn't be able to function if I didn't come to the bookstore." Holy moly, I hope he doesn't think I'm hitting on him. What I said almost sounds like I only come to work for him, which is not the case. Not even a little.

As I said, Andrew is too normal.

"Well, we will be here waiting for you when you come back tomorrow." He grins, rocking back on his heels and rubbing two fingers over his bottom lip as he grins.

How do I tell my boss I'm not interested in him because I think I'm falling in love with a man who lives in the dark?

I wave goodbye and start my journey walking two blocks, replaying the conversation I had with Tongue in my head. Why won't he talk to me? Like truly speak and have a conversation? He doesn't have to watch me from afar or from the corners; he can touch me if he wants, and love me if he wants.

I keep my head down, thinking about a million reasons and excuses for him, but at the end of the day, I truly don't know anything about him. For all I know, Reaper is right. No matter what I try to convince myself, Tongue is the night, and according to Reaper, his armor is caked in blood.

If he is so bad for me, why can't I rationalize that?

Thinking about him makes the time walking to my apartment fly by. The hairs on the back of my neck stand up, but the excitement isn't there, the heat, the anticipation. It's gone. This creepy feeling has my skin pebbling in warning and fear tearing into my stomach. Pausing mid-step, I look over my shoulder to see if anyone is watching me.

There's a mailman wearing a light blue shirt and navy shorts walking to his United States Post Office car. There's another woman who is walking her chihuahua. A few cars are parked along the street. They are compact, small, and I can see through the windows. No one is there.

A hot breeze has me turning my head in the other direction, so I don't choke on the dry heat. Studying another point of view, I don't see anything except trash cans and the shadows casting onto the road from the buildings.

The inkling that someone is watching me doesn't go away. The keys in my hand jingle, clinking together as tremors overtake my body. "Oh god, oh god, oh god," I chant when the feeling gets worse, like the evil is closing in, and I only have a second to get inside before it snatches me.

Tears blur the keyhole, but I've unlocked this door so many times that I can do it in my sleep. I let out a relieved huff of air as the doorknob turns. I turn my body and squeeze my way inside, keeping the door as closed as I can. I slam it behind me and twist the bolt until the lock slides in place. Covering my face with my hands, I laugh. Oh my god, I'm so ridiculous. It was probably nothing. I'm freaking out for no reason.

Everything is A-okay. I'm peachy. Life is good. I need to have a glass of wine and relax. My phone rings in my purse, and I scream from the unexpected sound cutting through my anxiety. I lay palm against my forehead and chuckle. "God, he really has you in a freaking mess, doesn't he?" If he doesn't approach me soon, maybe dating a normal guy will be better for my freaking health.

I pull my phone out of the side pocket of my purse, and a folded-up piece of paper falls to the floor. "Hello?" I answer, bending over to pick up the grocery list, receipt, or whatever it is. My purse isn't the cleanest, okay? I bet I have receipts in there from my damn birthday last year.

"Hey, sweetie," Aunt Tina greets me. "Oh, no. You stop it." She giggles to someone.

I grin. She's always been the life of the party. "Traveling sounds like it's going well." While Aunt Tina lives here in Vegas, she isn't here half the year. She's always traveling. Years ago, her daughter died a few hours after she was born, and Aunt Tina has never been the same. She doesn't like to stay in one place. She's always on the move. I think when she stands still long enough, she remembers holding her daughter for the first and only time.

I don't blame her for not wanting to be here. If that had happened to me, I'm sure I'd be moving all over the country too, flirting with men I don't know, and drinking yummy fruity drinks. She can afford it too. Apparently, the hospital was negligent and caused her baby to die. She was born a healthy, crying baby, but that's all I know. Details of her past are not something Aunt Tina discusses with me.

Aunt Tina sued the holy moly out of that hospital and got millions. It's part of the reason why I can work at a bookstore and afford this apartment. She makes sure I'm okay. She doesn't want me to live my life working; she wants me to truly live, but I'm only twenty-five. I have no idea how to live like she wants me to, so I work. I like working. I barely ever have to dip into the funds she left me. I'm thinking of going back to school too, and the little egg she left will help with that.

I have plenty of time to figure it out. If life keeps going the way it's going, I'm going to be an old cat lady by the time I'm thirty.

And I'm allergic.

"It's fun. I miss you. I think I might come home for a few weeks. I'd love to see you."

"Really? I miss you too. I want to talk to you about … someone I met."

"Oh my god!" she squeals, and then she grunts. "No, you get away. Fucking asshole." I hear a splash, and then she mutters, "What a waste of good tequila." The phone rustles, and the noise in the background fades. "Is it about a boy?"

I roll my eyes when I hear her smile. "It's about a man; thank you very much," I say, finally climbing up the steps. I unfold the piece of paper and think about Tongue and the way he makes me feel.

It's hard to explain, but it's that feeling you get when you're standing at the edge of a really high cliff, looking down at the lake or ocean, contemplating if you should jump. It's safe. All your friends have done it, but it's your turn. You're excited, scared, nervous, and nearly shaking because even though there is water at the bottom, the cliff is still high.

He's the butterflies in my stomach and the water beneath me, but he won't let me jump into him.

And I'm bound to the cliff with the feeling gnawing at my stomach. It's torture.

He's torture.

And I like it.

It's a weird, sick, foreplay, and it kind of turns me on.

This is why I can't do normal.

Tongue's weirdness calls to mine.

"Oh, what's he like? What's he do? I bet he's a sexy mechanic or something, isn't he?"

Or something.

"We just met. We're taking things slow. Super slow. No, sloth slow. In fact, Aunt Tina, I don't even know his real name, and we haven't had a conversation that is longer than one minute."

"Oh, life is too short for slow. Go fast, sweetie. Fast is fun."

"Your fast is too fast, Aunt Tina," I chuckle, placing my shoulder against my phone to hold it so I can open my apartment door.

Only to find it already open.

"Aunt Tina, I'll call you back," I say slowly.

"What? No! Tell me about this guy—" But the phone goes dead when it hits the floor with a hard thud, and then cracks spider across the screen. Bending down, I pick it up off the floor and swipe across the screen to get to my keypad to dial 911.

I drop the receipt on the floor to get my hand free when I notice writing on it. It isn't an old receipt. It's a piece of paper.

I open the last fold and gag when I see what it says:

Roses are red,

Dead lips are blue,

Stay away from him,

Or next it will be you.

I hold a hand over my mouth, stifling a sob, and dial 911.

"911, what's your emergency?" the operator asks.

"Someone is in my apartment," I whisper, taking my hand away from my mouth. "I have a note that was left in my purse too. I think someone is watching me." Is it Tongue? He did say he is always going to watch me, but I don't see him doing something like this. He wouldn't scare me.

"Someone broke into your apartment. Is anything damaged or missing?" they ask.

I lay my palm flat against the door and push it open, hoping to see nothing. My hand reaches inside and pats against the wall in an uncoordinated way. I flip the light switch, and my hand slides across something wet.

I stare at the red liquid on my hand, and the breath is knocked out of me. "Oh my god." I follow the line of blood across the wall. It looks like something was dragged.

"Ma'am? What is it? Are you okay?" the operator asks.

I don't respond. I follow the trail of blood, and what I see has the phone falling from my hand.

There's a tongue nailed on the trim of the window, dripping blood on the stack of books beneath it.

I scream at the top of my lungs and forget I have blood on my hands, smearing it across my cheek. I inhale a deep breath and scream again.

"Help is on the way, ma'am. I'll stay on the phone with you until the police arrive."

Reaper's warning about Tongue is a siren in my head, and

doubt starts to creep in. What if I've been obsessed with a monster this entire time? What if he's been staying away, not because I make him nervous, but because he's hunting me.

Holy moly.

I really need to evaluate my taste in men.

I run out the door and hurry down the steps, leaving the bloodstained apartment as fast as I can. I trip over my left foot and fall, tumbling down the staircase. My knee hits the solid hardwood that makes the steps, and my wrist bends in a funny position. When I get to the floor, the momentum of my body can't be stopped, and my head slams against the wall.

Groaning, I hold my arm against my chest as the door bursts in.

"Vegas Police Department!" one of them shouts. "Hey, I need a medic over here now! Ma'am, are you okay? Do you know your name? What happened?" he asks.

"I fell down the steps," I moan when I roll to my back. "Trying to get away from the blood." I wince when I try to move my knee, so I keep it in a bent position instead.

"An ambulance is on its way. You're going to be fine, Ms. Lace," he reassures me.

"You're going to want to see this, Officer Hodder," another cop says from the middle of the staircase.

Paramedics burst through the door and then quickly and load me onto a gurney and strap a brace around my neck. Is this really happening? Did I seriously fall down the steps because there is a tongue nailed to the windowsill? This can't be my life. If this is what living is like, how the hell do I slow it down? Aunt Tina jinxed me.

The paramedics roll me outside, and my vision starts to blur. The sun is too bright, and my head starts to pound.

"Wait!" Officer Hodder, the cop who comforted me, runs out the front door to stop the medics from loading me in the ambulance.

"We need to get her to the hospital now. She has a concussion," the female paramedic says with a bit of attitude.

"Hey, Ms. Lace." Officer Hodder leans down in front of my face, and there are two of him. I blink, trying to focus, but it doesn't work. He's mid-thirties, handsome, normal.

A guy I should date. And why am I thinking about that right now and not the disgusting tongue dangling in front of my window?

"Can you think of anyone who wanted to do this? Has anything been suspicious over the last few days? Anything at all."

"You can question her later."

"I need to ask her while she has her damn eyes open, Reynolds. Lay off," he snaps at the woman trying to help me. It's obvious they don't like each other. "Ms. Lace. I'm sorry, but can you think of anyone?" he asks me again, softening his voice.

I should tell them about Tongue. Everything points to him, but I don't say anything. My instincts, no matter how crazy they are, tell me he has nothing to do with this.

"No," I whisper. I keep my secret to myself, hoping I didn't sign my death warrant by trusting a man I hardly know.

CHAPTER SIX

Tongue

I SHOULDN'T HAVE SPOKEN TO HER, BUT I COULDN'T HELP IT. SHE looked so pretty. So *mine*. I got tired of being so far away. I wanted to be close for once. Just one time. When our fingers grazed, fuck, I could live off the feeling it gave me for the rest of my life.

How can I stay away from her when I think she was born for me?

She's mine.

She's coded into the DNA in my blood; she's a part of who I am.

Daphne doesn't hold the missing piece of me. She is the missing piece.

I crave her.

I'm dying to be whole because being half a man is killing me.

Reaper wanted me to talk to Mercy last night, but on the way out of my room, I turned right down the hall, pretending I needed to go the bathroom, and hightailed it out the door. I hopped on my hog and snuck into her apartment to watch her sleep.

It's my favorite thing to do. I love watching her chest rise and fall. I even sat on the bed, and she turned against me. It's like she could feel me there and needed to be close to me. When she left for work, I had to follow. I wasn't ready to be away from her for the day, but I had to come face the heat at the clubhouse.

Reaper is going to be pissed at me for leaving like I did. After I get my punishment, I plan on going back to watching Daphne. She's consumed my mind. She's an obsession that grows by the day. I can't even remember the last time I thought about a knife.

The bike grumbles beneath me, and I stroke the tongue whipping out of its mouth. I close my eyes and remember what it's like to cut, to hear people scream, to feel their blood. I miss it. I miss my swamp kitties. I miss my knives.

Maybe it's time I let Daphne go. She deserves more than me anyway. She loves books for fuck's sake, and I can't even read.

How pathetic is that? What am I thinking?

The front door opens, and Reaper is standing there with his arms crossed, a look on his face that can only mean I'm in deep fucking shit.

Whatever.

I'm not afraid of pain. I've had worse. Anything Reaper does to me won't compare to what I've already been through. I swing my leg over my hog and shut it off. I open my saddlebags and grab the books Daphne touched at the bookstore. I plan on taking all of them one day; every single one that has been lucky enough to touch her fingertips are going to be in a bookcase that I'll make her.

I climb the steps to the clubhouse, and Reaper doesn't move from the middle of the doorway. "Please tell me you weren't with Daphne, Tongue. Tell me you were doing what you love to do, and you mailed tongues to the fucking gators in NOLA."

"Is he back?" Mercy bellows from the inside of the house. "He needs to get in here now."

"What the fuck is going on, Reaper?"

He yanks me inside by the cut and slams the door.

"What did you do, Tongue?" Badge asks me as he types on his computer, frantic.

"What are you talking about? I haven't done a thing," I say slowly, sitting on the couch in front of the club as they surround me. I don't like this. I reach into my pocket and grab my knife, rubbing my fingers up and down the sharp blade. It calms me, but it doesn't change that I'm being backed into a corner.

Reaper points the remote at the TV and turns the sound on.

"This is Marsha Collins with LV Local News reporting what seems to be a disturbing stalker in our area. Earlier this evening, a young woman entered her apartment to find blood on the walls of her home, along with a tongue nailed to the window. That's right, a tongue. As of right now, there are no witnesses. The young lady who lives in this apartment building is at the hospital seeking medical treatment after falling down the steps. Anyone with any information regarding this matter, please contact the Vegas Police Department. I promise to keep you informed as more information is made available. This is Marsha Collins with LV Local News; stay ahead and stay safe."

I throw the knife across the room with a thunderous roar, and it lands next to Patrick's head. He freezes, not moving a muscle, and stares at the knife.

"If I walk further into the room, am I going to die? Tell me now so I can go in the opposite direction," he says, holding out his hand when Skirt tries to pass him.

I'm annoyed.

And when I'm annoyed, I tend to kill.

I grab my other knife and go to throw it, but Tool tackles me to the couch and yanks the blade from my hand.

"What did you do, Tongue?" Reaper asks so desperately; his voice is hoarse as if accusing me of this crime is hard for him.

I kick Tool off me and grab his wrist, twisting it to the left, and steal my fucking knife back. "You better watch who the fuck you're messing with, Tool." I bite the air, sneering in his face, and he takes a step away as my crazy starts to boil over.

I've been wondering where it went.

I need to get to Daphne. I have to make sure she's okay. How the hell can I get out of here? She's all alone in that hospital. She has to be afraid.

"Shite, who pissed off Tongue? Ye know better than to do that," Skirt says just as a pregnant Joanna walks around him to come into the living room, but Doc runs to her, whispering in her ear. She glances at me, then shakes her head before disappearing into the other room. I bet all the ol' ladies are in there.

I wish that's where I was. I only ever feel accused when I'm with the guys, but when I'm with the women, they secure me in a blanket of nurturing that I've never had before.

"Tongue, what did you do?" Reaper repeats. "I won't ask again."

I get up slowly and eye all of them. Mercy and Badge are standing next to one another, and the way all of them are looking at me, they think I did this. They think I'm guilty. They didn't ask me if I did it. None of them have any doubt on their faces.

Why is Mercy here anyway? Isn't he some 'has been' FBI agent? This isn't a federal issue. It's a psycho on the loose.

"We need to know. The police are going to figure it out eventually. What do we need to do," Reaper states, brushing a hand through his hair.

"Maybe we send him to NOLA? Just until the heat dies down," Mercy offers, which is bold considering he isn't even a King.

I lick the knife, letting the dangerous edge prick my tongue, and the metallic taste of blood flows across the taste buds I have left. I need release. The rage is at an all-time high as they talk about me as if I'm not here.

"You think I did this." I don't ask. I state. It's obvious they think I'm capable of going off the edge like this.

"Tongue, who else did it? I don't know another guy with the same M.O. as you," Mercy says. "When I heard what happened over the police scanner, I came right over. There has been another case just like it across the lake."

"You've been gone a lot."

I laugh at Reaper and suck my tongue over my teeth, leaving them bloody for all of them to see.

I might be a crazy fucking bastard, but hurting Daphne is something I'd never do. On my dying breath, if someone told me they could save me if it meant inflicting pain on her, I'd gladly die.

"Wow," I shake my head at my so-called "family," and my

fingers twitch, itching to cut one of their tongues out for the betrayal I feel. "You guys don't know me at all. You think I'd hurt a woman? When have I ever wasted a tongue? And why would I hurt Daphne? I need to go check on her." I slide my knife in my holster and try to walk out the door, but Tank stands in front of me. He's the only one here as big as me, but he isn't near as vicious.

"If you don't get out of my way, I'll slice your throat from right to left, Tank. No one will keep me from Daphne." I turn my head and tilt my chin down, lifting my gaze through my lashes. "No one."

"He's right. He doesn't waste the tongues he cuts out," Slingshot says, lifting his feet and placing them on the coffee table.

"These events both happened when you were out for long periods of time. Tongue, I love you like a brother, but I can't ignore the facts."

"And what facts are those, Reaper?" I reach for my knife and tap the tip on the front of my teeth. "Tell me the *facts*."

"I think you found a tongue you really like, and you're working her up, getting her scared. I've seen you do unimaginable things to other people. I won't let you hurt an innocent girl. No one else cuts tongues."

"The man left a note too," Badge says, printing out proof from the computer. "This was just logged in at evidence."

"Who has she been around?" Reaper asks, shoving the note in my face. "Why are you doing this to her?"

I stab the paper with my knife, then slam it on to the coffee table, locking the damn picture of the note I can't read in place. "She's been around me and that guy she works with at the boo-bookstore." No, I will not lose my composure now. I refuse to be weak. I refuse to be stupid. "I've been around her.

I've been following her. The only crime I've committed is stalking, gently, but she knows I'm there."

"Spoken like a true psychopath," Mercy mumbles under his breath.

I grab a short three-inch blade that I keep tucked in my boot and let it fly, nicking him across his neck. "She does know I'm there. I don't give a fuck what you say. I didn't write this note. I didn't leave a tongue in her apartment. I didn't do this, Reaper. Why can't you believe me?"

"Because of past behavior."

"You don't judge Tool every time he whips out his screwdriver. You didn't judge Poodle for being a serial killer for a minute. You didn't judge Boomer or Patrick for being a fucking drunk, but you blame me."

"Reaper, he didn't do it," Sarah says. She runs across the room and wraps her arms around my waist.

"Sarah, don't—"

"He didn't do it!" she screams at him with tears in her eyes. "He couldn't have written that note."

"It's okay, Sarah."

"Tongue, it isn't—"

I wrap my hand around my favorite knife and pull it from the coffee table. I need to be with Daphne, and I can't do this arguing my case in front of my brothers, the people who were supposed to have my back. "It's okay, Sarah." I push her toward Reaper with a good amount of force, then snag Tank from the front door, and stab the knife into his shoulder, with the note clinging to his chest.

He screams, and it sounds so sweet. I bet his blood is sweeter, but this isn't about my pleasure right now. This is about proving a point. "Is this what you're expecting from me?"

"Tongue! What are you doing? Get away from him." Braveheart tries to attack me, launching his leaner body against me, but one shove of my leg and he flies through the air, slamming against the couch.

"Is this better? Is this what you want from me?" I wrap my hand around Tank's throat, and a sharp cackle escapes me. The darkness is closing in and man, I've missed it. "Nothing personal, Tank. I like you. I'm just proving a point." I rip the knife out of his shoulder, and he falls to his knees. "Or maybe you expect this." I grip Tank by the back of the nape and tilt his head back, laying the bloody metal against his jugular vein. "Are you expecting me to bathe in his blood? Do you want to know how much I want to?"

"Tongue—" Reaper inches forward, nervous for Tank who is currently nursing a shoulder wound. He'll be fine.

"Ah, don't…" I reach into his mouth and pull out his tongue next. "We all know what happens when I get to this beauty." Tank whimpers. His eyes are wide with fear. I glance down, soaking up the terror like a sponge. He probably sees voids in my eyes, carelessness, and death.

I am all of those things.

But I'm only those things when I absolutely need to be.

I clean my blade against his tongue, letting him swallow his own blood. "Out of everyone in the world to not be on my side, I never thought it would be my brothers."

"We can get you help."

"He doesn't need help!" Sarah screams and stands in front of me, pushing Tank away from me with all her strength. She takes his place. "He can't read or write, Reaper. It wasn't him because Tongue doesn't know how to do those things. I believe him."

The room falls silent, and all eyes are on me.

"Sarah…"

"I'm sorry, Tongue. I'm so sorry. I couldn't let them think you did it. I know you didn't. I had to defend you. I know you wouldn't hurt Daphne. You've changed since meeting her. I've seen it. You have to be honest."

"You promised," I say, broken as I stare at the person who is supposed to be my best friend.

"I know. I know, but now, your name is in the clear—" She reaches for my hand, but I pull away, glaring at her like I don't even know her.

"His name isn't clear yet. A few cops know about him. They will come sniffing around," Badge says. "I can take care of it, though. Going to NOLA wouldn't be such a bad idea until this all blows over, Tongue."

Doc is on the floor, examining Tank's wound. I want to roll my eyes. It isn't even that bad. A few stitches and he will be as good as new.

"I'm not leaving Daphne, but I'm wondering if I should leave you," I say the words to all of them and step on the note the killer left Daphne. "For all we know it's the Groundskeeper, and the first person you think of is me. I might be… I might be…" I stutter again, the scars across my tongue throbbing like they always do when I think I'm about to experience pain. "I'm the monster to you all. I can't be with people like that again."

"Tongue, we can talk about this—"

I don't give Reaper the chance to finish his sentence. I leave all of them behind, Sarah included. I hop on my bike, not bothering to put on my helmet, and I peel out of the parking lot. My comets must be aligned tonight because the gate is open, and I pull back on the throttle to get the fuck out of here.

They have a point. Going to NOLA would be the smart thing to do. I'd leave Daphne behind, and she'd be safe. I'd be with guys who are more like me, and I'd probably feel more accepted. Maybe the killer leaving tongues in Daphne's home will follow me since I seem to be the issue.

I'll leave.

I'll see Daphne one last time. I'll say goodbye to the woman I couldn't keep safe because I decided to go home instead of watching her. The only woman who has ever managed to let the man rise from under the blood-soaked killer will be a memory.

After time passes, I'll wonder if my crazy made her up in my mind, a figment of my imagination. It would make sense dreaming up someone I couldn't have because I hallucinated them. Actually, that's probably what happened because what woman in her right mind would touch herself to a monster hiding in the shadows of her home?

Even villains know love, but I'm no villain, am I?

I'm worse.

Maybe me and the Groundskeeper are more alike than I like to think.

He should lay me down six feet under again because that's right where I belong.

The closer to hell I am, the better off the world will be. The flames will eventually stop burning my soul, and darkness will be there. That's what's so great about shadows. They are always there to welcome me home.

CHAPTER SEVEN

Daphne

I WAKE WITH A START, SNAPPING MY EYES OPEN WHEN I FEEL HIM.

It's dark outside, and it only makes the shadows darker in the room since the lights aren't on. I can hear the doctors outside, the roll of a gurney, and the beep of my heart rate monitor. The doctors wanted to keep me overnight for observation because of the concussion I received, smacking my head against the wall.

Of course, the maniac who left a tongue in my apartment didn't hurt me; I had to go and hurt myself trying to get away.

Holy moly, speaking of my head—it really freaking hurts.

But knowing he's here is making me feel better.

"You're here," I say to the left corner of the room.

He's quiet, not confirming or denying his presence. He doesn't have to. Tongue's presence is enough to wake me up from a coma if I were in one.

Tears prickle my eyes when I think about what I saw in my apartment. I never want to go back there. My home, my sanctuary, it's ruined. I won't be able to look at it the same again. "Where were you? I thought you said you'd always be there. You weren't there. Someone—"

Silence.

"Talk to me!" I shout, commanding him to speak to me. "Talk to me, damn it! Talk. To. Me. Why are you doing this? God, if you don't want anything to do with me, just leave me alone. Just go. Go away. I can't do this anymore. I can't feel you and know you're there and nothing happens. You're... You're... You're..." I'm trying to find the right words to say, but I can't. How do I tell a ghost that I never want him to disappear? How do I tell him I like the feeling he gives me?

"You're not hiding in the dark. You aren't fading into the shadows; don't you get it?" I say to him, pushing my glasses in place as they slip. "You've become my shadow. I need you everywhere or..." Or I feel lost. "I sound insane." I chuckle and tug the blanket up to my chin. "I'm talking to someone who probably isn't even here."

"I'm here," he says. The rough dips in his voice have me snapping my head up from where I'm staring at my hands twisting together.

I close my eyes, and a tear drips down my cheek, relieved. "Where were you today? I was scared."

"I had to go see Reaper."

If I hadn't met the man, I would have thought Tongue meant meeting death, which I guess in a way, Reaper is. "That's the guy in charge, right?"

Tongue grunts in response, and for some reason, I expect him to come out of the corner, but he doesn't.

"Do you not feel safe with me? Is that why you never show your face? What are you hiding from?" I press a button on the remote that controls the bed, and it slowly moves into an upright position.

"I hide you from me."

I shake my head and reach for the light so I can see him.

"Don't," he says. "Don't turn on the light."

"I need to know you're real."

"If you knew me, you'd wish I wasn't."

"Why? Was it you? Did you break into my apartment and leave that..." Bile works its way up my throat when I remember the tongue dangling there, dripping blood. I never knew tongues were so long. I guess I learn something new every day.

"No. I'd never do that to you."

The way he says it leaves it open to interpretation. "But you'd do it to someone else?" I ask, not afraid of his answer but afraid for him.

"I don't... I don't do what that person did to you. I don't waste tongues. I don't use them as scare tactics. I am the scare tactic."

"Tongue," I repeat the road name out loud when it hits me how he must have earned that title. "That's what you do then? You cut out people's tongues and silence them?"

"Yes," he agrees quickly.

"You like it?"

"Yes."

I swallow, and the heart rate monitor speeds up when I hear the truth.

"Do you like to inflict pain?"

"Yes," he says without hesitation.

"Um..." I wipe my undereye and sniffle. "Do you like blood?"

He groans in a sick, twisted way, almost like it's pleasurable for him to think about. "Love it," he states, short and sweet.

"Will you ever stop?"

"No."

"Do you want to cut out my tongue? Is that why you're so interested in me?" I remember the first time we met, and he stared at my mouth. I thought he was looking at my lips, which I had silently praised myself for wearing the new lip gloss I'd bought the day before, thinking that was the reason he stared at me.

"No. I never want to hurt you. I love your tongue. It's pretty and pink. I like your voice. Your silence would be my tragedy," he says sadly. "I'm afraid if I stay around, I'll be your tragedy."

He's weird. By far, he's not normal.

And I want more of him. He's different than any other man I've ever met in my life.

"What's that supposed to mean? What are you going to do?"

"I should have never... I'm not a good man. You deserve more."

"What are you saying?"

"I'm saying I should've stayed outside the window of the bookstore. I should've left you alone." He moves from the corner by a step, but it's all I need to see a glimpse of his face from the streetlight shining through the window. His eyebrows are creased in worry or maybe pain; I can't tell since I can't see his entire face, but I can see the tattoos along his neck.

I bet all of his tattoos tell a million stories, and if it meant getting to know Tongue, I'd sit down and listen to every single one of them.

"You're leaving?" I cut to the chase when I realize where

this conversation is going. "Do you watch all girls you take a liking to from spooky corners, and once you've had your fill, leave?"

"No. Only you. But to get my fill? Never."

"Please," I beg. "Don't go."

"I have to if I want to keep you safe."

"Take me with you," I blurt, surprised by my outburst for a second.

He takes another step into the light, but only half of his face shows. The one eye I see is dark, matching the abyss around us, and the drag of something along the wall has my eyes falling to the area beside him. A glint of something metal scratches, carving a line as his body seems to vibrate. "Don't joke like that. You have no idea what you will get yourself into with me. I'm not... I'm not..." he stutters and then stabs the wall. "I'm not the kind of man who changes. I won't stop being who I am."

"And who are you?" I ask him, swinging my legs off the side of the bed to stand. My feet land on the cold tile floor, and I limp as I take my first step. My knee is sore, and I can hardly put my weight on it, but it's better than nothing.

"I'm the man who cuts out tongues—"

"No, that's what you do. *Who* are *you*?" I take another step forward. I'm so close I can smell the leather, the cologne, and the hint of smoke from the exhaust of his bike.

I've found peace in a man who is anything but peaceful.

"I-I'm a Ruthless King. I stay in a corner. I feed my swamp kitties. I—"

"You aren't telling me who you are, Tongue." I lift my hand to touch his chest, but he takes a step away from me, further into the shadow. I can no longer see him. "You don't know, do you?"

"There isn't much to know."

"I think that's a lie." I keep all of my weight on my other leg and take another step forward. If he doesn't want to come to me, I'll go to him. "I don't think you've been given a chance to figure yourself out. I think you're expected to do certain things, and now you think they define you."

Tongue falls quiet again, and the closer I get to him, the harder his breaths fan across my face. My hand caresses his massive chest, and his heart jackhammers against my palm.

Bang. Bang. Bang.

The beat is wild and untamed, and like him, it has no idea of its true purpose. My breath catches when I rub my hand up to his neck, finally able to touch him like I've wanted to since the day I spoke to him carrying that box.

He said it dripped blood.

I laughed it off, but knowing him now, he told me the truth.

"Are you afraid of me?" he asks, flattening the body of the blade against my arm. He slides it up and down my flesh. I thought feeling a knife against my skin would scare me.

But it feels good.

The metal is cold against my skin and a shiver of the unknown trembles beneath my flesh.

"No," I state, tilting my head back and exposing the vulnerable part of my throat. The tip of the knife presses under my chin, and I gasp.

"I could cut you," he says, but the statement is weak and falls on deaf ears. "I could do so many things to you before you wished for death. You'd scream, and I'd get hard because that's the kind of man I am, Daphne. Fear feeds me."

"You won't hurt me. I think you would've done it already. You're trying to scare me away."

"Is it working?"

"No."

"It should," he states, gliding the knife down to my chest. "I should. My club should scare you."

"If you leave, put me out of my misery," I sneer, pushing my chest into his weapon. "Because I don't want to spend the rest of my life searching for my knight in the dark. You've made me expect you everywhere I go. You can't leave me now."

"I'm no knight," he growls, removing the knife from my chest. Leather crinkles, and I imagine he's opening his cut to put the weapon away. "I'm a nightmare."

My fingers glide over his chest, and I close my eyes, trying to memorize the feel of him. He's all muscle. His pecs are huge and swollen, his stomach has divots, promising abs, and strength. He's pure protection, the deadliest weapon, the bullet after it leaves the gun. I can sense the wrath under his skin—it's black and sour, damned, and unable to be saved.

"You aren't my nightmare," I whisper, skimming my hand up to his chest and neck, gasping when I feel the heat of his skin. He is hot, burning alive from the inside out, but he stands calm and collected, as cold as ice.

Maybe he is from Hell, but even the Devil is an angel.

And if redemption isn't possible, then what has the world come to? I'm not asking him to change who he is; I'm just asking him to take a chance on me. I want him to come out of hiding. There is no reason for him to hide from me. Everything he exudes is everything my soul is aching for.

I don't do normal because I know deep down I'm not.

I want sinister and wicked things. Tongue can promise both.

The invisible flames dancing along his skin travel up my arm and through my body.

"Y-you ... have no ... idea ... what ... you're asking," he says between shaky breaths as my fingers dip into the small craters along his neck.

I wish I could see him, but I won't push him into the light if he isn't comfortable. I can explore him from here. We can get to know each other in blindness. "What's your name?" I question again, letting my hand drop to his heart. "Let me in, please." My forehead lands on his chest.

"You don't want to know me." His thick fingers drag along my chin, the rough violence of his skin scratches against mine, vowing nothing but kindness as he touches me. "So pretty," he maps my lips, outlining the round shape. "I'll never do anything in this life to deserve you."

His palm cups my neck, his right hand almost takes up the entire right side of my face, and I'm dizzy from being touched by poison, but somehow, I've managed to survive.

The toxins he spits, I'm immune to.

Opening my eyes, I know he's close because the scratch of his scruff rubs along my cheek.

"You smell so good," he growls, burying his nose in my hair.

His erection is pressed against my thigh, long, hard, and thick.

"Did I smell good the night you watched me touch myself?"

He nips my jaw. "Yes. You have no idea how much I wanted to taste you."

"Why didn't you?" I moan, rolling my head back as he glides his nose down my throat.

"Because I'll ruin you if given the chance. It's something I can't risk."

"I'm already ruined," I admit, tears soaring across my eyes. The ratio of how I hold myself together day by day to how many hours I search for him in a day is astronomical. One clearly outweighs the other.

"Then let me save you from me," he whispers against my lips, and right before I think he's about to kiss me, right as his mouth lands against mine, he's gone. "Tongue?" I call out to him, but the air is different. The electricity that tingles my skin has vanished. "No." I search for his chest again, to feel his warmth, but I fall forward, catching myself on the wall. "No!" I cry, frustrated and heartbroken because he left me.

He always leaves me.

I limp toward the lamp and turn it on. The yellow cast falls along the white floor, and tears drip from my eyes when I inspect the room only to find myself alone.

I drop to the bed and cry, big shoulder shaking sobs. I bury my face in the pillow, feeling more lost than I ever have before. This is what he does to me.

I wasn't lying when I said he has ruined me.

His presence is just as earthshattering as his absence. He empowers me, and when he leaves, the power causes the strength to crumble, and I'm left in the devastation of his debris.

"Why!" I scream, slashing my arm across the nightstand. The lamp flies through the air and unplugs, slamming against the wall. It shatters. Small glass pieces hit my arms, and a flurry of doctors rush into the room when they hear the noise. "Why did he do this to me? Why?" Why am I addicted to the presence of a ghost?

The overhead light flips on, and the female nurse hurries to my side, helping me lay in bed. "Shh, it's okay. I know. What happened to you was so scary. It's okay to have nightmares. I'll have the doctors give you something to relax. You're safe here, sweetheart. You're okay."

"I'm not," I cry, clawing at the skin covering my heart. "I'm not." Is this what Tongue meant by ruining me?

Why play with my mind only to leave me obsessed?

I feel like I'm experiencing a mental break.

Maybe he is someone that I've made up. Is he real?

"Shhhh, sweetheart. You'll feel the medicine take effect any moment now. You poor thing. It's okay. You sleep. Everything will be fine in the morning."

Everything will not be fine.

Nothing is fine.

There was a tongue in my apartment.

There was blood on my hands that didn't belong to me.

The man I want, the man I dream of, the man I talk to in the corner, doesn't exist.

I think I've made him up.

My eyes hood and begin to close, sinking into oblivion. I'm about to be trapped in darkness, and the only thing I can think about is Tongue. If he wants to live in my mind, if he wants to stay in the dark, then I'm going to join him, and I never want to find a way out.

He has to be real. I felt him under my fingers. I heard his voice. What I feel is real, even if he isn't.

"Has she taken her meds today?" the doctor asks the nurse as he flips through my file.

"I need him! I need him, please, please! Bring him to me, please," I cry as the sedative tries to take me under.

"There's no one else here, sweetheart. You're okay. You're okay."

"She isn't having an anxiety attack. It's her psychosis if she hasn't had her meds today."

"He was here. He was right here. In the corner," I explain, so they don't think I'm crazy. I'm not crazy. I'm not. He was here. I swear.

"Oh, sweet girl," the nurses croons at me, brushing her hands through my hair.

"Tongue. I need…" I slur, doing my best to force the words out from between my lips, but I fail.

My psychosis…

I haven't had an issue with that for a few years. Of course, it would come back to play from one interaction with a man I only met once.

Tongue has no idea, but I was ruined before I ever met him.

CHAPTER EIGHT

Tongue

I'M THE DEVIL SHE DOESN'T KNOW, AND SHE STILL GRIPS ME BY THE horns, uncaring of the warnings I've given her. She doesn't understand. She can't seem to wrap her mind around just how bad I am for her.

If I stand on the steps of a church, I'll burst into flames. My evil cannot be contained, but I have a feeling, if she allows, she'll be the closest to a holy experience I'll ever get.

She's a saint.

A sweet, innocent beautiful woman who loves books, who is educated and happy. I'll dumb her down, hold her back, and have her worried about me constantly.

Maybe I need to watch her from a further distance. No, I have to go away. I have to get the person threatening her to follow me. She's in danger because I took an interest in her.

I lay one hand on my knee and keep one hand on the

throttle. The wind blows through my hair, and it reminds me that when I get back, I'm going to cut it. Even though I'm leaving, I still want to be everything Daphne desires, so when I come back, and I will come back, she'll want me.

I'll kill the man who ruined her home and made her afraid, and then I'll come back. NOLA isn't my home, but maybe it's where I need to be to get some space from my brothers here. For the first time in my life, when the driveway comes to view, I don't want to turn left.

I don't want to go home.

I rev the engine, and the exhaust rumbles, a sound every biker has come to love.

Blum, blum, blum, blum, the bike growls like a beast between my legs. The vibrations travel up my thighs, tickling the heavy sack that's filled with cum. My cock is still hard and leaking from how close she was to me at the hospital.

I could feel the warmth between her legs, the tight peak of her nipples against my stomach and her skin. *Mmmm, fuck, her skin.* I could rub my hands all over her body for the rest of my life, and it wouldn't be long enough. She's soft, like those silk sheets my uncle used to lay me on, but she isn't tainted like those sheets. Daphne isn't ruined. She's new and fragile. She's so small. When my hand cupped her face, and I saw just how much power I have over her, my cock leaked, and I swear, I came a little in my jeans.

I could pin her down, flip her over, spank her ass and overpower her…

I could inflict pain on her if I wanted to.

But I don't have the urge.

Never.

I never want to see her hurt. I always thought if I ever had sex, the only way for me to get pleasure was for me to cut them or worse. Sexually, I didn't know who I was as a man because the only time I ever got hard was when I saw blood.

That's not the case.

I only want to lay her down and be gentle with her. I've never been gentle; I wonder if I have it in me to be as soft as she feels. I want to be. I want to try.

The pothole in the driveway yanks me out of my thoughts as my bike dips. The cool night of autumn turning into winter blows against my cheeks, causing them to be red and raw. At night, the desert gets cold, to the point where every time you breathe, a puff of smoke leaves your lips.

I pull up to the front of the clubhouse, away from the other bikes, and sit off to the side, alone. I stare at the place that's been my home for almost as long as I can remember. When I was taken from my uncle's house, I didn't get charged with his murder because it was self-defense, but I was put in a rehabilitation center to try to improve my social skills.

I was hopeless.

Officer Lionel ended up taking me in and calling in a favor to a friend in Vegas. We upped and moved, he got a job at the police department, and I found the Ruthless Kings as I became a man.

I haven't spoken to Lionel in years. I left the moment I could, and I never looked back. I thought I was with my own people, my own brand of fucking crazy, but that is far from the truth. I am the crazy here. I am the outsider. Yearning to belong is something that hasn't gone away; it's gotten worse over the years because I've noticed just how different I am.

I can't control my impulses.

No one understands.

I need to cut. Every tongue I remove is another way of defeating my uncle. Every drop of blood is one step closer to ridding the world of rancid human beings. I'm one of those people too, but my time will come when it's meant to; that's something I believe whole-heartedly.

Until then, I'll ride my bike, want a woman I can't have, and contemplate my life choices.

The soot from Skirt's house can still be smelt if I really concentrate. The maze is still to the right from Halloween, and I don't see it coming down anytime soon. People are healing, the members need time, and the kids like it.

I bet that's enough for Reaper to keep it.

Leaning my arms against the handlebars, I stare out over the open land and the homes being built. We have really made something out of ourselves.

"Not wanting to go inside?"

I turn half my body and see Moretti smoking a cigarette. He looks like hell. He's been avoiding seeing his brother and his daughter because he can't remember them. I think he will one day, but he has his process he has to go through. In the meantime, he's being a prickly asshole.

"Not really," I answer simply, wishing I had a flask in my cut pocket.

"I heard you can't read and write," he states, blowing out smoke from between his lips. "That fucking sucks."

I grit my teeth together and swing my leg over the bike. If there's one thing I never want to talk about, it's my stupidity.

"How have you gotten through life?"

I crack my neck and pull out my knife. "Don't tempt me, Moretti. I've had a long few days. If I have to cut your tongue out to make you stop speaking, I will."

"Got it. Don't want to talk about it." He chuckles, throwing the butt of the cigarette on the ground. He smashes it with his foot. "I don't know how I got through life if it makes you feel any better. I can't remember a damn thing."

"It doesn't make me feel better," I say honestly.

"You're an asshole."

I sling my knife around before sliding it into my back pocket. "So I've heard." Heat lightning flashes across the sky. The small clouds rolling in might bring rain, but I doubt it. We don't get much of that around here.

Walking away, my boots slide against the desert floor, kicking rocks and broken beer bottles.

"I'm fine; thanks for asking," Moretti yells behind me.

My hand grabs the rail of the porch, and I turn to look over my shoulder. "I didn't ask," I state, not understanding why people are so damn sensitive about themselves. The steps creak as I pound up them. I stare at the door, wondering what I'm going to do when I enter. I don't have much time to think about it because the door swings open, and a crying Sarah appears.

Now this is where I become sensitive. Leaving her will be one of the hardest things I've ever had to do, behind leaving Daphne. Sarah's hair is up on top of her head, wrapped up in one of those messy buns. A few pieces of blonde frame her face, and her brown eyes are dipped in honey right now because of those tears. The tip of her nose is pink, and her bottom lip is swollen from where she chews on it while she cries.

"Tongue! Where have you been? You left. You can't leave like that again. Please, you can't leave."

"Sarah…" Maizey's sweet, high-pitched voice comes from beside Sarah. Maizey wraps her arms around Sarah's leg, then presses her cheek against Sarah's thigh. "Hi, Tongue. How are you?"

"I'm okay," I say, squatting to meet her big brown eyes. "You've grown since the last time I saw you."

"I'm a big girl," she says proudly.

"Yeah, you are. You'll be wielding your knife in no time," I tell her.

She grins, her front tooth missing as her eyes widen. She starts to bounce with excitement. "Really? Can you make it for me?"

"That's up to Sarah," I say, standing to my full height.

"Maybe when you're a little older." Sarah sniffles, rubbing her cheeks on her shoulders. She opens the door wider, and I make my way in. There aren't any cut-sluts here right now. Ever since Candy and Jasmine died, they've been too scared to come around. I'm alright with it. I think cut-sluts are a damn drain.

Well, there is Becks. She hasn't been around in a while because she's off at some massage retreat. I miss her. She's good at really getting in the muscle and working out the knots. I hope she's back before Christmas. I'm making her a knife.

There isn't anyone here as I walk through the living room. The TV is off. The dogs are on the couches. Yeti is snuggled up next to Lady. Tyrant is on his back, balls out, and Chaos has his nose buried in Tyrant's ass. Whatever floats their boats. I don't think I'd like the smell of ass.

Well, maybe if it was Daphne's ass...

I hear voices coming from the kitchen and keep my feet light, so I don't make a sound. I give Sarah one last look as she sits on the couch with Maizey. I stop in the hallway and step into one of the corners, so I can listen in like I always do. I take my knife out again and rub my fingers against the silver. My eyes land on the kitchen table where most of the guys are. They all seem to be looking at something, but from here, I can't tell what they are looking at.

"What are we going to do?" Poodle asks, flipping another page.

"Aye, my god, Reaper, this is horrible." Skirt leans back in his chair, and he has his daughter strapped to his chest. "My God, how does he function?"

I bend my head forward to listen to them, curious at who they're talking about.

"If this was his life, it's no wonder he can't read or write. We have to help him, Reaper." Tool tosses a book on the table and reaches to his left and grabs another.

"His drawings are in amazing detail. I had no idea he was so talented," Patrick states, hissing when he flips to a certain page.

It takes me a few moments to catch on when I realize the books they are looking at and the person they are talking about is me. I watch as they stare at my life's horrors, judging me. Sweat and panic grip my heart, my lungs, and my brain. I can't breathe. Fuck, they know. They know!

"Oh my god," Slingshot tosses the journal across the table and buries his face in his hands, shaking his head. "This couldn't have happened to him. We can't be looking at this. We are invading his privacy."

"I need to know what we're dealing with. Tongue has gone off the deep end. If it's him cutting those tongues out and scaring that poor girl..."

"It isn't. I think he likes her."

"I don't think he knows how to love," Badge states, sighing, staring at a page in my journal.

His words take my breath. It's been a long time since something has hurt so damn bad. They don't think I'm capable of love. Am I that much of a monster? A drop of water landing on my hand takes my attention away from them.

I'm crying ... I think. Again.

I don't understand why.

Ever since I've met Daphne, there has been this unwinding of pressure in my chest. I'm a lock, and I threw away the key to make sure I never felt a damn thing again.

But Daphne found the key and slid it into my chest, releasing years of suppressed emotions.

"A person who went through what he went through has severe psychological issues. I'm not surprised he is the way he is, but that doesn't mean he doesn't know how to love. Everyone loves differently, in their own way," Doc inserts what he thinks.

They went through my things.

How did they open my file cabinet? They can't without the key; unless Tool somehow found a way.

"His uncle was a monster," Tank says, leaning forward next to Bullseye. I'm surprised Tank cares after what I pulled earlier. Bullseye isn't doing too well since he got diagnosed with diabetes. He hasn't been taking care of his sugar, and he has lost a bit of weight and seems sorta out of it. He's in denial.

"I say we kill him," Bullseye says, polishing a dart.

"Tongue?" Slingshot gasps in horror at what Bullseye just said.

Like they could. I'd like to see them try.

Bullseye smacks Slingshot on the head. "His uncle, idiot. Tongue is one of us. I'm worried now. I didn't know ... I didn't know any of this," he says sadly, picking up one of the journals. "He must have been so angry."

"He is still angry. Can't you tell?" Tool scoffs.

"Looks like he beat us to killing his uncle." Reaper throws down the journal that shows the drawing of what I did to my uncle.

Tool whistles. "He cut out his tongue."

"Good," Doc agrees, and the guys around the table nod.

"Oh. Oh! This must be when he met Daphne. Aw, that's…" Slingshot turns the page and blushes. "Detailed."

I step out of the shadows and snatch the journal from his hand, slamming it shut. I have nothing to say to them. I feel betrayed. I'm to the point where I'm about to kill all of them. They want to peek into my past, fine. They want to judge me, feel sorry for me, wonder what to do with me, fine.

But they will not look at Daphne.

Daphne is mine. She's my heaven to look at, my paradise, my escape from my fucked-up reality.

"Tongue—"

"Don't," I cut Reaper off and gather my journals. I snatch another from Bullseye's hand, then one out of Doc's, feeling frustrated and out of my depth. I've never been so exposed. "Don't any of you fucking dare try to talk to me after this."

"I needed answers," Reaper says, a slight regret on his face.

"Answers? You wanted answers? For what? To understand me. You never had a prob-problem…. You never…"

"Take your time," Reaper says kindly, without agitation.

"Don't. Don't you dare fucking do that!" I shout, slamming my knife against the table near his hand. "Don't condescend me. You didn't even know… You didn't…." I try to take a deep breath, to relax, and remind myself I only stutter when I get ahead of myself. It isn't even a real stutter. I'm thrown back to the past when I had to explain myself to my uncle with a sore tongue. "Don't you fucking dare act like you give a damn now when both of us know better."

"Tongue, I care. I'm … I'm so sorry this happened to you. You've detailed your life with extraordinary talent."

I scoff, rubbing my fingers over the front of a leather cover. This journal in my hands shows what my uncle did to me. I take my knife out, lay the journal on the table, and puncture it as if it had a heart. The knife slices through effortlessly, sliding to the other end of the journal, and the tip of the blade lodges in the table. "Talent? Are you fucking kidding?"

Now I'm getting angry.

"You went through my journals!" I slam my fist on the counter, and Slingshot flinches. "You had no right! None! You just don't trust me, so you took it upon yourself to invade my privacy. These were my fucking secrets—mine!" I rip the knife away from the journal and charge Reaper, slamming him against the counter. The knife hovers just above his neck, and he doesn't move; he doesn't blink.

"You're right," he says.

"You doubted me."

"I know."

Tool stands next to Reaper, but the Prez holds up his hand to stop Tool from encroaching on us.

"You don't share. The girl, what happened in her apartment, I needed to make sure."

"You should have trusted me. Instead you went through my journals," my voice cracks, knowing what they saw. A tear slips down my cheek, and my chest feels … open. It's new to me. "You have no idea how out of place you are. I should kill you!"

"You would do that to Sarah?" he asks, leaning his neck into the blade.

Would I do it?

I'd think about it for a minute.

I know at the end of the day; I wouldn't do it.

"Melissa, Joanna, Dawn, not now," Skirt says to the girls who enter the kitchen from the hallway.

"What's going on? What are these?" Melissa asks, picking up a journal without thinking and opens it. "Oh, wow, she's really pretty. Who drew these? They are so talented."

I snatch the journal away from her, but as soon as I do, Dawn picks one up, then Joanna. I can't stop them all.

"You drew because you couldn't write," Reaper states to me.

"Leave me alone."

"You drew because you didn't know how to read," Slingshot says next.

"Shut up! You don't know anything! You don't fucking know!" I scream, slamming my fist on the table again. The journals bounce in the air from the force, but the men are blurry.

Reaper takes the journal that I took from Melissa and opens it to the first picture of Daphne. She's asleep, tangled in blankets, with a slight smile on her face. Her hair is cascading across the other pillow, where I deserve to be.

"You follow her. You watch her because you don't know how else to be."

"You don't fucking know anything!" I slam my fist against Reaper's face, unable to hold back my rage. "No one knows anything!"

"Tongue, you crazy fucking bastard. Get off him," Tool bellows, wrapping his arms around my torso, but he's nowhere near strong enough to take me down. I rip the knife from the journal on the table and rear it back, slamming Tool in the bicep with it.

"Fuck!" he cries, stumbling back and cradling his injured arm.

Bullseye tackles me next, then Slingshot holds me down, along with Knives. Tool stands over me, a stream of blood staining his flesh. "That's what you get for going through my shit," I snarl at him as three men hold me down.

"We aren't your enemy," Reaper tells me, kneeling by my head. I turn it back and forth, feeling crowded. Slingshot's face comes closer to mine, and it morphs into my uncle's. He's laughing at me. I can feel the cigarette ashes falling and searing my skin.

"You're a fucking idiot, aren't you? Always so dumb. You make it easy; you know that?"

"Get off me! Get off!" I shout, kicking and bucking.

"Tongue, you're okay."

"You need to step away from him, Reaper, Slingshot, Knives, Bullseye. Step away," Doc warns, slowly inching away from me.

"I can't wait to get my hands on that filthy little ass of yours, Wayne. If you'd listen. That is all it takes. You can't even call me by Justine, no matter how many times I've told you. Roll over."

"Get off." I tug against his hands, nervous and afraid. "Please, stop," I croak, breaking like I did when I was twelve.

"God, are you people deaf? Get off him!"

"Bend over and spread your cheeks."

No.

With one last effort, I roar, slinging my uncle off me. Everything is blurry. I see faces. They form into my uncle, laughing at me, curlers in his hair, and a silk robe hanging off his shoulders.

"Get on your knees. Suck my cock, Wayne."

"No!" I take my knife and bury it in his stomach, killing him once and for all. "You fucking bastard." A satisfied grin takes over my face, and the haze around my eyes starts to fade.

"No! What did you do? What did you do?" Reaper yells in my ear, and the flurry of chaos whips me back into reality.

I blink, the sweat stinging my eyes, and when I come back to real life, I see Sarah in front of me, hands cupped over her stomach, and blood spilling from her mouth. "No," I whisper. "No!" I shout and lurch for her, but Reaper pushes me away as he catches Sarah as her knees buckle.

"Sarah, I'm... I'm-I'm so sorry. I didn't .... know it was you." I fall to the ground, and Reaper holds his hand over the knife, surrounding the wound, but blood flows in thick streams over his hand. "Is she going to be okay?" The tears that leak from my eyes make sense now. "Doc! Doc, please, help her."

Everyone is screaming. The ol' ladies are crying, and Reaper is crooning to Sarah, telling her to hang on. Maizey is screaming, the dogs are barking, but all I can see is Sarah's eyes as they grow glassier and more vacant.

"You can't die, okay? You can't die, Doll. I need you here. I need you more than fucking anything, please," Reaper begs her, holding her limp body.

"Reaper," she gasps. "Don't—" Sarah wheezes. "Don't blame—"

"Shhh, it's okay. Don't talk. Just focus on breathing for me, okay? That's all I need you to do."

Doc swings open the basement door, and a few of the kids from NOLA run up the steps, chuckling until they see Sarah.

She's the only real mother here, and they immediately burst into tears.

"Get them out of here! Get them out!" Reaper orders, slinging a bloody hand in the air.

Slingshot gathers the two boys and ushers them down the hall where the gym is. Tank follows, along with Braveheart. Bullseye still has a tight grip on my arms, but he doesn't need to worry about holding me.

"Sarah," I crawl toward her just as Doc squats and evaluates her.

"Don't move the knife. I need it to stay inside. It's helping her not to bleed out."

"Not bleed out! Look at the blood. She is bleeding out. I can't lose her, Doc; I can't lose her. Please," Reaper begs, and the only time I ever see the Prez tear up is when Sarah's life is jeopardized. "Save her."

Doc slides his arms under her and stands, disappearing down the steps where his operating room is.

Reaper is on the ground, sliding his hand through the blood on the floor. Her blood. It's the first time I feel sick at the sight of it. I want to puke.

"If she dies, I'll kill you, Tongue." Reaper's cold eyes land on me and fear seeps into my core. I'm not afraid of anything, but right now, I have every reason to be. "I'll cut out your tongue and feed it to your fucking swamp kitties. You hear me, Tongue?"

"I didn't know. I-I didn't know it was her. I thought..."

"I don't give a fuck what you thought!" Reaper launches himself at me, wrapping his blood-soaked hands around my throat and squeezing.

"Get off him, Reaper! He didn't know. It's our fault. It's

our fault. Doc told us to stop," Tool tries to pull the Prez off me with his good arm, but it isn't enough. I'm not going to fight Reaper to survive.

"He was in a flashback; it was an accident," Bullseye defends me.

"Don't," I wheeze through choked and broken breaths. "Make … excuses." I cough, letting my hands fall to the floor in defeat.

"No." Poodle opens a journal and shoves it in Reaper's face. "Let him go." Poodle comes to my defense.

Reaper stares at the journal and let's go of my neck, snatching it from Poodle's hand. The blood from his fingers transfers to the paper, and a tear falls down his cheek. "Go to her," Reaper says, laying the journal flat against my chest. "I don't want you here for a while. When you come back, you'll get your punishment."

I'll take whatever he decides to give me.

I deserve it after that. There is no forgiveness in killing my best friend.

I'll go.

And this time, I won't come back.

CHAPTER NINE

Daphne

"**D**APHNE? DAPHNE? OH MY GOD, THANK GOODNESS you're awake. I've been worried sick," my Aunt Tina says, sitting next to the hospital bed and waking me up by brushing my hair. It takes me a minute to realize where I am. "I got on the first flight I could when the hospital called me. I can't believe someone broke into your apartment. They said the stress made you have one of your episodes. Are you okay, sweetie? Any more hallucinations since last night?"

I rub my eyes, blinking away the sleep, and sit up. The mattress is hard and uncomfortable. "I don't think so. I feel a lot better. They must have given me medication this morning." The sun is shining in the room, illuminating all the shadows, and Tongue isn't there. "I need to call the bookstore and tell Andrew what happened."

"He knows. He's already been by. He left you flowers. He's a handsome guy. Is he the one that you've been … you know," Aunt Tina wiggles her eyebrows and nudges my arm with her elbow.

"No, Aunt Tina. Andrew is a great boss, but he is … boring."

Aunt Tina's hands hold mine, and she pats them in concern. "Sweetie, you need boring. I'm worried about you. Your psychosis—"

"Is fine. It's under control. A lot happened out of the norm yesterday, and lately in general. I've been under more stress. I'm okay. I promise."

"I'm going to stay." Aunt Tina stands and walks toward the window, spreading the curtains apart to allow more sunlight in. "You need me here, and you aren't going back to that damn apartment of yours. You can forget that. That fucking freak. I swear, they better find the guy who did that. What if he's following you?"

Then I guess I'm screwed.

"Tina Mullins?" a nurse stops in the doorway, holding a clipboard. "We have a few questions about insurance."

"Sure," Aunt Tina tells her, straightening her spine. Her brown hair is over her shoulder in a long braid, and she gives me a sweet smile. "I'll be back. Don't go anywhere." She pats my ankle, then gives me a wink. "Maybe there are some single hot doctors out there." She tugs the front of her shirt down so more of her cleavage shows. "Wish me luck."

"Good luck." I give her two thumbs-up. Only she would be on the prowl while I'm in the damn hospital. I don't know how to tell her that I don't want to stay with her. The last thing I want is to be kicked out of my apartment, my home. I moved to Vegas to prove to my dad that I can live a normal life with my… issue.

TONGUE

I hate being reminded of my psychosis. My mental illness was at its worst when I was a teenager, but as I got older and accepted my fate, the doctors put me on medication, and I've lived a great life. There are good days and bad days just like with anything, and lately things have been amazing, until Tongue.

I rub my temples, annoyed at myself. It has to be my psychosis. I never see him out in the light and during the day except for that one time. One time is all it took for him to set his boughs in my mind, anchoring himself to my psyche.

I'm not having an episode.

Tongue is my psychotic break, and the longer I live without him, the worse the break gets.

"Are you ready?" Aunt Tina struts into the room, her black high heels clicking against the floor. "I brought you a change of clothes. Don't worry. You'll be out of that hospital gown in no time." She checks her watch as if she's about to be late for something and helps me stand. I hate feeling like a burden. It's one of the main reasons I moved away from my dad. I've always been a burden because of my psychosis.

You know what? None of this would have happened if I'd never met Tongue. I wouldn't be questioning myself. My home would be safe. I wouldn't be in this damn hospital, and what's even worse is I wouldn't be angry anymore if he just showed up and stayed.

"Hey, why the sad face? It's going to be okay. If you want, we will get you some help if you're not feeling like yourself."

I hold onto her shoulder as she tugs the sweatpants up my swollen knee. "No, I'm fine. Just tired. I'm ready to go back to sleep. You don't have to worry about me, you know. If you have somewhere to be, go. I'll be fine once I'm in the house."

I switch hands and press my weight against her other shoulder while she pulls my pants up and secures them around my hips.

"Don't be ridiculous. I'm not going anywhere. I'm going to take care of you. You're my favorite person in the world. I know I'm not here all the time, but it doesn't mean I don't love you."

I whip my head back and stare at her openmouthed, but she can see my face since she's pulling a shirt over my head. "I know that. I love you too. I'm saying don't feel obligated. I'm a grown woman. I don't have a huge handicap. I feel like you think I'm incapable, and I'm not."

"I know. I just worry about you; that's all."

I slide my flip flops on and stare into the corner one last time as I slip on my cardigan. It's cold in the hospital.

Or maybe Tongue brings winter, freezing life around me as I wait for him to come back to me. The corner is lonely, and I wait for my mind to conjure him up, but he isn't there. No matter how hard I try to focus, his darkness isn't here.

The nurse rolls in a wheelchair, and I sit down, the leather seat giving under my weight. Aunt Tina pats my arm, strolls over to the nurse outside of the door, and they share whispers. I try to listen, but I can't hear any words. I know what she's talking to the nurse about, and I'm worried Aunt Tina is going to suggest that I get committed for a few weeks.

I swear, if she does that, I'll never forgive her.

"Okay, are you ready?" She gives me a big, bright smile, her dimples peeking out on either side of her cheeks.

"I was ready yesterday." I'm willing to do anything to get me out of this room.

The corners are haunted, and yet the ghost isn't here.

"I bet. Hospitals are a drag," she says, wheeling me down

the hallway. "Want to have some fun?" she leans down and whispers in my ear.

"Always," I say out of the side of my mouth, keeping a smile on my face as doctors give us curious looks.

She speeds up her pace. We pass nurses, and one doctor jumps out of our way, dropping a medical chart. Aunt Tina doesn't apologize. She's running now, and if she lets go of the wheelchair, I'm going to go flying.

"Hey! You can't do that here," an overweight security guard yells at us as we zoom by him.

"Oh, crap. He's running after us!" Aunt Tina screeches, and right as we make it out of the double doors of the hospital, the roaring grumbles of Harley Davidsons have me searching the parking lot.

I'm searching for a speck of chrome, the shine of smooth black, a man in leather, but too many cars are in the way.

"That was fun…" Aunt Tina slows down, gasping for air.

"Hey! We need that wheelchair back," the security guard shouts at us as he leans against a supportive white beam. He holds his side from a cramp, and even from the parking lot, I can see the sweat shining on his bald forehead.

"Oh, right." Aunt Tina rolls her eyes. "They act like they don't have plenty of these pieces of crap. I mean look, the wheel is fucking rusted. It's a lawsuit waiting to happen." She holds up her finger to the guard, telling him to hold on a moment. "Sorry, I need to get my *injured* niece into the car. It will only take a moment." She fishes for the keys in her blue tote and points the black key fob to her Lexus. The clicks tell me the car is unlocked, and Aunt Tina opens the passenger side door for me. She lifts me up and supports me as I stand. My hand grabs the plastic 'oh-shit' handle to pull myself into the seat. "I'm going to roll that security guard over with this damn wheelchair."

"Aunt Tina!" I scold her and click my seatbelt in place.

"What? He was rushing us. I don't like to be rushed." She shuts the door, and I watch out the window as she approaches the guard who is now sitting on the curb. "Yoo-hoo! Mr. Security Guard." She waves at him, hiking her purse up on her shoulder.

"She's impossible," I mumble under my breath.

"You want your wheelchair? Go fucking get it, dick!"

She pushes the chair, and it rolls away from us and even farther away from the guard. He stands and runs after it, his pants falling down his ass, showing the top of his butt crack.

Aunt Tina spins around, dark hair flowing over her shoulders, and her plump lips spread into a wicked grin. She dusts off her hands. "All in a day's work."

"You're horrible," I mouth from inside the car.

She shrugs, uncaring, and walks around to get into the driver's seat. That's when my eyes catch a sea of black entering the hospital. I sit forward, staring straight ahead to see if I can recognize any of the men, but all I see before the automatic doors close is the skull.

"What is it? Did you forget something?" Aunt Tina asks as she starts the car by pressing a single red button.

"No, I just thought I saw someone I knew. It's nothing."

"Oh, okay. As long as you're sure," she says as she backs out of the parking space, then puts the car in drive.

I lay my head against the window, the warmth of the sun teasing the glass. It makes me sleepy. The flowers Andrew bought me sit in my lap, and as I stare at them, I wish they were from Tongue.

A man who doesn't exist.

I rub a rose petal with my thumb, and my brows crease when I see a black card nestled in the roses. That's not like Andrew. Red and black are too gloomy for him. He'd never choose those colors. He likes muted tones, beige, brown, navy blue, things like that. I pinch it off the tiny piece of clear plastic and open the small envelope. I inch the card out and grin when I see the simple statement.

"I'm always watching you."

It's Tongue.

I know it is.

Tucking the card back in the envelope, I shove the sleek, expensive paper in my pocket and let my eyes fall closed. The flowers smell sweeter now that I know they are from Tongue. I'm happier. This makes him real. I'm not imagining him. My psychosis isn't messing with me. The last episode I can remember having is five years ago where I was speaking incoherently. My aunt couldn't understand what I was saying, and I pointed to the ceiling, trying to talk about the stars shining, but apparently, that wasn't what I said.

Psychosis wasn't always a part of who I was. I used to be normal, but trauma affects everyone differently, and for me, sometimes I lose touch with reality. Sometimes, it isn't so bad. Whatever my mind decides to conjure up can be a vacation from real life. I've never imagined something violent. It's almost as if I ate a bunch of pot brownies, and my mind goes on a trip.

What's the trauma?

I wish I knew.

No one seems to know. The doctor says my brain is blocking it out, so I can live a normal life.

If he calls psychosis normal…

The car comes to a slow stop, and in the distance, I think

I hear the snarling of a motorcycle, but when I peer over my shoulder to see out of the back window, there's nothing there.

Nothing ever is.

Nothing ever will be.

Then I stare at the roses and know I have to be wrong.

"Okay, we are here," Aunt Tina says as she parks in her driveway.

It's been a while since I've been here, but I'm still blown away by how large the house is. It's a Spanish style home, white with dark red shutters. A bunch of cacti lines her sidewalk, and she has a koi pond in her yard since she can't grow grass. The bench is still there, and I grin knowing my initials are still carved in the wood from when I was seventeen.

"For someone who lives on their own, I still don't understand the massive house, Aunt Tina."

"Well, maybe I won't always be alone. Maybe I'll have my own harem of hot, sexy men, and they will need rooms, right?" she teases, giving me a wink before she exits the car.

"She's a mess." I follow her with my eyes as she rounds the car and opens the door. Her hands are cold as she helps me up and out of the low Lexus. The air is sticky with humidity, and the sun is no longer shining because it has been replaced with gray skies promising rain.

It hasn't rained in the desert in a while. We need it.

"Come on. Let's get you set up in bed, and you can get some rest. I need to call the cop who came by the hospital. He said he needed to speak to you. Officer … Hod … something," Aunt Tina informs me, wrapping her arm around my waist to take the brunt of my weight.

"Hodder? He was the cop that found me at the bottom of the steps."

126

"He's handsome."

"You think everyone is handsome."

"Hey, when you get to be my age, you can't be picky."

"You're young, Aunt Tina," I remind her. She's only in her forties.

"Yeah, but these boobs aren't getting any higher."

"Wha…" I stop walking and stare at her in shock, then burst out laughing. "You're too much, Aunt Tina."

"You love me."

"If only I had better judgment."

"Brat. You can help yourself to the bed." She lets go of me, and I teeter, grasping tight to the vase, so the flowers don't spill.

"Okay, I'm sorry. I'm sorry," I chuckle, reaching out to her before I fall over and bruise my other knee.

With a loving smile, she helps me to the guest bedroom on the main floor. I slide my bad leg across the beautiful oak floors, and when we get to the teal door, I hold my breath thinking I'm about to see a whole new world. I get that way every time I enter the guest bedroom. The hinges squeak as the door flings open, and I hop away from Aunt Tina's tight grip and cold hands, place the vase on the nightstand, then plop on the bed.

"It's like floating on a cloud," I say.

She fluffs a few pillows and stuffs them under my leg to keep it elevated, then pulls the fluffy comforter up and over my body, tucking it under my chin. She sits on the edge of the bed and traces the bruises on my forehead gently. Tears swarm her eyes, and I reach up and take her hand in mine.

"I'm okay."

"I know," she looks down, then away. She focuses out the window and presses my hand against her cheek. "You're all I have. I worry about you. And now…" She sniffles and let's go of my hand to wipe under her eyes. "Look at me; I'm a mess." She bends down and kisses me on the cheek. "Get some rest, okay? If you need me, scream. The walls are thick. I won't be able to hear you."

"I'll text you instead. Okay?"

She nods, still trying to hold herself together. She still won't look at me.

"I love you, Aunt Tina. Thank you."

"I love you too, Daphne. Your mom would have been very proud of you."

I don't talk about my mom. She killed herself when I was eight-years-old, and I don't know why. She's the one topic I never want to talk about. "I'm really tired. I think I'm going to go to bed."

Aunt Tina wants to say more, but she knows better. I'll get angry talking about my mom, and I don't have the energy to be mad.

"Sure. Sleep well, sweetie." Aunt Tina presses a kiss on my cheek and gently closes the door behind her.

I let out a huge breath, tuck my hands under my cheek, and stare at the roses on the nightstand.

Roses are red...

The note I was left enters my mind as I stare at the vibrant red petals and bright green stems. The beauty is a contradiction to the painful thorns decorating the side. So enthralling with the rich color, yet so daring. A droplet of water pops on a thorn as it tries to drip, proving the danger that resides in such an elegant flower.

They remind me of someone.

Tongue is a red rose dipped in thorns, and the only way to get to his heart is to prick my fingers and bleed.

CHAPTER TEN

Tongue

THE VALLEY OF DEATH ISN'T AS DARK AS PEOPLE THINK. IT ISN'T the valley that's so dangerous; it's the souls of the dead that linger. I believe there is more to this world than we know and not accepting it will lead us to be surprised with how we die, what we see in the afterlife, or the challenges we face.

See, I'm not surprised about anything I've ever done. All the people I've killed, all the shadows I've haunted, all the blood I've spilt—I expected. But there are two things that have happened recently that I have not understood.

Daphne and Sarah.

Sarah.

God, I stabbed her. I'll never forgive myself if she dies. I'll walk myself into the swamp in NOLA and let the swamp kitties feast on me, and then I hope my soul finds its way to the valley of death where I'll linger forever without peace.

I'm standing outside of Daphne's aunt's house, knowing my only form of comfort is behind those walls. I want to go inside; I want to say goodbye because I'm leaving, and I don't know when I'll be back. Reaper doesn't want me around the clubhouse right now, and all I can stare at is the blood on my hands.

It's never bothered me before. I love blood. I love how seductive it is as I watch it flow. I love the smell, even the taste.

But this is Sarah's blood, the blood of an innocent. The blood of my best friend. I almost can't fully think of a proper thought. My phone buzzes, and I dip in my pocket and grab it, swiping the screen. I'm hoping it's one of the guys to let me know how Sarah is doing, but it isn't.

It's a picture of one of my swamp kitties in NOLA. Gator is sitting next to the beast, petting its head, and giving me a thumbs-up. I look for any amount of happiness inside me when I see the picture, but I don't feel anything. I press the button that takes me to my home screen, and I press the number three that calls Slingshot.

"Hey, it's Slingshot, leave a message or don't. I don't give a fuck." The beep after that has me hanging up, and I press the palms of my hands against my eyes, feeling a fucking break coming on. I need to leave. What if I hurt Daphne next?

I cut through the trees, one of the only woods that Vegas has, and keep to the shadows. A gust of wind blows in my face, rustling my hair, and it reminds me that I haven't cut it yet. I whip out my knife, grab a chunk, and slice. I let the hair fall from my hands and do the same to the other side. I grab the last piece of hair in the back and cut it, watching it fall to the ground. I run my hand through it and feel that it is uneven.

Who cares?

Daphne will like it, and she will see how much I tried for her before I have to go away.

Just a quick goodbye, that's all. I'll go inside, say my goodbyes, and leave. It's that simple. I can do that. I can have some form of control. I check my watch and turn the side on, letting the face become green and it reads...

Three? I think. And since it's dark it means it is three in the morning, not three in the afternoon. Everyone should be asleep. I inch out of the trees and creep around the side of the house. My boots crunch against the rocks, the stars are out, twinkling false wishes, and the moon is high, promising deceit.

When I get to the back door, I grip the handle, and turn it as hard as I can, breaking it. The door opens, welcoming me into a home that isn't mine, and I step inside. The floorboards creak from my weight, and I shut the door behind me, but it opens again.

Annoyed, I push it closed.

It opens.

I close it.

The creak tells me it opens ... again.

I growl at it, take my knife out, the widest blade I own, and stab it between the door and the trim. I grin, satisfied with myself. *Fucking doors.*

But then I'm reminded of the blood on my hands, and the smile fades. I'm not allowed to smile. I'm not allowed to feel happiness, not when my best friend is hanging on for dear life. I glance to the right and notice the kitchen. I see the block of knives, and I'm tempted to take one for my personal collection but think better of it.

I have plenty.

I take a step forward, entering the living room since it's an open space. There's a big sofa, a sectional, and a TV that takes up the size of the wall. On the far side of the room, there is a huge spiral staircase, but I remember her limping at the hospital, so I don't think she'd be upstairs. Looking left, I see another hallway and disappear into it, becoming one with the darkness. My heart pounds, adrenaline rushes, and the quiet ignites my temptation to cause pain.

That's what's so beautiful about silence; just because it's quiet, doesn't mean something heinous isn't happening. Maybe the reason why someone can't scream is because someone like me ripped their tongue out.

I'm usually that something heinous.

But right now, I'm lost.

My mind, my heart, my soul, everything I thought I knew I was, everything I am, what's it for? Am I made for anything else except a killer with blood-caked hands?

Maybe in another life, I could be made for Daphne.

I open one bedroom door to find it empty and stare at the other end of the hall. That is where she has to be. With determined strides, I march down the hall and push the door open since it isn't closed all the way. The room is drowned in night, and the moon is shining through the sheer curtains. It's as if a spotlight is being shined on the object of my obsession. She's laying in the middle of the bed, and she's mumbling something again.

I close the door to her room and lock it, wanting to be alone and uninterrupted. I tilt my head to the side, admiring the curves of her body the comforter gets to touch. I step forward, and there it is again, that deep yearning for something more than I've ever been.

Bending down, I take one of my bloody hands and pick

up her hair, bringing it to my nose so I can smell her. My cock hardens when I get a whiff of coconut and sunlight. She smells like the beach, and I want to lay in her waters for the rest of my life. I rub my face against the soft strands, grunting when my erection thickens. She feels so good. I want to feel the strands tickle my chest as she licks down my pecs while teasing a knife against my skin.

She whimpers in her sleep, and I let go of her hair to not wake her. I let out a haunted breath and turn away from her beautiful, porcelain face. That's when I see the roses. Who the fuck gave her those? Those were not there when I visited her in the hospital. Fuck, why didn't I think of bringing her flowers? Women like flowers.

I can give her a knife. I'll make one for her. She'll like it. And she'll be able to protect herself. Flowers fucking die. How is that a good gesture to get well? A knife is much better, and she needs protecting. Daphne falls down the damn steps. She needs all the help she can get.

Maybe...

Maybe I can slide in against her. To hold her. To know what it's like. I've never held someone before, not like how I want to hold Daphne. I walk around to the other end of the bed, keeping my eyes locked on her prone form, never wanting to miss a second of her chest rising and falling. I unlace my boots and kick them off, deciding if I do this farewell, I'm going to do it the right way.

A horrid thought flashes in my mind.

What if I kill her so she can't be with anyone else, and then I kill myself? Then we can be together forever without the stressors of life holding us down. We can haunt the valley of death together.

"I can't," I whisper to myself and crawl onto the bed. I reach my fingers out and stroke the apple of her cheek. I can't take someone so beautiful out of this world. The universe is too lucky to have her. She's the kind of person who makes the world a better place. I know that because ever since my eyes have landed on her, she's made me want to be better.

I lay next to her, and the bed dips so far down her side raises because she's so light. My god, I could throw her around, manhandle her, do whatever I wanted to her with ease. I rub a hand down my chest and unbutton my pants. My cock is dying to get out. I'm surrounded by her scent, by her. I need her.

Turning to my side, I watch her lips as they part, exhaling cute puffs of air as she sleeps. She has a bruise on her head where she smacked against the wall, and a tendril of guilt worms its way through me. I wasn't there when she needed me. The one time I wasn't watching her and something bad happened.

Of course, I have a feeling she'd be better off without me. She'd stay safe, but I can't stay away. Daphne is the madness healing my brain. We can change together, morph into something no one expected.

"Tongue?"

Her voice is unexpected, and my heart jumps in my chest. I roll to get out of bed, but I fall on the floor with a hard thud, smacking cock first into the unforgiving wooden slates. I groan in pleasure. Some would think a fall like that would hurt, but I'm on the brink of coming. I love pain.

"Are you okay?" She hurries to the side of the bed and looks down at me on the floor. Her hair becomes a waterfall, cascading down her shoulders. The ends sway and dance above me, like a mobile for a baby.

Daphne is my devil's lullaby, the only thing known in existence to tame the evil inside the hell in my heart.

I open my eyes, and she hurries to turn on the lamp near the bed. The light turns on, and I flinch. I feel caught. I don't have the darkness anymore to hide who I am.

"You're real," she says in awe, tucking her brown strands behind her ear. "I thought … I thought you were … a dream."

"You'd be better off if I was, Daphne." I push off the floor and grip the bed, using it as leverage to stand.

Only I don't straighten like I should. I don't take the moment to walk out the damn door like I should. I don't say goodbye.

Like I fucking should.

Instead, my dumbass inches forward because I'm entranced in her blue eyes.

"I can't see you," she says, reaching for her glasses.

"That's not necessarily a bad thing. I'm not that great to look at."

"I think you're the greatest thing in the world to lay my eyes on," she states, stealing my breath. No one has that ability. She slides those black-framed glasses on her face, and my heart melts when I see how happy she is to see me.

Me.

She must be fucking crazy.

Her eyes roam my body, and she almost seems … hungry as she checks me out. The smile fades when she sees my hands. She gasps, grabbing the sardonic palms, uncaring of the blood. It's obvious what it is, yet she doesn't flinch. "What happened?" The way she rubs her hand over mine has my cock jerking. I don't deserve pleasure. Not after what happened to Sarah.

"Something bad," I state. "Something really bad."

"Tell me." She pushes off the bed and starts to limp toward another room.

I stop her, not wanting Daphne to hurt herself. "Where are you going?"

"The bathroom to get a rag. You don't just have blood on your hands," she says.

"Don't," I say. "I deserve to feel it. What I did is unforgivable. I came here to tell you goodbye—"

"What!" she yells and then realizes how loud she's being. "You can't leave. You can't leave me. You can't go. You can't just…You can't. Okay? You can't leave me. I need you. I search for you in all the corners. Every shadow I see, I want to see you, and when you aren't there, it hurts. It hurts so much. Please don't go. Don't leave me."

"You don't know me. This"—I hold up my hands for her to see—"this is nothing compared to what I've done. I'm not a good man."

"I don't believe that."

"I stabbed my best friend tonight. She might be dead right now. I don't know. That's the kind of man I am."

"You didn't do it on purpose."

There is no way she can know that. "Maybe I did."

"You didn't. I don't know how I know that. I just do." She flinches in pain, and I swing her up into my arms and carry her to the bed.

"It doesn't matter how I did it. What matters is that I did, and I need to leave for a while, until Reaper says I'm allowed to come back."

"What happened?" She cups my face, searching my eyes for the truth.

I'm too afraid to give it to her.

"You want to know me? You want to make the decision for yourself?"

"Yes," she says. "More than anything."

I take a step away, shrug off my cut, and begin to undress. "You want to see the monster you allow to look at you at night?" I toss my shirt on the floor. "You want to see the man you touched yourself in front of?" I hiss, unzipping my pants. "I'm no fucking angel. I don't say that with wiggle room for you to think there is hope for me. I'm hopeless, Daphne." I'm becoming angry. What does she see in me? Everyone fears me. Why can't she?

I toss my pants on the floor and stand in front of her naked as the day I was born. I turn, holding out my arms to show her the ruin of what is my body. Sure, I have tattoos, but the scars aren't impossible to see. "You want to know what made me a man?" I charge at her and grab her hand within my blood-stained grasp, then run her fingers down the front of my body. Her eyes are locked on my straining cock hanging between my legs. I'm throbbing for her, dripping pre-cum down my thigh with her fingers on me.

"Holy moly," she whispers. I *think* she whispers. She says it so soft that I'm not sure if it was an exhale of air or what.

I never thought a woman's touch could feel so good. I never thought any touch would feel good, but I want these slender fingers to wrap around my shaft. I want her to bite me. I want her to threaten me. I want her to promise harm.

And then I want her to make me come.

"What..." She swallows. "What are those bumps? There are so many."

"Cigarette burns."

She gasps in horror and yanks her hand away, but I snatch it

137

and spin around, slapping them onto my lower back. Her hands shake as they glide up my shoulders, then down over the globes of my ass. I whirl around and snatch her wrists in my hands, tightening my fingers around them like cuffs.

A simple flick and I can snap her in half.

"No one touches me there. No one."

"Why?"

I sneer, bringing my face closer to hers, debating if I want to tell her the truth. I've never said the words out loud to anyone besides Sarah. My eyes land on the dried blood on my hands, and I realize it's the least I can do for Sarah. She'd want me to confide in Daphne.

She leans closer to me, not fighting the hold I have on her wrists, and lays her cheek against my chest. I inhale the sharpest breath when I feel another person against me. I freeze. I don't know what to do. What do I do?

The air coming out of her nose tickles the hair on my chest. My eyes roll to the back of my head, and a piece of me breaks. I gasp. I can't seem to find a way to breathe. And then she does something I would never expect.

She lays a kiss in the middle of my chest.

Another piece of me dissolves, and I tilt my head back, my eyes burning with how … intense she's making me feel.

"My uncle… My parents died in a car accident when I was a kid. He took me in. He … did things to me." I gulp. "He liked to dress up in women's clothes, and if I didn't call him by his female name, he'd make me bend over. He liked to play first. He always told me not to make a sound. It took me a long time to learn to speak because he would burn my tongue." I stick it out so she can see, and she has tears dripping down her cheeks.

"What's wrong? Are you in pain?" I ask her, and she nods.

"For you. I'm in pain for you."

"I killed him when I had the chance. I cut out his tongue. I slit his throat, but living with him changed me. I don't know how to read or write. I learned how to count because of Sarah and how to write my name, but she's... I stabbed her because my club found my journals. Since I don't know how to write, I got really good at drawing, so I'd draw the events of the day, you know? A way for me to express myself. They found them. They thought I put that tongue in your apartment. They thought I'd hurt you. They held me down, and I was reminded of..." I lay her hands on my shoulders, and she slides her fingers down the swell of my arms. The fury building like a raging fire simmers down from her touch. "I only saw my uncle, and I thought I'd stabbed him, but I stabbed her."

Daphne wraps her arms around my neck, and her eyes are like neon oceans with how bright they are right now. "You only thought you were protecting yourself. Surely, Reaper knows that. I'm sorry all of this happened to you."

I lift a shoulder, uncaring, but I'm realizing that I care a-fucking-lot. "The last thing any member does is fuck with the ol' ladies," I state. "People have been killed for far less than my crime."

A few moments of silence pass, and she strokes my skin with her fingers, her knuckles, brushing her lips against my chest, and I can barely fucking focus. I need to leave. I need to tell her that her life is better off without me.

"You can't read or write? Why take the books from the bookstore?"

"Because you touched them," I answer honestly. "I never thought I'd experience your touch, so I wanted the closest thing to it."

Her breath breezes over my nipple, and I feel it constrict. "And how is it now? Is it … is it what you thought it would be?"

I look down and arch my brow at her, confused about why it matters to her so much. Can't she see I'm bad for her? "It's more. I've never…I've never had a woman's touch, so I wasn't sure what to expect."

She rears back, cocking her head in confusion. Daphne eyes me up and down, those blue orbs widening when she sees my cock again. "You've never…"

"No. I only got hard when I saw blood. I thought I was just sick in the head. I never wanted to have sex because of what my uncle did."

"And now?"

"You're all I can think about wanting," I say. "Daphne, I'm not allowed to want things. I'm dangerous."

"I'm okay with that." She grips my hands, lacing her fingers with mine; not caring about the blood. "I'm not perfect. I know what you see, but it is what you don't see that matters."

I cup her face, rubbing her wet cheek and smearing the tears. I have the urge to lick them off. Are they salty? Sweet? I want to know, but now isn't the moment. "You can tell me anything."

"I have a form of psychosis," she whispers, ashamed. Daphne bends her head, placing her forehead on my chest. "I thought you were a form of my darkness inside me. It was the only thing that made sense because you were there one minute, then gone the next."

Psychosis… I'm not too familiar with it, but I have heard of it before. It's mostly when people lose touch with reality.

Her admission makes me feel … bad. I don't usually feel bad about how I make people feel, but Daphne is different. "I'm sorry. I never wanted you to feel that way. I'm very real. I'm the man who followed you, stalked you, and watched you, and I don't regret a fucking thing."

"You don't care?" she asks with wet lashes, blinking at me with an innocence I want to ruin and own.

"I hope you lose sense of reality when you're with me." Because my reality is completely different than what I thought it could be. My thumb brushes over her bottom lip, and I inch forward, wanting to kiss her for the first time when I remember the blood on my hands. "Fuck, I'm sorry. I need to go wash my hands off. I just touched your mouth with…"

Daphne leans into my tainted palm which causes my fingers to press against her mouth again.

My eyes zero in on what she's doing. "I have blood on my hands," I remind her.

Her tongue flicks out along my thumb, and I growl when I see the pretty pink muscle licking the pad of my finger. I know she had to taste blood. Sarah's blood.

I'm guilty.

I deserve a thousand deaths for allowing this to happen, but something about the woman I'm obsessed with, tasting the only other woman I've ever cared about has me almost coming unhinged. I want to get my knife and cut my wrists. Would she drink me down? Would she want our DNA to combine?

The thought has an orgasm blitzing through me. My cock pumps thick streams of seed, splashing on her arm. I grunt, not apologetic at all for what just happened. I crack my neck, roll my shoulders, and glare at her, daring her to question me.

I won't apologize for how she makes me feel.

She meets my intensity with her own. Daphne surprises me, dragging her fingers down her arm and then she brings

141

her fingers to her lips. The little she-devil rubs my cum over her mouth like fucking lip gloss. "You taste good," she purrs. "I want more."

I do something I've never done before.

I slam my lips against hers and kiss her as if I'm about to die.

For all I know, I might be.

But right now, I know what it's like to finally live.

And I've been missing out.

CHAPTER ELEVEN

Daphne

I DON'T KNOW WHAT GOT INTO ME.

He brings the woman I've been suppressing for far too long out.

His tongue is long and thick, just like his cock, and he licks his cum off my lips. His fingers grip my chin before flattening his palm over my neck and squeezing. I gasp, the threat of the lack of air beading my nipples as he claims my mouth.

There's no way he has never kissed a woman because he is in complete control right now. He snags my bottom lip in his mouth, growls, and bites down. I gasp, feeling the throb between my legs as he leans me back against the bed.

My knee aches as he spreads my legs with his hands and settles between my thighs. His shaft is hot and heavy against my thigh, rubbing in the remainder of his cum that's dripping from his slit. His hand dives between us, and he rips my panties from my body. I'm so damn glad I took my pants off before I went to sleep.

"Yes," I hiss when he roughly cups my pussy, rubbing his thumb over the sensitive bundle of nerves. "Tongue."

"Wayne," he whispers into my mouth in between kisses. "My name is Wayne."

My arms wrap around his back, the scars that hide under his tattoos rub against me, and knowing I can touch him, smell him, and taste him. It makes all of this real.

I'm not crazy.

But he makes me insane.

"Wayne," I repeat his name to him, and his shoulders bunch in response. He freezes above me, and he usually does that right before he vanishes into thin air. I hold onto him tighter, so he doesn't move.

"It's been a long time since I've heard someone say my real name."

"Do you like it, or do you want me to stop?"

"Does it feel like I want you to stop?" He rocks his hips between my thighs, and I feel more cum on my leg.

He orgasmed again.

Tongue steals my mouth in a fiery, passionate kiss. It's sloppy. It's clear neither of us have much experience, but I'm happy because I think I've been waiting for someone who can accept me for me.

Psychosis and all.

I break away from his kiss, and he snarls at me, digging his fingers in my cheeks to force me to look at him. I reach for his hair, the strands I've wanted to feel since I saw him, but my hands hit short, choppy pieces.

I rip my mouth from him, he sneers, showing his straight

white teeth like a mad man. "I'm not ready to be done with you."

"You cut your hair," I say with horror, wondering how in the hell I didn't recognize it sooner.

"Do you like it? I thought you would."

"Don't ever cut your hair again, Wayne. Do you understand me?" I clench my fingers on the side of his head, gathering the hair from the root and pull. "I asked you if you understood me." I threaten to rip his hair from his scalp, tightening my hold.

A sardonic slip of a chuckle escapes him, and the tilt of his lips turn sinister along with the shape of his eyes. Pools of endless, black ink stare back at me. His hand leaves my throat for a moment, and he bends down to pick something up off the floor. The moonlight shines against the silver metal of his blade as he slides the flat side down my body.

"Don't forget what I can do to you," he warns, and a gush of liquid heat escapes me, and my virgin hole flutters for his cock. "You have no idea the danger you've allowed in your bed." My shirt is in the way of his pursuit, and he digs the tip of the metal into the shirt, ripping it in half. "The danger you've allowed between your legs." He dips the blade down and presses the cold, flat side against my clit.

I let out a shaky breath, filled with fear and anticipation. Goosebumps prickle along my skin, my body warning me, but my insanity likes it.

"I think you're interested in the blood," he states, rubbing my clit with the knife.

I arch my back, gripping the sheets in my fists.

"You're interested in the chaos."

He plunges a bloody finger inside me, and a rumble

matching the sound of his motorcycle vibrates his chest when he feels how wet I am. He pulls the finger out, then shoves it in my mouth. My nectar mixed with the blood on his hand has me moaning. I wrap my tongue around the wide digit and lick him clean.

Iron and honey, a combination that does not mix, yet belong together.

He continues to circle the knife along my clit, and the sense of danger looms. He could slip, he could cut me, kill me even. I trust him. I trusted him the moment I saw him, and if cutting me is what he wants to do, I'll let him.

My thighs begin to tremble, my belly burns, and I tilt my head back, gasping for air. I try to hold out for as long as I can. I don't want this to end. He parts my ripped shirt and exposes one of my tits, cupping the small curve in the palm of his hand. Tongue bends down and sucks the red bead into his mouth and bites down hard.

It hurts.

Tears prickle my eyes, but it's glorious. I shove my hands over my mouth to silence my screams as I come long and hard. A sliver of pain stings my thigh, and my orgasm is prolonged. I climb to another height, soaring over a peak I had no idea existed. Another sting happens on my other thigh and when I glance down, I see blood.

Fresh, dripping, red blood.

The cuts aren't big. They are thin, but it's enough liquid for Tongue to use to massage into my skin, staining me with my own life liquid.

He inches his way down my body, and I think he's about to eat me out, but he doesn't. Instead, he licks the blood clean off my legs, lapping his tongue over the wound he gave me.

"Would you leave with me?" he asks, and I watch as he licks the knife clean, a line of red laying over his taste buds.

"I'd go anywhere with you," I say, drunk off pleasure, high off Tongue.

Bleed me dry and dump my body if he has to; as long as I experience this feeling, life can't get better.

He puts the knife in my hand and guides himself to my entrance. My thighs sting as our flesh rubs together, but I love it. I never want this to stop. Is it possible to want to be so close to someone that you want to bathe in their blood? To live underneath their skin. Because that's what I want to do with Tongue.

Close will never be close enough.

"I've never…" I start to say.

"I trust you," he tells me, leaning over to take my lips in a wicked kiss, promising a life of new manic experiences.

All he said was three words, but with the fractures in his eyes from his soul being broken, I know those words aren't easy for him to say.

I press the tip of the knife against his shoulder right as the tip of his cock enters me. I gasp from the intrusion, and my hand slips causing the blade to tear into his skin. His neck tendons protrude as he feels something other than pain for the first time in his life.

I'll soothe his soul. I'll give him everything he needs.

I've found sanctuary in the kind of crazy, my crazy was looking for.

He grips my throat, and I slice another line into his skin. With a curl of his lip, he roughly shoves inside me, breaking through my virginity without the gentle thrust normal guys give. He yanks out, then fucks himself back in. With every rock of his hips, the knife cuts into his shoulder, and eventually his blood drips onto my chest.

Tossing the knife aside, I lean up on my elbows and latch my mouth onto his wound, cleaning him up like he did for me. I moan, wishing we were something other than human so we could be bound together for eternity.

I pretend our blood joins, are DNA mixes, and I'm his.

He throws my head against the bed by keeping his hand around my throat and kisses me. He fucks me harder, and his balls slap against me with every thrust. His hand grips my leg, keeping it around his waist, and he sweeps me into another kiss, tangling our tongues together.

"So fucking tight," he rumbles into my mouth. He glances down, watching his big cock saw in and out of me, owning me, possessing me.

That's what he and I need. We both need something that is beyond love. We need someone to possess our souls in the most forbidden, unacceptable, taboo way.

"You're fucking mine, Daphne. You're mine. No matter where you go, no matter where you run, I'll fucking find you. You can't leave me."

"Never."

"You can't fucking leave me. I will follow you. I will bring you home. You're mine. You belong to me. Say it, Daphne. My Comet, tell me."

"I'm yours," I moan, scratching my nails down the plains of his strong back.

He lifts up and wraps the other hand around my throat. I cough, unable to breathe, but I'm able to feel every inch of him powering inside my channel with my other senses being on alert. "You don't get it," he sneers with a hint of disdain. "You can't get rid of me. If you leave me…"

"I'll let you kill me," I tell him, and the statement has him gripping the headboard, using it as leverage to put more force in his thrusts. For a man who has never had sex, he sure knows how to fuck. "And then, I'll let you cut out my tongue," I whisper into his ear, sucking the lobe into my mouth.

Our mouths lock again, desperate and needy, failing to try to get closer, but physically we can only do so much. All I taste is blood and the sinful aftertaste he leaves in my mouth.

"Say you'll marry me." He flips me over, my knee somehow on the damn elevated pillow to give it cushion, and he bites my ass and sucks the flesh in his mouth. He bites the other side, then plows inside me once more. "Fucking marry me!" He slaps my ass with his palm as a loud, pleasurable cry escapes me.

Saying yes would be crazy.

"I'm going to come," I warn him.

Not happy with that answer, he pulls me against my chest by gripping my neck, choking me. "I said marry me."

"Yes!" I scream, clenching on him so tight, he has no choice but to fill me with his seed. "Yes, more. Give me all of it," I moan, loving the heat filling my pussy.

He bites the meat of my shoulder, thrusting one more time as he fills me to the brink. I wish he could stay locked inside me forever.

"We will get married tomorrow," he tells me. "You're mine. Need you to be mine."

It's a good thing normal doesn't belong here.

"Now you can tell that asshole who gave you those flowers to fuck off." Tongue's voice turns to nails as he spits hatred toward the roses.

My eyes land on the flowers, Tongue's cock still flexing inside me when my body goes rigid. "Those aren't from you?"

"Fuck no, Comet. If I'm going to get you something, it isn't going to die. Well, at least, no so quick." He lays a kiss on the side of my neck, chuckling.

"Wayne?" I say his name to let him know the seriousness of the situation. "If they aren't from you..."

He doesn't wait another moment. Tongue yanks out of me and stalks over to the vase, grabs them, opens the window, and tosses them outside. He's fucking furious. He grabs my good ankle, pulls me to the side of the bed, and slams his cock in me again. I'm scared. Tears drip down my cheeks, but I'm not afraid of Tongue.

I'm afraid of what will happen to me if he isn't around. If this man is always watching me, anything can happen.

Tongue bends down and licks the tears off my face, and I cry more because I want to give him what he wants.

"I'm going to rip the tongue from the depths of his throat," Wayne whispers the filthy words in my ear, a whole new level of dirty talk.

And he gives me what I want.

CHAPTER TWELVE

Tongue

"**S**ARAH MADE IT OUT OF SURGERY. SHE'S GOING TO BE OKAY. *Reaper doesn't want you back yet. Let things calm down. I'll let you know when it's safe.*" The read-out-loud option on my phone reads the text from Slingshot.

I'm equally relieved and saddened, but I understand. I'm so glad Sarah is okay. I was scared, and that fear was what led me to see Daphne at three in the morning. I should feel regret, especially after what happened with Sarah. I don't deserve happiness after what I did to her, but there's a part of me speaking to me that's been silent for so long.

I wasn't in my right mind.

It doesn't make it okay, but it makes the guilt a little easier to burden.

If Reaper doesn't want me there, it's the least I can do. I wish I could grab the books from my room, the journals too.

I don't fucking know if I'm ever going to be able to show my face in that clubhouse again after everything that has happened.

NOLA might be the best place for us right now. We can stay there for a few weeks, and maybe things will fall into place.

After we get married, of course.

I wasn't kidding when I asked her. I'm a possessive man. I know what I want, I take it, and I want to take her. Forever. I never thought I'd find a woman who wants me for all of me, yet here I am, in bed with one.

I love her intensely, unhealthily, obsessively, dangerously, and to the point where it fucking hurts.

I'll always be watching her from the shadows, though, because I have an inkling it's going to be our 'thing.'

Rolling out of bed, I walk to the bathroom to take a piss and glance at myself in the mirror. Jesus Christ, my hair is fucked up.

And she doesn't even like it.

I don't like it either. Good thing hair grows back.

I turn my hands over next, seeing Sarah's blood. Some areas are clean; some aren't. I trace the wounds on my shoulder with my nails, and dried blood is smeared along my chest. I look down. My no-longer-virgin-cock hangs low, plumping when I think about how good last night felt.

My shaft has blood on it too from taking her virginity. Was I too rough? I don't know how else to be, but maybe she can teach me. I can learn.

A knock at the bedroom door has me tensing.

"Daphne? Are you okay? I'm going to San Diego. I won't be back until tomorrow night," her aunt calls through the door.

"Okay," Daphne answers sleepily. "Sorry, naked!" she warns her aunt, giving her a reason why the door is locked.

Damn right she's naked.

Mine.

I've never felt so primal before.

"No worries. Glad you're okay. I'll text. Love you." Her aunt finally leaves. Damn, that woman is annoying. She's been around so much. Well, only the last few days, but that's too much. I don't want to share Daphne.

I flush the toilet, scrub the blood off my hands, dry them off, and reach my arms up to grip the upper trim of the door.

Daphne is in bed, looking fucking delicious and exhausted. The knife is on the floor, blood still on the silver, but Daphne doesn't seem to notice it. She stretches, yawning as she tries to shake the morning. When she sees me, she blushes. "Hi," she says, shy and soft.

"Hi," I say in return, cocking my head at the interesting creature that's stolen the man I thought I was, only to give back the man I'm supposed to become.

"Um…" She bites her lip, and my eyes fall to her mouth. Her lips are still red and swollen from how much we kissed and how hard. I want to feel my cock slide down her throat. I want to feel her gag and choke. I've seen Bullseye with a few cut-sluts, and he seems to like it when they do it, so why wouldn't I? "Last night was…"

"Did I hurt you?" I cut her off. My eyes land on the slightly pink bruise around her neck where I choked her. I didn't know I gripped so hard.

"No." She sighs as if she's thinking of a daydream. "Everything was perfect."

I walk over to her and pull the blanket down her body. Bruises are everywhere, and there are two shallow wounds on either thigh. Fuck, she looks beautiful dressed up in my marks,

153

but if she's in pain, if it's too much, I need to know. Being gentle is a touch I've never known, but I do want to learn how to do it. She'll need to be patient with me. "Are you sure?" I ask her, tilting her chin up to meet my stare. "I'm willing to learn how to be different."

"I don't want you to be different, Tongue. I want you. This morning was more than I could have ever imagine, and seeing you in the sunlight during the day, I'm happy. I'm happy you aren't a dream."

"If I was, I'd find a way to escape your mind and be real for you." I mean it. I don't believe anything could ever keep me away from her, not even something like fantasy and reality.

"Well, I'm glad you're here, and now that I see that horrible haircut, we need to fix it before we get married. Unless, you don't want to, which I get; last night was so intense that I know—" I shove a finger over her mouth to silence her.

She's cute when she babbles. Her tongue doesn't stop. Usually I find it annoying, when someone talks so much, but not Daphne. I want to listen to her speak forever.

"I'm not the kind of man who jokes, not intentionally any-way. People laugh at things I say or do, but I never play. I'm marrying you."

"You realize how crazy that is, right? People aren't going to be happy."

"It's a good thing I don't give a fuck about people, and if they piss me off, I'll just—"

"Kill them," she finishes my sentence for me, and I grin.

I take her chin in my hand and press a kiss to her lips. "You're learning quick, Comet."

"Why do you call me that?" She blinks up at me, curiosity singeing the blue irises.

"Sarah read to me one night, about comets and how rare they are. I've never seen one, but then I saw you through the window of the bookstore, and I knew for sure comets existed."

"You know what a comet is, right?" she questions, a frown of concern between her brows.

"Yeah, I know. Some comets burn for hundreds of years, and that's how I felt when I met you; like I could burn *for* you for the rest of time."

"That would make you my comet." Her fingers dance up my chest and tap my chin.

"We can be each other's comets."

She has no idea how true it is.

"I like the sound of that." She wraps her arms around my waist, and another piece of me falls, shattering onto the floor. The old me is being replaced by someone new.

New-ish. She's teaching me how to love; she isn't taking away the bloodthirsty killer.

"So where are we getting married?"

"Elvis," I state. Vegas is the easiest place to get married in. I don't care where or who marries us as long as it is legal, and she has my last name.

"You're funny." She giggles.

"I'm not kidding." Why do people think I joke all the time? I don't understand.

"Oh… Oh! You're serious. Okay, can we make sure the impersonator is a good Elvis? I don't care about cheesy, but a bad Elvis is disrespectful to the true king."

"Anything my Comet wants, she gets."

She slides on her pants, and a black envelope falls out of the pocket. I bend over to pick it up, and the matte material feels good under my fingers. Daphne tries to take it away from me, but I open it and pull out the card, keeping it higher than she can reach.

I try to read the simple sentence, but I can't. "This is from him?" I ball up the card and throw it onto the ground. I'm seething. My breathing is quick and the urge to cut, to kill, is strong.

"It says, 'I'm always watching you.' I'll make sure to teach you how to read and write. You don't ever have to worry about that again. Not as long as you have me.'"

I'm not mad that she caught me struggling. She doesn't seem to care about my hindrances. She wants to help me with them. She isn't trying to figure out why I can't; she just

gets it.

I bend down to pick up the card and unfold it. The crinkles ruin the gold letters, and I stare at the sentence to see what it looks like. I can see why she thinks it is from me.

This has to be The Groundskeeper. He didn't kill me on Halloween, so he's pissed off and trying to make sure he does, indefinitely.

That man has been nothing but a pain in the ass since he set his sights on the Ruthless Kings.

I'm going to chop him up into little fucking bits and feed him to my swamp kitties. I'll personally drive him to NOLA and feed his body parts to the gators.

My phone rings, and I crumble the card up again, then shove it in my mouth and chew it. I'll be damn if this bastard gets the upper hand on me. Again. The card crunches, and the paper becomes soft. I swallow it. Letting his warning note settle in the pit of my belly, feeding the beast inside me, fueling my blood to kill.

I snatch my phone off the dresser and slide the green button to the left to answer. "Hello?" I grunt.

"Tongue?" Sarah's voice whispers sleepily through the phone.

I lose my balance and fall to the bed. "Sarah." I hold my hand over my heart. My soul is so relieved that it hurts. "You're okay." My voice breaks when the emotion chokes my throat. "I'm so sorry. I'm so sorry." I begin to rock back and forth, and Daphne crawls onto the bed behind me, wrapping her arms around my chest to comfort me.

I never knew touch could feel so good and make me feel so complete, but with every stroke of her hands along my shoulders, every glide of her lips along my neck, her hard nipples teasing the curve of my spine, I realize being in the light isn't a bad thing.

It's darkness that has swallowed me whole, and now I'm making the climb to get out. Her sun feels good shining against my face, and I know if I keep climbing, eventually she'll engulf me.

I've already lost myself in Daphne, but it's the good kind of lost. I want to wander around and learn new things about her. I want to go on a journey and hope life can show me how good it's really supposed to be.

"It's okay. I don't blame you." Sarah's voice is hoarse, and I can hear the pain I've caused.

"You should blame me."

"Reaper doesn't know I'm calling," she admits, keeping her voice quiet. "I love you, okay? Don't come back yet. Let me wear Reaper down. He's pretty pissed." She grunts, and I hear someone mutter something in the background. It isn't Reaper, but I'm sure they are warning her to hurry up, so she doesn't get caught talking to me.

"I love you too. I'm so sorry. I'll never forgive myself." The image of the knife piercing her stomach is something I'll never be able to forget.

"Nonsense. You have to," she slurs with sleep. "Forgiveness is the only way to achieve happiness, Tongue."

"Okay, come on," Doc's voice interrupts our conversation, and the static on the other end deafens me. "Tongue, she's fine. We can't be caught talking to you. Reaper has forbidden it. Stay safe, man."

I've always been the outsider. I've always liked isolation.

But it's been a long time since I've felt like I don't have a home, and the dial tone reminds me of how alone I am.

Daphne skims her hands down my arms reminds me that while I don't have my usual family, I have her.

I have no one to talk about my newfound happiness with. Everyone has turned their backs on me, and rightfully so.

"What do you need?" she asks the right question, one that has me thinking about my darkest desires. She's scratching the itch inside me. Her fingers trace along every burn, and I shut my eyes, relishing in the touch I've never had.

I need to cut a tongue out, but I don't know where to go for that. I don't know where The Groundskeeper is. I don't know how to go about finding him. There isn't an abundance of a threat like there was with the attack on the club. I got to cut so many tongues out. It was such a good day. My swamp kitties were well-fed because of that.

My phone rings again, and I almost throw it across the room, but the wizard emoji pops up, and my brows shoot to my forehead. It's Seer.

I ignore it. I'm not in the mood for anything out of this world right now.

"You aren't going to get that?" Daphne asks.

"No. I'm too tired to care what he has to say." The phone stops ringing only for it to start chiming again. I sigh, seeing the wizard emoji once more. I ignore it. NOLA is probably expecting me to come there. I bet Reaper called them. I'm wondering if my patch is about to get ripped off, or I'm about to get traded. Damn it, that would really fucking suck.

The phone falls silent, and it lights up again, ringing. Annoyed, I answer it and snap, "What?"

"Nice of you to finally answer."

"Been busy, Seer."

"So I've seen."

Great. He probably knows everything about me now. How the hell do secrets get out in the open so damn quick? "What do you want?"

"I saw a note this morning while having coffee."

The hairs on the back of my neck stand up, and I clutch the phone so tight that the cheap plastic cracks from the force. "And?" I push when he doesn't fucking say anything. "What the hell did it say?"

"The roses are red. Did they find their way to you? You didn't stay away from him. Your lips will turn blue." Seer recites the note from memory.

My heart stutters, and I reach up to lay my hand on top of Daphne's. "Did you see anything else?"

"An old building, brick, falling apart. He wrote it in blood. Listen, I got to go. I saw what will happen. I'm sorry. I was going to stay away from you Ruthless Kings, Mon Amie, but I can't deny a vision when I see one. Sarah will be okay. I've seen that too. Everything will be fine, Wayne. You'll see. I can tell you're on the fence about coming here, so your indecision doesn't let me know if I'll see you or not. If I see anything else,

159

you'll be the first I'll call." The dial tone has me wishing he didn't hang up. He knew my name. No one knows my name besides Daphne.

"Who was that?" Daphne asks, rubbing her hands down my chest, petting me to calm the beast.

"Seer. A member of the Ruthless Kings down in NOLA. He has visions sometimes. He warned me about a note he saw about you over his morning fucking coffee."

Her hands stop rubbing my shoulders, and I immediately miss it. I don't know what's happened to me, but the man I am with her? The man who suddenly loves touch, the man who wants to please her, the man who wants to focus on something other than vengeance? I like this man.

I know I have my issues, alright? I'm far from fucking perfect. Happiness used to be something wished for, something that happens to people, who aren't me. The emotion was earned, sought out, and bought most of the time because it sure as hell isn't what makes the world go 'round.

Being with Daphne makes me realize it isn't about happiness but finding the person you want to search for happiness with. I can have that with her. Everyone blinks at me when they realize how fucked up I am, but Daphne doesn't. She embraces it. My crazy Comet wants to experience it with me.

Would she want to torture someone with me? How far would she go to know what it's like to be with me for a day? Would she get her hands bloody? Would she want to fuck in a pool of someone else's blood?

See, I think about those things. My deepest, darkest desires, my secrets.

In the middle of my soul's séance, the universe answered, and she gave me Daphne.

"What do you want to do?" Daphne moves off the bed and stands in front of me. My eyes lock on her breasts, small with a slight curve. "I'm not strong enough to fight him, Tongue. I'm … I fell down the damn steps when I saw the…" She gags and holds her stomach.

I chuckle. She's cute.

"Tongues freak you out, huh?" I tease, then wink. She blushes and bites her lip. "After what happened last night, I didn't think it would bother you."

She scoffs, then points at me. "Cut me some slack. I've never seen one before. Out of a mouth, that is."

"You don't like it?" Dread swirls in the pits of my stomach.

"I … I don't know," she says, perplexed. "I mean, seeing it was shocking, and it scared me, but if I ever came across the person who did it…"

I lean forward, placing my elbows on my knees, "Yes?"

"I'd want to scare them the way they scared me." Her blue eyes meet mine swirling with newfound obscurity, and another chamber locked in my soul opens for her, swinging wide open like a door. That's all I need to know.

"Get dressed, Comet." I stand, and my cock points at her, hard and aching for her wet cunt to wrap around me.

"Where are we going?"

"Don't think I forgot binding you to me. It's happening. Today. Now. I'm not waiting for another moment."

"I don't even know your last name," she sasses, throwing her hands on her hips.

"Hendrix. You'll be Daphne Hendrix," I moan and reach down to squeeze my cock. "That sounds so fucking sexy." I bet I could come if I chanted her new name.

"Middle name?" she asks, her voice husky with arousal.

"Don't have one."

"Birthday?"

"Don't know," I say, gliding my hands up the curves of her hips. "You?"

"Ellen. June 6th. You really don't know your birthday?"

"I know I'm probably too old for you, but I don't give a fuck about that. Favorite color?"

"Purple." She straddles my lap and rocks her wet cunt against me. "You?"

"Blood." I tilt my head back when she kisses along my neck and slides her pussy down on me, and then she jumps off, leaving my cock wet and shining with her juices. I snap my eyes open and watch her giggle as she slips on her panties. "What the hell are you doing?"

"I thought we were going to go get married. But first, you need to feed me. We missed breakfast and lunch. We can't do either of those things if we get distracted—again."

"I like distractions," I growl, "but you're right. The next time I take you, it will be as my wife. And then we will go to NOLA, away from here to keep you safe." I bend down and grab the black jeans off the floor and slip them on. I'm careful tucking my cock in so the zipper doesn't catch. Bending over, the knife glimmers one last time before I pick it up and turn around, showing her the blood on the blade.

I show her our combined fluids that have dried along the knife and lick it, flattening my tongue along the body. God, we taste good. It's better than whiskey after a long day. She shrugs a simple summer dress over her shoulders and grabs a green cardigan. I love how different we are. She's all bright and shiny while I'm dark and stormy. She saunters up to me and wraps her hand around mine, pulling the knife to her face.

TONGUE

Holding my breath, I wait to see if she's about to do what I think she's about to do. Her pretty pink tongue laps across the metal, tinting her taste buds a beautiful shade of aphrodisiac red.

We aren't ever going to leave this room, which is a problem, because I need her to be bound to me. I want her to get an ol' lady tattoo, right over her heart.

It isn't only her body that's the Property of Tongue—it's her soul too.

I'll get one, but instead, I'll have her carve her name into my skin, and it will be the only scar that has ever mattered.

She smirks at me, then grabs a pill bottle off the nightstand to put in her purse. I don't

want her to take medication. I want her to be herself. Her mind isn't broken. It's beautiful, and I want to see every nook and cranny of it.

In her despair, in her confusion, I'll be there.

And I'll be everything she needs.

Even if it means letting go of my own insanity.

CHAPTER THIRTEEN

Daphne

"**S**O WHERE ARE WE GOING?" I ASK TONGUE, HOLDING HIS hand as we walk down the Vegas strip after eating an early dinner.

"I know a guy," he states, stopping in front of a club.

"Here?"

"No. The club owns this." He stares at it from across the street longingly. It takes a strong man to admit he's afraid to go home.

The windows are blacked out and the sign is neon green flashing "Kings' Club." There's a crown hanging off the K, and I can hear a beautiful voice pouring out the door singing Janice Joplin.

"You want to go inside?"

"Can't. When Reaper says I'm not allowed at the club-house, he means here too." Tongue rubs the spot over his heart, looking confused at the pain he feels. "Come on, let's go," he takes my hand and drags me down the sidewalk without a parting glance at the club.

I look over my shoulder at the line that is spilling out the door and anger blooms in my veins. I hate how they are treating Tongue. He deserves better.

Sure, he stabbed Sarah, but I bet that isn't the worst thing that has happened in the club.

"We need to get you a ring before we go see Maximo."

"Maximo?" That name reminds me of a guy that shoots people for a living.

"He runs a casino. His brother, Matteo Moretti, is at the clubhouse because he was in an explosion and fell into a coma. He just woke up but can't remember anything. So his brother, Maximo, took over the family business."

"We are going to a casino?"

"There's a chapel in every casino here," he says with a maniacal smirk. "Maximo will marry us and then there is a fighting rink under the casino. If you're into that sort of thing..."

I can tell he wants me to be.

I giggle, jumping and wrapping my legs around his waist and my arms around his muscular neck. Damn it, I could fuck him right here in the middle of everything and everyone just so they can be envious of me.

"Nice haircut, freak." A frat boy with his collar popped throws a drink on us, and Tongue sets me in the alleyway we are near.

"Tongue, no," I whisper, but I know it's too late.

That frat boy has popped his last collar.

Indefinitely.

"Is that right?" Tongue grips the man who spilled his beer

all over us and his friend by the neck. People who are walking by us don't even blink an eye. They are drunk and not paying any mind to what we are doing. "Let's take a little trip, boys." Tongue pushes them into the black alley. "You're stupid, aren't you?"

"We were just on our way by. We won't bother you again," the innocent one says, whispering something out of the side of his mouth to his friend.

I'm not sure what gets into me, but I flank Tongue's other side, wanting to be there for him. We reek of beer.

Frat boy pushes his friend, who falls in a pile of trash that is sitting in the corner. Who knows how long it's been there? The ground underneath the black garbage bag is wet. "Fuck that. He's just some weirdo with a hot piece of ass. Does he share, baby? I promise, you've never—" his eyes go wide when Tongue shoves his knife in the middle of the guys throat.

I inch closer, gasping when I see him choke on his own blood, gasping for air.

"Holy shit," the friend of his says, cowering in the corner. "Oh my god. Oh my god."

"You fucked with the wrong freak," Tongue lowers his voice and twists the knife in the frat boy's throat, then gives it an extra shove until a slight crunch has the knife exiting out of the back of the head. "Apologize to my wife." Tongue pulls the young guy forward and he coughs blood. It drips down his chin. "I said apologize or I'll kill your friend here too." Tongue licks the blood off the guys chin, and I know I should be disturbed, but I'm not.

All I want Tongue to do is kiss me now.

"You taste like fucking bitch," Tongue says.

The smell of piss fills the air and the guy hanging on

Tongue's blade slides his vacant eyes to me. "I'm—" he wheezes, spitting out another mouthful of blood. "—Sorry."

"Sorry won't save you." The words slip out of my mouth at the same time Tongue pulls the knife free of the man's neck. He falls to his knees, and Tongue opens the man's mouth, pulls out his tongue, digs the knife in the back of his throat, and cuts. "Now you won't be able to disrespect women from the dead."

My crazy man tucks the bloody tongue in his cut pocket, and I lift a brow in question. "My swamp kitties."

"You have kittens?" I ask with excitement. "Oh, can we get one?"

"Anything my Comet wants, she gets," Tongue says simply, then stares at the man in the corner sitting on the trashcan, crying his eyes out.

"Please," the guy begs. His jeans are wet with garbage juice and pee. Snot is running down his lips, and his eyes are swollen from sobbing. "Please, don't kill me. I don't think you're a freak. My friend was an asshole. I'm not like that."

"I don't believe you. Birds of a feather and such..." Tongue spins the ten-inch blade around, but it's a different one. I haven't seen this knife before. The blade is black, and the handle is ivory. There is something carved into the side, but I can't tell.

"No, I swear, I swear, I don't share the same thoughts. I won't tell a soul what happened. I..."

"I wouldn't care if you did," Tongue says, taking a step closer.

I follow him, stepping in a pool of blood. An idea flashes in my mind, but it's crazy. I can't, but I want to ask Tongue to step in it as I kneel to suck his cock.

"Tell my wife she is beautiful," Tongue orders, sliding the obsidian metal across the man's cheek, cutting the flesh open. "Tell her!" he roars, and the anger in his voice has a gush of heat pooling in my panties.

"You're very pretty," the man trembles, licking the snot off his lips. He turns his watery gaze to Tongue and whimpers. "Please. I'll do anything. I'm a senior in college. I have a fiancé. I'm not a bad guy. I'm not."

Tongue drags his knife down the man's throat. "Every guy is a bad guy."

"I'm not. The worst thing I've ever done is litter. I swear, please," he sobs, squeezing his face in agony as he begs for his life.

I can see what Tongue likes about it. There is so much adrenaline when it comes to taking a life.

We're in the shadows. Night has fallen. The only lights that shine are the ones of the Vegas strip. I can hear low hums of conversation at the start of the alley, but I can no longer see the crowd of people walking.

We can do whatever we want, and no one will know.

"I don't know if I believe you," Tongue taps the tip of the knife against his tooth. "I think you're just saying that, so you don't end up like your buddy."

The guy widens his eyes and shakes his head. "No, no, no, I'm not. She's very beautiful. If I weren't engaged and she was single, I'd ask her out."

"You'd ask out the woman meant for me? No one else is allowed to have her."

"Of course not," the man nods in agreement. "If you didn't exist, that's all I'm saying, and if my fiancé didn't exist. Different worlds."

"What do you think, Comet? Let him go?" Tongue onyx orbs land on me waiting to see if I can make the decision. I feel like I have to do this.

"Yeah, let him go, my Comet," I say sweetly, swaying the hem of my dress. "We can have fun with this one," I point to the frat boy who is still bleeding out fresh rivers of blood.

I can't tell if Tongue is disappointed in me or not. His facial expressions give nothing away. He blows me a kiss and stares at the guy again. "You heard her. She's in charge. You're free to go."

"Really?" the guy's wet cheeks shine in the light of the moon.

"Really," I say with reassurance, sliding my hand over Tongue's shoulder.

The man doesn't say anything else. He pushes to his feet and leans against the brick wall, then inches his way around us. I can hear the material of his shirt being pricked by the stone as he drags himself across it. "Thank you," he says. "Thank you so much." He gives his friend a sorrowful stare and then throws up when he sees all the blood.

He stumbles in a zig-zag pattern, slamming against the right side of the wall. "Ouch, you okay?" I ask him and he doesn't give me an answer. His eyes are on the exit.

"Hey, kid," Tongue flips the knife in the air and catches it. "You know what I hate?" And with a flick of his wrist, the blade slices through the air and lands with a sickening thud in the middle of the guys forehead.

My hand grips the swell of Tongue's ass, more turned on than ever because Tongue knew I didn't want the guy to escape.

The guy lifts his hands and touches the ivory handle, then yanks it out. He tries to come at us, but he is only a second away from death. He trips, slamming into Tongue. Tongue croons gently at the dying college student and rips the knife out of his hand.

"I hate liars," Tongue whispers in the victim's ear, then with the gentlest push, the sharp tool effortlessly pierces the throat. "You're in Vegas without your fiancé with frat boy over here. That tells me you're up to no good. No good man travels without the love of his life. I'd never go anywhere without my Comet," Tongue explains to him and eases the shiv out of his throat. He gags like his friend, spews blood into Tongue's face. "Mmm," Tongue licks his lips and chuckles, dipping his hand into the man's mouth.

There's no fight in the stranger. He doesn't make a sound.

Even if he wanted to, he can't now, not with his Tongue in my Comet's hands. He opens up his cut pocket to tuck it alongside the other one, but I stop him. "Can I?" I hold out my hands, wondering what it's like to hold one.

"You sure? These go to the swamp kitties, Comet. I'm not going to be mad if you don't want to. It's an acquired taste."

"Please."

"Another time, Daphne. I don't want you to ruin your dress. It's pretty on you." He tucks my hair behind my ear. "I like that color on you, it brings out the creamy tone of your skin, Comet."

I glance down and blush, swaying my dress from side to side.

"Come on, let's go get married." Blood drips from his cut pocket, dripping down his jeans. It reminds me of the box he held when I first saw him. He wasn't lying when he said it was dripping blood.

Holy Moly.

He's a maniac.

And I'm in love with him.

"Let's go get married." Our bloody hands lock together, and he slips the knife into another pocket where it can be seen. We walk out of the alley, and I wait for someone to notice the mess on us, everyone is laughing, drinking, and ignoring us.

We pass the Bellagio, and the fountain is putting on a show with different colored lights flashing. Tourists are stopped, pointing at the tall sprays of water. We pass a sad-looking Elvis who is overweight, and the wig is crooked, but people are paying him for pictures anyway. There's a man painted silver, standing stock still.

I think it's a man.

I don't know. He's really convincing. I lean forward as we walk by, and his eyes follow me. I jump, holding my hand to my chest and laugh, then wave as Tongue pulls me behind him. I'm thirsty, and my skin is sticky with sweat from the humidity in the air. When we stop in front of the hotel, I'm surprised when I notice the Circus Circus Casino, but the name is gone, blank, and everything is under construction.

"Maximo is rebuilding this piece of shit. The inside is classy. Perfect to marry you in. Then, we can get a room, maybe after we visit the underground fighting ring. Shit! Your ring. I haven't gotten you one."

"It's okay. I don't need one. I just want to be with you."

"No, no! You need a ring. Fuck."

"Tongue? That you? You crazy son-of-a-bitch!"

I dip behind Tongue's back to hide behind his massive back and peer around his shoulder.

"Maximo. The man I wanted to see."

"Really? That's interesting. What can I do your for? You

want to get in on some fighting action? God, you'd make me a lot of money."

"Can I cut out tongues?"

"You can do whatever the fuck you want. You do that for me, anything is yours."

I tighten my hand around Tongue's and push up my glasses with my fingers. Maximo leans to the left and eyes me, smiling.

"Well, look at you, Tongue. I had no idea a man of your caliber was interested in women."

"You never asked. Don't look at her or I'll fucking kill you."

"How can I not look at her? She's cute, a little geeky, which I'm surprised because you're big and scary," Maximo laughs, pulling out a long cigar from his pocket. He rubs it under his nose, sniffing it, which reminds me of how Tongue smells books.

"Mine," Tongue snarls at him and pushes me behind his back more to completely block me from Maximo.

Maximo rolls his eyes, and he snaps his fingers in the air. Immediately, a guy the size of Tongue lights a match and places it on the end of the cigar. Maximo puffs until the orange glow is constant. "Don't be a caveman. I'm not interested in your librarian. What do you want? Why is a lone Ruthless King on my property? Is this about my brother?"

"No. I'm here because we are getting married. Can we do it here? Penthouse Suite, the works. I need a ring too. I'll pay any price."

"You fight three fighters, and it's all yours."

"I'll kill them," Tongue states. "I don't fight to wound, Maximo."

"I know. That's what I love about you." Maximo brushes off the lapels of his expensive suit. The lapels are black but the suit itself is blue. He's a good-looking man. Tan skin, pretty hair that's combed back in waves. He points the cigar at Tongue's hair. "You aren't getting near anything expensive with that hair. I have a reputation to uphold."

"It isn't that bad."

I chuckle when I hear the pout in Tongue's voice. He isn't the kind of guy to pout.

"It's bad. You did it, didn't you? I swear to god, a guy cuts for a living but can't cut his own damn hair. How does that make sense?"

"You want those fights or not?" Tongue marches forward, and I yelp when I'm jerked forward unexpectedly.

"Hey!" Maximo snaps his fingers. "I'm serious. You aren't going in there with that haircut. I'm building a business here. I can't allow just anyone in. You have fucking blood on your shoes. You aren't tracking that in. Jesus, did you kill on your stroll over. I'm going to call Reaper and tell him his psycho fled the building."

"Don't," Tongue warns, the hint of the playful side of him gone. "Don't call him."

Maximo tilts his head up to meet Tongue's eyes, grinning like a scum who just figured out something he could use for himself. Knowledge is power and the only way to get ahead in life is to use it for your advantage. Maximo knows this. "Oh, what did the favorite do?" Maximo tsks, his teeth glimmering white in the flashing casino lights.

I push my hands under Tongue's shirt and rub his back when he tenses.

"Five fights and your secret is my own." Maximo blows out stinky smoke and lays a hand on his heart. "What do you say, Tongue? Want to make a deal with the devil?"

Tongue whips out his knife and presses it against Maximo's chest. The goons surrounding Maximo whip out their guns, and I move from behind Tongue and stand in front of him, ready to take all the bullets.

"Oh, why don't you look at that," Maximo pushes the knife away, more interested in me. "You found someone who is crazy enough to take a bullet for you. Isn't that sweet. I had no idea psychos could love."

"We love harder," I spit at him. "And you're nothing like the Devil I know."

The Devil I know is the one you wish you didn't.

CHAPTER FOURTEEN

Tongue

I WANT TO FUCK HER RIGHT HERE, RIGHT NOW.

I can't believe she stepped in front of two men with guns to protect me.

Me.

I never knew I was worth it, but she's shown me I'm worth it to her.

"Well, let me show you the way to hell, beautiful," Maximo spreads out his arm to the front doors of the casino, showing us the way inside.

Please.

Slot machines and blackjack tables are a far cry from being burned alive.

"Take a left. Do not go in there looking like a serial killer. I do not need customers fleeing because they see you," Maximo informs me, walking ahead of us.

K.L. SAVAGE

The lights inside strobe with every pull of a handle from a slot machine. People are shouting as they win and groan as they lose. Suckers. I'd never give my money to Maximo. The chances of winning are slim to none when it comes to casinos, but when it comes to killing?

I always win.

"Here," Maximo opens the door to a private hallway, and when Daphne is tucked safely at my side, the echoing sound of a lock sliding into place bounces off the empty hallway. The noise of the casino fades away, and the only noise is the thud of our footsteps as we follow Maximo. "I want the cut off, shirt off, and you can have your knife in the ring. Anyone who volunteers can fight you."

"Why does his shirt need to be off?" Daphne's jealousy has my erection pressing against my zipper. I need to have her soon.

"Because he is a big, bad biker with tattoos, beautiful. Sex sells, and I want to make money."

Daphne's fingers push her glasses up the bridge of her nose, narrowing her eyes at Maximo in discontent. I love this side of her.

"I don't like you," Daphne tells Maximo, the temporary boss of the Moretti mafia, while his brother heals.

"Such a shame because I really like you," Maximo purrs, opening a black door with a gold handle.

"Watch it, Maximo. I just killed two men for less," I warn him, feeling the itch to kill him. I can't do that, or I'll declare war and right now, I have enough to worry about right now, like if I have a home to go to. And I need to find the man threatening Daphne. If someone takes her from me, they don't want to see what I'll turn into.

There will be no saving me or anyone in my way. No one understands how my mind works except Daphne.

When I say she is mine, I don't mean it in a sweet way. I mean it in the worst way possible. The kind that scares people. The kind of way her friends would be worried about her because I'm so possessive of her. I'm beyond obsessed.

"Just getting you worked up for the fight. I'll get my stylist to fix that mess. Be ready in twenty minutes," Maximo says.

"Don't bother. I can fix it," Daphne enters the room and I follow.

"A woman that takes charge—"

Daphne slams the door in Maximo's face, silencing him from talking. "That guy gets on my nerves."

I shrug off my cut and one of the tongues slips out and falls to the floor with a sickening slap. "You do know he is the head of the mafia here in Vegas, right?"

"So?" she scoffs. "Doesn't mean I have to like him." She bends down to pick up the tongue, but I stop her by placing my boot on top of it. "It's okay, I got it," she says, blinking those sapphire eyes at me.

Testing her, I lift my leg off the tongue and watch in fascination as she slips her hand under it. "Wow," she says, staring in awed interest. "It's heavier than I thought it would be." She leans down and sniffs it. "Uh, this guy had bad breath." She pinches the tip and hands it back to me and I can't help but chuckle.

"You're perfect," I state simply, staring at her in fascination. How did I get so lucky? I lift my cut off the chair and tuck the tongue inside the pocket. I'll need to clean this cut. There's a ton of blood on it.

"I just want to be everything you want me to be," she

whispers, forgetting she has blood on her hands as she pushes her glasses up her nose again.

I shrug off my shirt and invade her space. I grip the back of her neck with my hand and bring my head down, teasing her with the promise of a kiss. "You're already everything I could ever want, Daphne. Don't force yourself to be someone you aren't for me. I wanted you from the moment I saw you and that is never going to change." I press a kiss to her lips and one taste has me losing the shredded thread of my control. I deepen the kiss pushing my tongue forcefully between her lips and licking the roof of her mouth. I want to devour her. I want to crawl underneath her skin and become one with the better half of who I am.

Some people would say it is sick to be so entranced by someone, but I call it love.

I pick her up by the thick meat of her ass and plop her on the counter. Pushing her legs apart, I settle between the space and get comfortable because I'm going to fucking live here. I break the kiss, moving my lips down her neck and growl in satisfaction when I see the pink bruise created by me.

I lick it, and she tosses her head back, moaning my name, "Wayne." My real name. I love that she uses it when she's turned on. It makes me feel different when I'm with her instead of the killer I am every day.

"You sure I didn't hurt you?" she hisses when I place my hand on her knee. I glance down and see the black and blue bruise swelling her knee. That isn't from me.

Fuck. How could I forget? "I'm sorry. I shouldn't have been so rough with you last night, not when you're healing from the fall."

Daphne lifts her dress up and slides her arms free from

the straps. Her red nipples tighten when the air hits them, and I lick my lips, wanting a taste. Her finger pop the button of my jeans then pulls the zipper down. "You better be rough with me because if you aren't, I'll find someone who will be."

The thought of someone else touching her body, another man being in her tight cunt, has me seeing red. I pick her up, spin her around, and slam her against the mirror hanging on the wall. Small pieces crack and fracture while she gasps, her cheek digging into the glass. I keep a tight hold between the space where her neck and shoulder meet, fish out my cock, and slam home. "Don't ever threaten me again. I am everything you need."

"Yes, you're everything," she replies as I slide out, only to punch forward again.

"I would kill them," I warn in a hushed, vile tone against her ear. "I would kill them, bathe you in their blood, then I'd fuck you and show you who owns you." I press her head against the glass harder, watching the cracks spread and grow along the mirror, then I yank her back and our eyes meet in our reflection. Our faces are broken from the imperfect mirror but letting us view how perfect we are together.

It's fitting.

My shattered soul and her shattered mind are one.

Her hands fall on either side of the gold frame as I fuck her.

"Do I need to carve my name into your skin for you to understand that no one else will exist for you?" I peer down where we are joined, and her honey has my cock shining to the high heavens. It's about the only thing holy between us because the only halo that exists is the one between her legs.

The wide tip of me lodges into her right before the flared

crown slips free. She screams when I fill her up again with a sharp thrust, then slip out again.

"Yes," she hisses. "Mark me." She ruts her ass against me, and I groan, letting my head roll over my shoulders as she uses me, trying to fit every inch inside her, but she can't.

I'm too fucking big for her small tight cunt.

Flipping her around, I hook her legs over my waist, my fingers brushing the soft skin of her thighs as I grab hold.

"Yes, Wayne. Yes, harder. More. I want more."

I slam her against the mirror, and she cries out, digging her nails into the muscles of my shoulders until the skin breaks. Glass falls onto the floor behind her and a few diamond-shaped pieces fall from above, landing on her tits.

Picking her up, I slam her against it again and blood smears across the mirror just as her pussy tightens around me, clenching as she comes from the pain. "Wayne! Oh, god. Yes."

My head falls to her left breast, and I suck the beaded candy between my lips, then bite down causing her to cry out again. Something demented comes to mind as I'm sucking on her tits. What if I can get her pregnant? What if I can bind her to me in every way? I can be a good father. I'll never do what my uncle did to me. I'll protect what is mine and I'll love them in the only way I know how.

Intensely.

She smells like sweat, sex, and sin. Speeding up my thrusts, I power drill her with every ounce of strength I possess. My orgasm hits me, squirting out of my cock in thick jets, painting her womb with my seed. I hold her close to me, thrusting with every rope of come leaving my body and pushing it further inside her.

"Mine," I gravel, raking my teeth across her chest.

"Yours." She claws her nails down my back and comes again. I imagine her spasms forcing my cum deeper into her body, so her womb drinks me up until the thirst for my children is satisfied.

I sag against her, my body shaking from the intensity of our union. Her legs are trembling too, and I ease her off the mirror and the release of pressure has more glass cascading to the floor. I set her on the counter, cock still plunged deep, and go to a mirror that isn't broken.

Three pieces of glass are embedded along her back. Two near her right shoulder and one on her lower back. I pluck one out and toss it on the ground and she moans. "You like that?" I ask her, wanting to file the information away for later.

"Love it," she slurs, drunkenly from the post-orgasmic high.

I yank the second one out and she falls against my chest, gasping for air. "Wayne, oh god, I'm going to come again." Her pussy flexes around me, plumping the semi-hard shaft to full mast in a second.

There's only one piece of glass left and it's the biggest one. I pinch my fingers around it and a grotesque squishing noise of her flesh trying to hug onto the shard has my cock flexing, pouring another around of come into her needy body.

"Wayne," she gasps, scratching a row of love marks down my arms, ruining the expensive tattoos as she orgasms.

If I had known I would have met her, I wouldn't have gotten any tattoos. I would have let Daphne scar me in any way she liked.

I smash my lips on her again, sucking in the air from her lungs to fill mine. Her glasses are crooked, and there's a cut on her lip, probably from a piece of glass, and I suck the plump flesh into my mouth to swallow the blood.

Delicious.

"Wow. I can't feel my legs," she giggles.

I lock my eyes on her pussy, combing my fingers through the brown tuft of hair and watch as I pull out of her. A white gush of cream leaves her tight, swollen hole and drips down to her asshole. I don't like that I'm spilling out of her, so I thrust inside again, and she moans. My fingers brush against her puckered star, and she inhales a sharp breath. Would I be interested in owning her there? Yes. I want my come in every hole, so she is ruined and too fucked up for anyone else.

Selfish? Wrong?

Yes.

I don't care.

The toxins in my heart have wrapped their venom around her, choosing her as mine and killing any hope in her heart that wanted normal.

She's apart of my poison now.

"You have no idea how much I want to carve my name into your skin." I grab the knife I made myself, teasing the pointed black tungsten against her creamy skin. Her wild heart pumps with so much intensity, it bounces the blade. Daphne's skin gives and turns a shade lighter as I press, but not hard enough to puncture.

Pity.

"As long as I can do it to you too, you have a deal." Daphne pushes her chest out and a tiny droplet of blood pebbles, seducing my taste buds.

And I'm suddenly dying of thirst.

The urge to scar her skin with my property patch

overwhelms me. Right as I'm about to drag the knife across her skin, a knock at the door interrupts me. I sling the blade through the air, and it lands on the door with a hard thud.

"You guys better be ready in five minutes," Maximo yells inside the room as he cracks the door open.

I wish the knife would have landed between his damn eyes. The next one will if he takes another step into the room. Daphne isn't decent. Her tits are out, her underwear are ripped to pieces, and my cock is nestled insider her hot cunt still. "Don't move another muscle, Maximo. I'll kill you."

"I swear to god, you Kings find a pretty piece of forever ass and won't stop fucking. I have a business to run. Zip your dick up, cut that fucking hair, and make me some goddamn money!" He slams the door, and Daphne's laugh is music to my ears as she lays her head against my shoulder.

"I guess we should get going. The sooner we do this—" she leans away from me, and her fingers play with the uneven strands of my hair "—the sooner you can make me your wife, if you want. If you're still wanting that..." She clears her throat, and her uncertainty about us makes me wish I had the time to show her.

"I want nothing more," I say, taking the edges of her jaw in my palms. "I would have made you mine the moment I saw you, but I convinced myself you were better off without me. It's why I watched you from the corners."

"I felt you," she whispers, leaning into my touch. I can't believe I have someone who actually wants to feel me.

"I know because I felt you too." I kiss her again and do the one thing I don't want to do; I slide out of her warmth. She has no idea just how much I felt for her—feel—for her. My love for her is bigger than the space that holds the stars above us, brighter than the moon, and hotter than the sun. She's inside my veins. She lives in me.

I can't be without her now that I've had her. I can't live that way. I'm an obsessive person. I have to have the compulsion that follows.

I have an obsession with killing.

My compulsion is to cut out tongues.

Daphne is my compulsion.

I zip up my pants, then button them, and bend down to pick up the black satin panties I ripped off her. I dangle the scrap in front of her face as she slips her arms through the thin straps of her dress. She reaches for the panties, and I bundle them in my fist, stuff them under my nose, and inhale.

"These are mine, Comet," I say and rub them over my face, letting her scent soak into my skin so I can smell the sweet perfume of her pussy on my face while I kill. Exhaling and buzzed from her scent, I stuff her panties into my pocket.

"That's fine. Easier access, right?" she flirts, jumping down from the counter, and taking my shirt off the back of the chair. I take it from her, brushing our fingers together to get another jolt of electricity, and pull the oversized t-shirt over her head.

Damn, it covers her entire body.

I never want her to wear anything of hers again. Only my shirts.

Fuck, I really do want to ruin her in the worst of ways.

She opens the drawer and finds a pair of clippers. "Ready?" she presses the button and the clippers buzz, mimicking the bees stinging my bones as I stare at her.

Hell no I'm not ready.

I want to stay in this room with her for the rest of time.

TONGUE

When I think about happiness, I think about being alone with Daphne. That's peace.

Running my fingers through my chopped mess of hair, I sit down in the chair and stare at her through the mirror. "Do your worst," I say, gripping the armrests. I'm not one that cuts my hair. It's how it got so long in the first place.

"When it comes to you, I'll only ever do my best."

The first inch of hair falls to my lap and it's liberating. The past is disintegrating, and the future has come, and her name is Daphne.

My Comet.

CHAPTER FIFTEEN

Daphne

HAVE YOU EVER SEEN SOMEONE THAT TAKES YOUR BREATH AWAY and you stare because they are so beautiful, you wonder how they exist?

That's how I feel right now. I can't keep my eyes of Tongue as we walk down the hallway toward the casino again. He is power, strength, fear, and intimidation rolled into one. His height, his build, his tattoos, his menacing snarl that is permanent on his face creates a threatening package I can't get enough of.

Yes, he is all of those things, but there is something else, one detail no one will know about him except me.

The snarl on his face doesn't exist when he watches me. He is every terrifying word a person can think of, but he loves madly, and he has set his instability on me.

I love it.

I'm sure people look at us and see a million reasons why we can't be together. I'm so much more different on the outside than he is, but on the inside? He answers every call my body has. Maybe it's wrong to some, but he is right to me.

And that is all that matters.

"You're going to make me a ton of money," Maximo says with so much glee he nearly bounces on his heels as he walks.

Tongue slides his hand into mine, his palm swallowing me from its massive size, and holds on tight as we walk. Not a single part of me is worried about Tongue entering the ring. I have no doubt he is going to win. No one stands a chance against him.

He's vile.

Even the Devil wouldn't dare to challenge this level of sin he has created.

As Maximo opens the door that leads into the main casino where all of the pretty women are dressed to the nines, and the men are wearing black-tie suits buying expensive drinks, they all turn their heads to stare at me. My shirt might be cheap, but the man it belongs to could kill their men with a snap of a finger.

Who needs money when I already have power?

I feel like I'm on top of the world and better than them when my hand is in Tongue's.

Until my knee gives out.

I almost fall and slam it against the floor again, but Tongue is there, lifting me into his arms without effort or breaking a sweat.

"You need to rest," Tongue says, and his chest vibrates from the whiskey notes in his voice. "Because I plan on doing more to that delicious body." He sucks my earlobe into his mouth, and my head falls onto his shoulder, an arousing sigh escaping me.

"You're gaining an audience," Maximo states, pressing the button to the elevator.

The elevator doors ding and slide open. Maximo is the first one to enter, then Tongue, then the goons. I tilt my head to the left giving Tongue the access he needs to kiss me.

"What the fuck do they put in the water over at the clubhouse?" Maximo fixes the gold cufflink attached to his sleeves, and his initials are etched in the elegant gold. "I need to get me some," he mutters under his breath, but no one hears him but me.

I act like I don't because I value my life, and I know he wouldn't be happy if he caught me staring at him. Maximo slides his card over a black scanner and the lights turn from green to red as we descend. After we pass the basement, the elevator doesn't give the floor or a hint of where we are going. We come to a smooth stop and the doors open, revealing a dark, poorly lit place.

Tongue must feel right at home because he hums in appreciation, like a cat purring when it's relaxed.

I thought the fighting ring would be fancier, but it's bare-bones and basic. The hallway leading to the ring is narrow and the floor is dirt. When we get to the main room, it's reminds me of a big garage since there is metal door leading outside where people are coming in and out of. The ring itself is fenced and there are bleachers on either side.

Above the ring, there is a dull yellow light and to the right is a stage with a microphone. I'm going to assume that is where Moretti stays since a throne-like chair is in the middle. Only a man in charge would sit in that chair. It's painted gold and the cushions are a dark red, like blood. I read somewhere red is a power color. If so, Maximo and Tongue are a lot alike.

Conversation is running rampant around us, so loud it's nearly giving me a headache. Smoke clings to the ceiling, similar to rainclouds and they block the light like the moon does the sun during an eclipse.

"She can sit in my chair since she is injured, Tongue. I will not let a lady suffer." Maximo holds out his hand, wanting me to take it so he can help me from Tongue's arms.

Tongue doesn't seem to like that idea, so he climbs up the steps to the stage and places me gently on the chair. He pushes my hair behind my ears, and I run my fingers through the new haircut we gave him. The pieces are still long, slightly curling around his nape, keeping it shaggy with a careless appeal.

He smashes his mouth against mine, kissing me senseless in front of everyone. We break apart, and he lays his forehead against mine. "Every kill is for you," he says.

"For us," I correct him.

"Okay, five fights. That's the deal. You have to win, or the deal is off, and I call your Prez and tell him all the dirty details."

Tongue straightens and his abs flex. His tattoos come to life, moving and dancing over the natural detailing of his body. There is one spot that is bare and it's right over his heart. It's easy to assume why, but I wonder if he was waiting for something special.

"I won't even break a sweat by the time the last one falls," Tongue says, then jumps on the fence and climbs up it like a monkey. When he gets to the top, he stares at me over his shoulder, winks, and jumps ten feet to the ground.

Everyone falls silent when the thunderous boom shakes the floor from Tongue's weight He looks like a superhero as he drags his fist across the dirt. A sandstorm dances around him as he straightens to his impressive height.

He is a furious storm ready to unleash catastrophe.

I don't feel bad for whoever gets in the ring with him because whoever chooses to go against him is a dumbass.

"What are you going to do if your psychopath dies?" Maximo asks, leaning against the throne. He dips into his pocket and pulls out two cigars. He hands me one.

I shake my head. "No, thank you. And he isn't going to die."

"What if he does?"

"He won't," I snip, annoyed that Maximo is testing me.

"If he does, you're more than welcome to stay with me. I'll give you all the riches. Your beauty deserves to be dripping in all the diamonds. Your body deserves to be bathed in cash and lavish oils." Maximo is closer now, his lips almost brushing against my ear, and I lean away.

Tongue is against the fence, clenching the chains with his fingers as he stares at Maximo. His chest heaves and his nostrils flare.

"The only thing I ever want my body bathed in, is Tongue."

Maximo twirls my hair around his finger, and I whip back, astonished he would touch me. "I can have that rearranged."

"I'd rather—" Maximo grunts, falling backwards onto his ass when I see the familiar ivory handle sticking out of his shoulder.

I snap my head toward the fence and see Tongue sitting on top of it, pissed off, but satisfied he hurt Maximo.

The crowd gasps and doesn't dare to cheer when they see the man that runs this show on the ground, yanking the knife from his shoulder. "That bastard fucking stabbed me," Maximo grits, tossing the knife on the ground. Blood spatters along the dirt and I bend over and pick it up.

It's lighter than I thought. I grip the handle tight and stand. "Be glad he didn't kill you. Maybe now you get the point. I am his and if he dies, I'd rather die than be with anyone else." I toss my hair over my shoulder and sit down on the ledge of the stage, then hop down, careful to put my weight on my good leg.

Tongue grips the top of the fence with one hand and then hangs his torso down, then stretches an arm out to take the knife that's still warm with blood.

"I thought you said he was mafia. Doesn't that mean you're as good as dead? What were you thinking? You better be glad his goons didn't shoot you."

"He knows what he was doing, and I'd like to see him try," Tongue cackles, then grabs my wrist and yanks me closer to him. I can smell the sweat and see the dirt clinging to his face. "Kiss me."

"After you win." I slither out of his hold and the torment and challenge in his golden-brown eyes tell me he is excited about the present he will receive after. I watch him climb up the fence again and jump down on the other side.

The hairs on the back of my neck stand up in warning. I'm getting that feeling again, the one that says someone is watching me. I know it isn't Tongue because the emotion I get is different. The wickedness slides over my skin like an invisible, sexual touch I don't want. I pretend not to notice and head back to the throne, limping up the steps to sit down. Maximo looks pissed as he holds a silk handkerchief to his shoulder, but he doesn't make any moves to hurt me.

"I deserved that," he says through pained huffs. "If I saw a man talking to my woman like that, I would have killed him. I'm glad he didn't. I'll have to apologize." The lights flicker and the crowd goes wild. This must mean it is the start of the show.

I cross one knee over the other and try to relax. I can't say there isn't a small part of me that isn't nervous. Maximo walks to the microphone and a few stragglers come in off the street, dipping under the metal door of the garage.

"Welcome friends. Foes. Tonight, I have a special treat. You're looking at the most notorious Ruthless King in Vegas. This is a one-time event. You will most likely never see him again. Place your bets. In three minutes we begin." He steps back from the microphone and sways from the pain in his shoulder. I hold back a laugh.

He deserves it.

"You want your chair back?"

"No. Please, sit." Something about his smile doesn't sit right with me, but I ignore it. He has something up his sleeve or maybe I'm pessimistic these days.

The lights strobe again, and I flinch from the quick pace. One of Maximo's men comes up to him and whispers in his ear.

"Fantastic," Maximo says. "The first fighter is here."

The room falls silent as the metal door lifts from the corner, showing a massive man with knots of muscle across his shoulders. I can only see the outline of his body and behind him, rain is falling, hitting the concrete.

I never thought I'd see a man bigger than Tongue, but I should know not to ever be surprised being submerged in this world. I rip my eyes away from the monster and see Tongue pacing the ring, staring at his opponent.

Now, I'm nervous.

I scoot forward on the seat and hold my breath as the lion sized fighter climbs the fence. The chains groan from the heavy weight, and the crowd murmurs. Did they place their bets on Tongue? Are they disappointed? Are we in over our heads?

We should have run away and never looked back. We don't need anyone but ourselves. Damn it. I could throw up.

Tongue tilts his head up as the man jumps down about to crush Tongue with his weight. My crazy comet doesn't move. He slings his arm in the air and the body of the knife slides right between the man's chest. Tongue lets go of the handle and the fighter falls to the ground, chest down, shoving the blade even further.

"Yes!" I whisper and squeal, clapping at his victory, but it isn't over yet. I cup my mouth with both hands as I watch Tongue circle the giant, who is trying to get up, but can't. He is on his hands and knees, gasping for air, but can't breathe because of the waterfall of blood leaving his mouth.

I try to stand, but Maximo holds me down against the seat by grabbing my shoulder. "You never know what can happen or what weapons can leave the ring. You're safer here. He would want you in this seat."

Maximo is right. Tongue wants me here, waiting for him when he is done. My excitement is soured by that eerie feeling again. I glance around the room, searching for something, anything to explain this, but all I see is blood-hungry people cheering on Tongue to kill a man.

I would feel bad, but the giant was going to do the same thing to Tongue. It's survival of the fittest and my man is the strongest of them all.

"What is it?" Maximo asks, staring out into the crowd, following my line of sight.

"Nothing, I thought I saw someone I knew." It's a lie, but what can Maximo do for me? He'd probably throw me in the ring given a chance.

No, thank you.

I wouldn't survive.

I'll cheer on the killer any day of the week, but I know my limits.

"Holy Moly." I'm in awe when I see Tongue kick the giant to his back, rip the knife from his heart, and dive into his mouth to cut his tongue out. He tosses the appendage to the side, then from right to left slices his opponent's throat.

Blood. Is. Everywhere.

A loud roar leaves Tongue, and from where he is standing, he points the knife at me as it drips his victim.

"Does he get a break now?" I ask, hoping I can get him some water or something, but Maximo throws his head back and laughs.

"Oh, you sweet, innocent thing. No. The fights will only get harder as time goes on. Only the best of the best survive."

I'm about to argue, but two fighters come out from the hallway at the same time and they both have samurai swords. I stand and stabs my finger in Maximo's chest. "That wasn't apart of the rules! That isn't fair."

"Oh, darling. Nothing is fair in love and war; don't you know that? People pay for a show."

I'm panicking now. They have fucking swords, and they scale the fence fast and agile, as if it's something they do every day just for the hell of it. Tongue doesn't seem worried and that must be nice because I'm freaking the fuck out. He licks the blade, then spits the blood out onto the dirt floor, gesturing the men with the much bigger swords to come at him.

They circle one another for so long, the crowd start to boo and become restless.

"What is he doing?" I ask myself, watching Tongue's eyes dart from one man to the next. He doesn't attack first. He is waiting for one of them to.

One samurai cuts through the air, and Tongue takes the opportunity to dive left, grab the man's arm, and without hesitation, controls the enemy's arm, slicing the sword through the air. For a minute, no one sees what happened.

Until the head of the second samurai falls to the ground. Tongue uses the guy's hesitation as he watches his friend's head roll across the ground and uses it as an advantage. Instead of using his own weapon, Tongue kills the man in his arm with his own sword, stabbing him right through the heart.

The crowd shouts in Tongue's victory, but he ignores the attention. He straddles the dead's lap and from here I can see the large erection tenting his jeans as he cuts out the tongues of the fallen. He tosses them to the side next to the giant's.

"Three down, two to go," Maximo informs.

Tongue wipes his forehead with the back of his hand, spins his weapon around as he searches for his next kill. "Who is next?" he yells, the boom from his lungs is louder than the shouts of the crowd.

A tall man wearing a grey hood comes out next, and his weapon is a gun. He climbs up the fence and jumps down, aiming the weapon at Tongue.

"No!" I cry and try to launch myself at the fence. I will do anything to get between the bullet and Tongue.

When the hood drops, I gasp, my stomach cramping at the man I see.

Andrew.

My only friend.

"It gets better, sweetheart," Maximo's sly words slither down my spine like the dangerous snake that he is.

I can tell Tongue is surprised, but not for long because he laughs, and his laughter quiets the excitement of the crowd. "Oh, my-oh-my, is it good to see you."

"Shut up!" Andrew hisses and when his eyes land on me, then Maximo, I know how he got here.

"What did you do?" I spin around so fast, I forget my knee is injured and almost fall forward, but Maximo catches me.

"I upped the stakes. Everyone wins some. Everyone loses some. Andrew came to see me for a favor about a year ago. He opened his own bookstore and he had issues paying me back, so I kept tabs." Maximo's finger slides under my chin. "I learned about his fascination with you. I told him he could fight tonight to help pay off his debt, and then you and Tongue showed up. It was like stars aligned."

A tear drips from my eye as I wrench my face away from his touch. I turn toward the ring, and Andrew is staring right at me. He has bags under his eyes, and his face is pale. He looks terrible. "What happened to him?" I ask.

"You did," Maximo says just as Andrew points the gun at me. "Oh, now there is a twist I didn't see coming."

"Andrew," I choke out his name, staring at a man that I thought was my friend.

"I loved you," he yells, "and then you started talking to him! This fucking psycho who followed you. Watched you. I knew, I fucking knew I'd lose you to him because good girls like you always fall for the assholes. I could have been good to you! Look at yourself, Daphne. He abuses you."

"No," I explain, inching my way toward the fence, but stopping at the edge of the stage. "He doesn't do anything I don't want him to do."

"That isn't good enough."

"It's going to have to be. It is always going to be him, Andrew. Always."

The barrel of the gun gets bigger as I stare down it. "I won't allow it." His fingers flex, and I shut my eyes when I know he is about to pull the trigger, but it never comes. After waiting a few seconds, I open my eyes to see Andrew on his knees, the gun pointed to his head.

His hand is chopped off, and he is holding it to his chest, cradling it as he sobs. Tongue is standing there with his dead opponent's sword in his hand, then places the tip against Andrew's throat.

"No!" I scream. "I don't want him to die, please, Tongue. Please. He's my friend."

"I don't want to be anything to you," Andrew replies, and the sharp bang of the bullet leaving the gun has me falling backward. I witness bits of brain, skull, and blood spew out the other side of Andrew's head.

I can't even hear myself screaming as heartbreak shatters me. I can't breathe. I didn't love him, but I cared for him. I looked forward to work every day because of him. This can't be real. It all happened so fast. Maybe that wasn't Andrew, and all of this is a sick joke.

He wouldn't have gotten into bed with a man like Maximo, would he? Did I know him at all? He was going to shoot me, but Tongue stopped it by slicing off his hand. There is a lot I can handle, but I don't know how to process this.

Andrew died because of me.

Because he wanted me, and I didn't want him.

Does friendship mean nothing? Is friendship not good enough?

The thought has me narrowing my watery eyes at Andrew's dead body, wishing his heart would pump for a few more minutes so I could spew my anger at him. If friendship wasn't enough, then what the hell would have been?

Tongue starts to climb the fence to come to me, but Maximo holds up his hand, stopping him. "You have one more fight."

"Fuck the fight," Tongue sneers, staring at me through the chain fence. He wants to come to me.

"Then you don't want to get married," Maximo reminds us. "One more."

"One more. One more. One more," The crowd chants and stomps their feet in equal rhythm.

What is love if there can't be different versions of it? Love is meant to be flexible, mendable, pliable to form what the heart yearns for in a certain person. There is a friendship love, a lover's love, a mother's love, a father's love, and so on, but there is one emotion people forget.

Out of love, hate is born.

And there are different versions of hate.

Right now, my love for Andrew is turning dark and twisted. A part of me is glad he is dead because I would have learned eventually that my version of love would not have been what he wanted.

And all there is left, is hate.

"I'm okay," I tell Tongue, wiping my cheek. "I swear."

I can tell he is torn. My wicked warrior wants to come to

my side, but right now, I'm filled with so much rage toward Andrew that I need Tongue to finish this once and for all. I want to move on with my life because now I realize how stagnant it has been.

"The last fighter. May the best man win," Maximo announces, a knowing smile on his face. Was Andrew not enough to torment me with?

Tongue's murderous smile fades, and I follow his line of sight until I see a familiar redhead wearing a kilt.

Both men stare at each other in shock and that's when I realize what Maximo has done.

Ruthless King vs. Ruthless King.

And only one man can come out alive.

CHAPTER SIXTEEN

Tongue

I'VE LIVED THROUGH A LOT OF NIGHTMARES, AND I'VE KILLED A lot of men. I've lost count of the number of tongues I've cut out and how many of my victims begged for their life. I've laughed in a dying man's face because it was deserved. I've bathed myself in blood and I've been so turned on by death, I've jacked off to the memory of inflicting pain.

But this…

I don't think I can survive knowing I killed Skirt. My brother. My family. I know there is a rift between me and the club right now for what I have done, but that doesn't mean I won't ever have their back.

"What the fuck is this Maximo? You said you had a fight for me. You didn't say this," Skirt sneers, clenching his fingers around the brass knuckles. I bet he is holding himself back from beating the living shit out of Maximo. I know I am.

"I'm not fighting him," I state, and the crowd boo's me. I flick them off, not giving a fuck what they have to say. I was doing this for Daphne, but I can afford to buy her my own ring and we can get married anywhere. I was only doing this because Maximo made a deal. I've hurt the Kings enough by hurting Sarah. Skirt has a little girl now, a wife, a son, and he is my family.

I'd have the power to kill him, but truth be told, I'd let him kill me if it meant him going home to see his family.

I'm vicious. I'm cruel. I'm fucked up.

But the one thing I've learned I'm not?

Heartless.

Daphne has made me realize that.

"If you don't do this, you do not get what you want," Maximo warns, wrapping his hand around the back of the throne.

I shrug and walk around the ring to pick up the tongues I've cut out. My swamp kitties are going to have a nice treat waiting for them when I overnight these bad boys. "I got what I want," I say simply, sliding the appendage in my cut pocket and staring at Daphne.

She gives me one of those smiles that makes it seem like everything is going to be okay.

"Fight or the girl dies," Maximo says, snapping his fingers. One of his goons presses a gun against Daphne's head and that beautiful, brilliant smile fades.

"Let her go or I swear to god, I'll fucking kill you," I warn Maximo.

"She'd be dead before you could. I refuse to lose money because you can't nut the fuck up and fight."

"He is my family!" I roar, spit flying out of my mouth as the rage turns to lividity.

"I thought she was your family?" Maximo runs a finger down her cheek, touching her.

Only I can touch her.

"I've stabbed you once. I'm not afraid to stab you again."

"Tongue, it's fine. We fight until one falls, not dies," Skirt says, walking toward the fence. "Just don't cut out me tongue. I need it. Dawn likes it too much," he winks, trying to lighten the mood, but I'm furious.

No wonder they call Maximo the damn Devil. He should name his resort Hell's Playground because that's all Maximo really likes to do, play in the fires until someone burns.

"I'm not fighting you," I tell him and grip the fence in my hands, blood dripping off them as I try to get as close to his face as possible. "Please, Skirt." I'm not the man to beg, but I am right now.

I can't handle the guilt.

He climbs the fence and lands beside me. "Ye girl is in danger right now, and if we don't fight, Maximo would probably kill her."

"He'll start a war," I whisper. "Why would he do that? It makes no sense."

"Business doesn't have to make sense when the person holding all the power wants something. And if we don't fight, I have a feeling he will kill her or take her. Unless ye can kill his goons at the same time, is it something ye want to risk?" Skirt looks around at the carnage and whistles. "Damn."

I spare another glance at Daphne, who is trembling in the arms of a man I want to add to my list to kill.

All I wanted to do was marry Daphne.

"Sorry, brother. I'm only doing what is best for ye," Skirt tells me right as he throws his professional UFC fucking fist through the air, slamming the brass knuckles against my jaw.

"Wayne!" Daphne screams my name, my real name out of fear as I fall into the fence, becoming someone else's victim for a change.

My own brother.

"Wayne? Shite, how did I not know that?" Skirt nails me again in the stomach. "How did I not know anything about yer past?" he says with a bit more resentment than I thought he'd have. He hits my jaw with his other hand. A smooth uppercut to the jaw has blood spewing out of my mouth. "Ye say we are family, ye call me yer brother, but I know nothing about ye," he says bitterly, kneeing me in the stomach next. "I would have fought ye demons with ye, Tongue." He grips me by the thick of the hair, yanking my head back.

I know I look weak in front of Daphne, but I know I'm not weak. I've won a thousand wars, but this battle, this is a defeat I deserve to feel.

"Fight me," Skirt sneers, throwing me across the ring. I slide through my fallen opponent's blood, soaking my jeans and clogging my fingernails.

"No," I croak, spitting, and feeling the side of my mouth swelling. No one has ever gotten the upper hand on me.

But this one time, this one time, I'm not going to fight.

"Fight me!" he roars, slamming his foot against my ribs, but I know it isn't as hard as he can kick or hit. He is going easy on me. "Why?"

"Because" I spit again. "Because I deserve this."

"Ye don't," Skirt chokes, gripping me by the back of the head again. "Sarah is okay. Reaper is pissed. He wants his punishment, but come home, Tongue."

"Not until he says."

Skirt sighs in anger, curling his lip in displeasure from my answer, then knees me in the face. The crowd roars when their favorite Scotsman pours blood. When Skirt fights, he always wins.

Always.

"Why?" he asks, again, slamming down against the dirt. I inhale a cloud of dust, choking, tasting the earth sticking to the inside of my mouth. The grit of the sand lines my gums. He slams his fist across my stomach again and Daphne cries my name. "We would have helped ye. We would have taught ye how to read and write. We would have—'

"Don't," I sneer, pushing him off me. I stagger to my feet. I point a finger at him, nearly crying again. I don't like crying. It confuses me. A man like me does not feel that deeply. I don't know how. "Don't you dare talk to me about my Uncle or what you saw in my drawings. You invaded my privacy." I throw my fist in the air next, slamming my knuckles against the side of his face. "Those were my secrets. That was my pain." I elbow him in the gut, take him by the back of the neck, turn around, and sling him over my shoulder, throwing him onto the ground in a pool of blood.

It splashes around us. Half of his face is covered in blood reminding me of a true warrior. His kilt is ruined, and the silver of his sword is swirling with red.

"That's it. Get mad, Tongue. Let's see how crazy ye can get." Skirt wipes the blood off his mouth, flashing his white teeth at me.

I crack my neck, holding in the need to snap Skirt in half. The restraint is hard. He has no idea how badly I want to break, but the sane side of me knows Skirt is family and we are being forced to do this to each other.

I pick him up by his neck the edges of my vision blurring,

the madness winning. All it will take is a quick flick of my wrist and he'll be dead.

"No! He's your family. Wayne, look at me. Look. At. Me." Daphne's desperate voice has me turning my head and Skirt is clawing at my hands, trying to make me let go of him. My eyes seek sanctuary, finding her blue eyes staring back at me. Even through her fear, even through her pain, she's giving me her strength. "He is family," she says again.

I tighten my grip around his neck and Skirt's face morphs into my Uncle's. All I see is him sneering back at me, hating me, judging me, making me look at him in women's clothing. I see a man that touched me, used me, hated me, hit me, burned me.

I hate the man in front of me.

I want him to die.

"Look at me," Daphne is on the other side of the cage, gripping the fence, and coming eye to eye with me, hoping to calm me. "Look at me, Comet."

I force myself to look at Daphne, not that my mind is helping me realize that I'm not with my Uncle, but my heart is guiding me. My Uncle's face is staring at me too when I look at her, but one thing powers through the haze, one thing that has never happened before.

Her blue eyes.

When I see them, my Uncle's face fades away, and the glasses appear on her face, her red pouted lips have my mouth watering and my cock hard.

"There you are," she whispers, pushing her fingers through the gaps of the fence. "There's my Comet."

I reach my free hand out to touch her, and when our fingers glide together, I'm taken back to the bookstore when I grabbed the book from her hand. Daphne.

I let go of Skirt, and he falls to the ground, gasping, choking, and coughing. He rubs his throat, then crawls to the side of the fence and leans against it. "I thought ye were going to kill me."

"I thought I was too," I answer honestly and his eyes round for a minute. "You have her to thank for your life." I step forward and lean against the fence, wrapping her fingers around mine. "Thank you. I love you, Daphne. I fucking love you." I can't stop the words flowing out of my mouth as I regulate my breathing, trying to come back down from the adrenaline rush.

"I love you too," she says, just as the lights go out and the metal of the garage door clanks, showing a dozen flashlights.

"Vegas Police Department!"

"FBI!"

I don't give a fuck about the law, but what I do care about is why I can't feel Daphne's fingers anymore.

"Daphne?" I call out her name in the dark. "Daphne!" I shout.

"Fuck, we need to get out of this ring before they find us!" Skirt whispers as he pulls me away from the fence.

"No, I'm not leaving her. Daphne!" the lights come back on and it's too late for me and Skirt. We have red lasers pointed at us that are attached to rifles.

"Get on your hands and knees! Now, drop the brass knuckles."

"Okay, okay," Skirt says, holding his hands up in the air to show we are innocent.

Jokes on him.

I'm anything but innocent, and I don't see Daphne, which breaks that little bit of sanity that was left in me. I dive to the left, sliding against the dirt, and grab the gun from that Andrew tried to kill Daphne with, aim, and fire.

I expect them to fire back and I feel a blazing heat in my thigh. It's a flesh wound. I aim the gun at each cop and fire. I have ten rounds left and ten cops.

I can't miss.

They drop like flies. Skirt army crawls through blood and dead bodies, grabs one of the swords, and stick it through the fence, gutting a cop where he stands, but not before he can get one last shot in, piercing me right in the shoulder. The gun drops from my hand and it's the most pain I've ever felt.

I can't feel my arm.

I try to flex my fingers, to grip the gun, but they don't move. They are paralyzed.

Still, it doesn't compare to the fear gripping thought that Daphne is injured. "Daphne?" I try to call out, but the searing pain grips my vocal cords.

"Aye, Tongue? Ye, okay? Yer fine. Yer going to be fine. Fuck, that's a lot of blood. I don't know if it's yours or the rest of the dead bodies."

"Daphne," I wheeze and dig my nails into his forearm. "Where is she?"

"I don't know."

"Find her!"

"No time, Tongue. We have to get out of here. Calvary is on the way."

"No, I need Daphne." Grunting, I roll to my side, my thigh burning and the hole stretching even further. "Comet!" I somehow manage to shout, but she doesn't answer me. "Comet!" I roar, slamming my fist down onto the ground. "Why isn't she answering, Skirt?" I wince when I roll over again and try to get up. I try to put my weight on the arm I can't feel, but I fall, and my shoulder hits the ground, radiating pain through my veins. "Skirt, please, look for her. I swear to God, I'll owe you my life." I'm not below begging when it comes to Daphne. What if she is hurt? What if she is scared? I need to find her.

"Okay, okay. Don't move."

I deadpan him, agitated.

He falls back before climbing up the fence. "I'm sorry. Ye know what I mean." He scurries up the fence and jumps down on the other side. Skirt cups his hands around his mouth and shouts for her, "Daphne! Daphne? Ye, here?" his Scottish accent echoes throughout the mostly empty room.

I swear to god when I get out of here, I'm going to kill Maximo. This was all his fault. I never should have agreed to fight for him. I never should have never walked her through these doors. Even I know that most people that come into this casino to fight never come out.

"Shit, Tongue!" Reaper's voice yanks me out of my regrets. The metal of the fence grinds the headache forming in my head. Black dots turn my vision to static as I search for Reaper. I'm surprised he is here. His boots land next to my head and sand flies, making me close my eyes from the sting. "Damn it, Tongue. What happened? Skirt dialed us 911. I have no explanation. It's a fucking bloodbath in here."

"Daphne," I clutch his shirt with my good hand and yank him down. "Please, if you can push your damn hate for me aside, find her. She's...she's..."

"I know buddy. She's your Sarah," Reaper pats my chest. "We're going to get you out of here. God, you look like shit."

"Skirt beat the shit out of me."

"You let him?" he asks, then snaps his fingers at Tool. "Get us out of here. He can't climb the fence. It's only a matter of time before someone comes looking for these cops, and we can't be here."

"We need to clean. We can't leave DNA evidence," Knives says.

"That's going to take too long. DNA is everywhere."

"Daphne!" I say with impatience. What the fuck do I need to do for people to get off their ass and look for her?

"We have to do what Boomer will do," Reaper states. "We're going to burn it."

"Burn down the casino again?"

"You have a better idea, Knives?"

"Nope," he pops the P. "I'll call Boomer to see what he would do."

"Jesus Christ, Knives. Get fucking gasoline, get a match, light the place on fire. Use your fucking head."

"Got it, Prez. Sorry." Knives runs out the garage door to get the supplies.

"Reaper, I can't feel my arm. I can't feel it."

"It's okay. Doc will fix you up, alright? This doesn't get you out of your punishment, you know."

"I wouldn't dream of it," I chuckle, then groan when the jostling from my laughter pulls at the wound on my shoulder. "I just wanted to marry her." That burning in my eyes tell me that losing her will kill me.

She's my sanity and without her, the thread keeping me human will break. My soul will be lost, and I'll be damned.

And I won't care.

"Tool is getting us out of here. I promise, we will find her, Tongue, okay? My Enforcer isn't going to live the life he's been living anymore. No more being in the corners and if she brings you out of them, then that's all I could want for you, *Wayne.*"

I squeeze my eyes shut when sweat drips down from my brows. "You knew? All this time?"

"Yeah, I knew. That's all I knew, I swear," he reassures.

My chest rises as I inhale, nodding, and relieved that's all he knew until lately.

"I'm sorry for not trusting you," Reaper says. "I'm sorry for invading your privacy."

"Okay, step back! It's falling," Tool hollers his warning as apart of the ring falls to the ground with a heavy bang.

"Let's get out of here," Reaper says, then points his chin at Slingshot. "Come get the other side of Tongue. Son of a bitch, he is heavy."

Slingshot runs to my side and lifts me. Reaper throws my dead arm around his shoulders and my knees buckle, but I keep myself up. Fuck, being shot hurts. "Daphne?" I stumble over my own two feet over the fence on the ground.

"We can't find her," Skirt runs to my side, sweating. He has dried blood on his face, a bruise across his cheek, and his knuckles are purple from the brass. "I looked everywhere, Tongue. We searched high and low. Maximo is gone, along with his goons. The only people in the casino are the ones gambling."

I'm going to kill Maximo for taking her and when I do?

I'm going to take my fucking time.

Bit by bit, cut by cut, piece by piece, he will know my wrath.

CHAPTER SEVENTEEN

Daphne

HOLY MOLY.

I feel drunk.

I sit up and smack my head against something hard and unforgiving. I blink, trying to gain some form of sight, but it's dark.

Really damn dark.

My heart rate kicks up when I realize it isn't my vision that's the issue; it's the space I'm in. I pat my hands along the carpet. It's thin, cheap, and scratchy. A whimper escapes me, but I swallow my panic just in case someone can hear me.

Deep breaths. *Everything is going to be fine. Everything is going to be fine.*

I try to calm the blood rushing through my ears, but the only way to do that is to calm my heart. A tear leaks from the corner of my eye when I hear the bass of speakers pounding beside me from music. I know we are moving. And by the size of the space I'm in, I'm in a trunk.

I'm going to die.

"No, you aren't going to die," I whisper to myself. I have too much to live for now. Tongue's face appears in my mind, menacing and intimidating, yet fiercely beautiful and loving. I need to get back to him.

I slide my palms along the curve of the trunk, trying to find a latch, or something that can get me out of here. I don't feel anything. "Come on!" My eyes fill with hot tears and fall one after the other as I search for the taillights next. I remember watching a video in high school about being trapped in the trunk of a car. Something about taillights. I can't remember. I know I can somehow loosen them or push them out to stick my hand out of the hole to flag down a car.

Why is it in stressful situations, I can't seem to remember anything? I even took a few self-defense classes. Look at the good that did me. The lights went out in the underground garage and someone wrapped their arms around me and what did I do?

I blanked.

I couldn't think of anything. All I knew was that it was dark, and someone was touching me. How useless could I be?

And now I'm in a trunk.

Just like my high school health teacher warned us about. I knew I should have paid for the few extra classes, but I wanted this classic first edition of Oliver Twist which cost an arm and a leg, so I didn't take the classes. I got the book instead.

I'm starting to wonder about my priorities.

When I get out of here, the first thing I'm going to have Tongue do, is teach me how to think on my feet.

"Oh!" I say when I feel the taillight, but I can't find how to push it out.

And that's what I get for reading in health class while I should have been more focused on the video.

Squeaky brakes sound and the car comes to a stop.

Holy Moly.

This is happening.

Do I fake being asleep? Do I play dead? What do I do? What's about to happen? I only have a few seconds of peace left before the person comes around and takes me out of the trunk. I need a weapon.

I wish I had the freaking knife Tongue wants to make me. I'd keep it strapped to my thigh, right where he cuts me and licks me, so I know he is always there. I rub my fingers over the thin scab along the cut between my legs, wishing he were here right now.

I love him.

God, I hope he is okay.

We have finally found each other after a life of being so lost, we can't be pulled apart now, but that's life isn't it? Life can only be so good before it's bad.

Balance.

I've never been good at balancing.

A door slams shut, and the vibrations of the engine stop when the driver shuts off the car. In hurried motions, I feel around for a weapon, a tire iron, a damn shoe, a water bottle, anything someone throws in the back of their car but there isn't anything.

Oh, wait! I wrap my hand around something long, skinny, and round. It feels like a stick or a rod of some sort. I hide it against my side and the trunk unlocks. The one thing I want to see is the face of the man who took me.

But I don't get the chance because when the trunk opens and the night is revealed, the man is wearing one of those creepy baby masks with a hint of blush on the cheeks and a smile that would give someone nightmares.

He grips my arm hard enough to bruise. It isn't like when Tongue touches me, bites me, cuts me, because it's what we both yearn for. I need him to mark me like that so I can feel his love for me, so I can see his love for me.

This man is hurting me.

"Come on, kitty. We have a long walk." He yanks me out of the car and my injured knee hits the inside of the trunk, right against the latch, and I bite back a cry of agony. I keep the stick to my side as he drags me out of the vehicle, and when my feet land on the ground, I fight.

And I fight like hell.

I lift the weapon in the air and slam it against him. "You bastard!" I keep slamming the wooden stick against his head, neck, then shove the end in his stomach. When he grunts, doubling over in pain, I do what every woman does when they need to run. I swing the rod between his legs and nail him right in the damn crotch.

He falls to the ground, cupping his cock, and I freeze, watching him gag from the pain scorching his balls.

Holy moly.

That worked.

Shit. Run, you fucking idiot!

I drop the rod and run down the dirt road. I'm surrounded by desert, rocks, and trees. I follow the road, deciding it's the best bet to stay on a path. Paths are good. They lead in...a direction which is better than where I was before.

My foot hits a rock, and I crash face-first into the ground.

Rocks cut along my cheek, but I don't stay down long. I inhale a few pebbles, chew on a few grains of sand, but don't bother spitting them out. There isn't time for me to think to spit. I stumble as I try to get up, the palms of my hands burn from the rubbing of the rocks.

My lungs are balloons, inflating and deflating with every inhale and exhale as I run. Tears fly down my face, and I pump my arms so I can run faster. My knee throbs, but I can't give in to the pain. There isn't anyone here.

It's me.

And him.

The oddest thing I'm noticing right now is the sky. I'm scared out of my mind, sweat is a blanket over my skin, and I'm running for my life, but the night sky is gorgeous right now. Blue and black hues are so deep and crisp, I feel like I could jump and touch the stars with how bright they are twinkling.

I guess if I'm going to die, out of all the nights, I'd rather lose my life under a beautiful sky instead of a rainy one.

I'm tackled from behind, and I hit the ground again. This time, my teeth pierce my lip and there is a high-pitched ringing in my ears. Someone grips my shoulders and flips me over. I struggle to open my eyes, but I manage, tasting blood from the cut across my lip. My hands lifted into the air and zip tied.

All I see is the baby mask. It's a clouded pale flesh color. I can see hues of his face, but not enough to make an I.D. It's something someone wears on Halloween.

"Do you know how long I've been watching you?" the man's voice is garbled, but not naturally, either from smoking cigarettes or damage to his throat. All I know, is it's a sound I'll never forget for the rest of my life.

I'll hear him when I close my eyes. It's the kind of voice

that's rememberable. If I'm surrounded by a crowd and he speaks one word, I'll hear him, and I'll know.

My arms are bound, but the rest of my body isn't. I kick, trying to push him off me, fling my elbows, but he straddles my lap and holds me down in the middle of the dirt road. In between my whimpers, I hear the rubbing of wings of crickets singing.

Fear is a paralytic controlling my body, but somehow the world finds a way to go one.

It's impressive, shocking, and more terrifying when you realize you're about to die, but all you can hear is the life around you. I can feel the breeze against my skin, the dry air, but the promise of cold nights approaching. A bird caws in the distance, a rattle of a snake shivers, and those damn crickets are getting louder.

"I told you not to go near him. I told you. I warned you what he did and yet you were with him anyway. What did I have to do, kitty? To save you from him."

"Why? So you can have me to yourself?" I sneer, gathering the blood in my mouth to launch it at his face.

"No. No, I don't want you. I'm trying to do you a favor. I'm trying to save you from his madness!" he roars so harshly; I can smell the coffee on his breath. "I'm trying to save you from him. Why can't you see that? He isn't good for you. None of them are. You are...you are..." he says the words again, this time, like he is fascinated with me. He hovers his hand over my jaw, then slides his hand down to the bruise across the middle of my throat. "He did this. He hurt you. I knew he would. I've been watching them and then Tongue got away from me. He got away!"

I turn my head away when he rubs his nose in my hair,

then across my jaw. My chin wobbles as I do my best not to cry, but it's impossible.

"I told you, I sent you the roses. I gave you clues about what would happen if you didn't stay away and look at you. They aren't good people. Especially, Tongue. I've watched him—oh, yes—I've watched him. I buried him, and I hate that he lived! Everyone loves him, but they don't see him as I see him. Sick recognizes sick, and he is a sick fuck, isn't he?" the man says softly against my cheek. "Look what he did to you. I wouldn't do this to a woman if I had one. Too pretty."

I keep my mouth shut. I'm not about to tell him I like every single thing Tongue does to me because what he and I have is love. It's intense. We give each other everything we need. Maybe he is a sick fuck, but you know what?

I am too.

"I did a little research on you too, you know," he chuckles, then taps the side of my temple. He brings his lips down to my ear and the warm air against my cheek reminds me of the heat kicking on in the middle of summer, suffocating me for a second. "You. Have. Psychosis." He taps three times against the side of my head. He lowers his voice, "Do you think I'm real? What if I'm not? What if this is all a delusion in that twisted head of yours? It's okay," he shushes me as I cry, petting the side of my head. "I'll take care of you. I'm going to help you. Okay? I'm going to help you."

"I don't need your help. I'm fine. I'm healthy." *Unlike you.* I want to say, but again, I swallow my tongue and stare at the road fading into the night.

"Mmm, is that why you're on medication? Because you're fine?" he rolls off me and zip ties my ankles together next. "We don't need medication. Nothing is wrong with us. You need to accept who you are. You don't have an illness. You have a gift."

It doesn't feel like a gift when I'm driving, and I hallucinate I'm about to drive off a cliff or my dead mother is talking to me from across the dinner table. There have been worse breaks in reality, sometimes suicidal thoughts, sometimes my mom would ask me to join her.

Sometimes, I'd want to.

Until I got on the medication.

"It's why I've switched your pills out with a placebo."

"No," I shake my head in denial. That can't be possible. I would have had symptoms. I think. Maybe.

"You'll see. You're going to feel so much better instead of living in a fog, unable to be yourself because society thinks you're broken!" he yells, sliding his arms under my body and slings me over his shoulder. He trudges out from the side of the road and, steps up on higher ground, and begins to walk into the trees.

Vegas is mostly desert, but there are some areas that are wooded and rocky. I bet I'm about to get thrown off that cliff I used to see when I had breaks in my reality. At least it will be a quick death.

"We are going to be great friends. I found a place. It's close to the Ruthless Kings, you know. I like to keep an eye on them. They can't be trusted. Especially Tongue. I buried him. I told you that, right?"

I lift my head to see where we are going, but I see a ton of land, and it's hard to decide where I am when I am seeing everything upside down. I open my mouth and start to scream at the top of my lungs, "Help me! Someone help me! Help me!"

He flings me to the ground, the thin skin around my

elbow pierced by a cactus. "Why did you have to go and do that? I thought we were friends. I've been doing you so many favors." He sighs, clearly not happy with me. He rips a section of his shirt off, squats, and carefully wraps the material around my head after stuffing it in my mouth, then ties it, tight.

"That ought to do it," he says proudly, patting my cheek. "Now, what was I saying?" he lifts me up and over his shoulder again. "Right. Tongue, your little boyfriend. I buried him. Six feet under. The chances of him surviving were…slim," his voice darkens. "He was so stupid, walking around, all scary and badass, yet he couldn't read the back of a milk carton."

I mumble around the mouth gag, "He isn't stupid!" not that it matters. It sounds like nothing, but I can't sit back and let him talk about Tongue like that. Tongue is smart, he is brilliant, and I can't wait to teach him the things he has missed out on because he will own the fucking world if given a chance.

I'm going to give it to him.

I lift my arms and slam them against my kidnapper's back. I'm sick of this nice guy act. He isn't nice. Nothing about him is fucking nice. I want to go home. I need to know Tongue is okay. I want to live my life waking up to Tongue licking my skin and promising a world filled in his shadows.

"Will you stop? That hurts. I have feelings."

I scoff and mumble, "I don't care." It doesn't sound that way, again, I'm sure he can't understand me, but it's worth a try. I keep hitting him, hoping I punch a kidney, or I paralyze him somehow, but he keeps walking as if he is in a field of damn wildflowers, casual and happy.

Holy Moly.

This is exhausting.

"We are here." He slings me over his shoulder again and holds me like a baby. "See, this can be our new home. We can get people like us. We can have our Asylum. It can be a place of safety where we can all be normal."

I tremble, slowly moving my neck until I'm looking at an old, run-down brick building. The windows are bashed in. There are plywood sheets over the door with a big red X to warn people to stay away. I bet this house is hundreds of years old. It's beautiful.

Or it was.

Until this creep found it.

CHAPTER EIGHTEEN

Tongue

"D APHNE," I MUMBLE HER NAME AS I WAKE UP SLOWLY, THE sound of machines beeping interrupting my dream. Daphne was there. She was beautiful in a long white dress, wearing my ring, and that night, while we were alone in our room, she let me carve my property patch into her skin while we fucked.

It's a dream that needs to become a reality.

But she isn't here.

"Daphne?" I croak, then yank out the oxygen tube hissing through my nostrils. "Daphne!" I yell through the cold, dark room. I used to yearn to live in the shadows, to be in the place I call home, but now, there is no appeal without the light at the end of the tunnel.

The light is Daphne.

"Hey, Tongue. Woah, it's okay. You're at the clubhouse

You're safe." Doc's voice has my eyelids trying to open but they are sandbags, heavy and full of grit.

"Daphne."

His face comes to view after he flips on the lamp and even though he has pretty boy looks, his back is carved up like a Thanksgiving turkey. We all have our fucking demons, and some are worse than others. A disappointed and dreadful line appears on either side of his lips. "I'm sorry, we haven't found her yet."

The heartrate monitor beeps quicker as my worst nightmare takes hold of my body. I turn my head to the right so Doc can't see the glassy mirage in my eyes, but then I see Sarah in the bed next to me. She's awake, staring at me with a kind smile.

"Sarah." Her name is broken on my tongue. A tear drips onto my cheek and this time, I understand my emotion. I'm thankful she's okay, and I'm scared out of my mind that Daphne is not. "I'm so glad to see you alive."

"Ah," she waves her hand dismissively. "It's going to take more than a knife wound in the stomach to bring me down." Sarah chuckles, then lays her hand over her stomach from the pain.

"I thought you were my Uncle," I admit. "The guys they found…"

"I know," she cuts me off and reaches her hand across the space between us. With my good arm, I meet her hand with mine and hold onto it. She frowns, and her lip trembles as she begins to cry. "I don't blame you. I'm so sorry, Tongue. I'm so sorry that happened to you." She studies my chest, no doubt trying to see the burn scars under the tattoos.

"Stop saying that. You knew before everyone. It isn't your fault."

"I'm still sorry," she says. "And I'm sorry about Daphne. Is she—"

"—She's mine, Sarah. Mine. She's everything. I need her. I need to find her."

"We will find her. Reaper won't let her be away from you."

I hope not, but I know punishment is still in my future from Reaper for what I did to Sarah. I'll never forgive myself. If Reaper decides for Daphne to be away from me, I'd have to leave the club because Daphne is what I need to survive.

Surviving used to be as easy as breathing, but now it isn't so simple. There's more to it than that. It's emotion. The damn thing I used to want to ignore because it can blind you. It isn't so bad though, fighting while blind because the heart leads you to what you need to do. I've been fighting all my life to breathe, but I haven't been fighting all my life to live.

Daphne has taught me the difference.

"Tongue," Doc says my name with a heavy burden as he sits down in the chair next to me. "We need to talk about your arm."

"I don't care about my arm." I yank the needle from the top of my hand and then pull the wires off my chest. "I need to find Daphne, and I can't do that from this damn room. It feels more like a graveyard than a hospital with all the traffic that's been through here. Sorry, Doc."

"No, I get it, but you can't leave."

"You aren't going to stop me," I reply, getting more pissed off by the minute.

"Nope," Badge stops at the bottom of the steps and twirls handcuffs in the air. "But I can."

"And I can make sure you can't feel your entire body." Doc moves too fast for me to notice and presses something sharp against my neck. "This sedative will knock you out for days, Tongue. Do not test me."

Badge whistles as he struts over to my side of the bed and instead of cuffing my hands like a normal person, he slings the metal over the left ankle and traps me against the bed. "What? I wanted to make sure he wasn't going to go anywhere," he defends himself as Doc and me both stare at him in discontent.

"I didn't want him to feel trapped," Doc explains, dropping the needle from my neck.

"Well, he brought it upon himself," Badge states, leaning against the wall and crossing his arms over his chest. "You know we can't trust him to stay."

"I'm not a fucking dog," I yank against the cuff attached to the bed, a brief, quick reminder that I'm more like a dog now than I ever have been before. I'm fucking chained. I might as well sleep outside in the fucking mud and be useless because that's how I feel.

"Hey!" Slingshot says with too much cheer. All of us turn our heads to the happy-go-hungry guy, and the smell of tacos has my stomach grumbling. He jumps down the steps and hands a bag to Sarah. "I got your favorite. I know how much you like the little taquitos with that spicy dip. And Tongue, I got you the macho box of carnitas with extra cilantro." He points a finger at me and shakes it. "Don't think I didn't notice how much cilantro you used. Anyway, I got you ten of them. Thought we could share, like we did on Halloween." He lifts his arm above his head and scratches his shoulder. "I—uh—I'm sorry."

I sigh, close my eyes, and roll them so no one can see. I have a feeling every single member is going to apologize to me for what they saw in my journals. It is exactly what I wanted to avoid.

"About Daphne," Slingshot hurries to explain his apology. "I'm sorry about Daphne. I know how much you like her."

"Love her."

"What?" he asks, coming around the side of the bed. Badge and Doc share a look. I know that shared glance. They think I'm crazy because not much time has passed since I met her. A guy like me loving a girl like Daphne, isn't good, is it?

"I love her," I correct Slingshot, sounding out each word slowly so they understand me. "Shocker, isn't it? That a monster like me is so capable of feeling something other than the urge to kill."

Doc opens his mouth to say something, but he is interrupted by the basement door opening again. Slingshot sits the bag of tacos on the nightstand, then plops down in the recliner beside me. He laces his fingers over his stomach as a stampede of boots clobber down the steps. Reaper, Bullseye, Tool, Knives, and Skirt appear. Skirt has a bruise on the side of his face and a blue bruise decorates his throat from when I nearly choked him to death.

"Skirt—" I begin to start my apology, but he holds up his hand. "Don't worry about it. I know. I'm sorry Maximo set us up like that."

"Yeah, he's officially on my shit list."

"About time," Moretti says from the bed all the way at the end. Shit, I didn't even know he was there.

"You don't even know anything about him," Reaper replies to Moretti.

"So. I still don't like him."

"I don't have the energy to deal with you right now." Reaper grips the end of the bed and his cheek jumps as he tightens his jaw. He rubs a hand over his mouth, walks between the beds, and kisses Sarah on the forehead. "Hey, Doll."

She hums as her eyes close, relishing in his touch. I should have relished in Daphne more.

"How are you feeling?" he asks her, rubbing his fingers over her cheek.

"Like brand new," she jokes, which only has me feeling worse.

"Good." I can tell he doesn't believe her and that's when he turns his sights on me.

And damn, they are full of damn fury.

"You up for talking, Tongue?" he asks, sitting on the edge of Sarah's bed.

The crinkling of paper has everyone turning their head to Slingshot. He is digging into the taco bag, and when he feels a dozen eyes on him he pauses and glances up from peering at the tacos. "I'm hungry," he says.

"No," Reaper orders.

"Reaper, I haven't had any today. I've been waiting on Tongue so we can share."

Reaper rubs his temples and takes a deep breath. "I said no. I'm not dealing with your gassy ass today."

Slingshot scoffs. "I...I...I took my pill."

"Yeah, we all know that doesn't matter," Bullseye mumbles and Tool elbows him in the gut. "What? It isn't like we aren't all thinking it."

"Okay, focus." Reaper places his palms together in a steeple position, exhaling. "Please, for the love of all things vile, fucking focus. The lot of you. For five goddamn minutes!" he shouts, his composure breaking. He grabs the lamp and throws it, submerging us in darkness. "Damn it! Someone turn on the light," he barks.

"Got it," Tool says, then a few seconds later, we hear a thud. "Shit. Stupid goddamn wall."

"Any day now, Tool."

"Got it. I got it, Prez." Tool flips on the light above and the sudden brightness has me turning my head and holding my hand over my eyes.

"Okay." Reaper pinches the bridge of his nose and there are footsteps running across the floorboards above. Hearing it makes him smile because it's the kids running around the house. "Damn it; I'm so tired. Too much has been going on. The corn maze is still up for fuck's sake. Skirt still doesn't have a home. Tongue killed ten cops."

"Nine," Skirt mumbles. "I killed one."

"Don't argue semantics with me. I'm really not in the mood," Reaper warns and Skirt nods, swallowing nervously. "Tongue, first thing is first, I need every detail about Daphne. Do you know anyone that would have taken her?"

"The same asshole that buried me alive," I say off into the distance, staring at the playroom door behind Skirt's shoulder. "He's been leaving her notes. You know because you thought it was me. He is coming after me, Reaper. The Groundskeeper is still here in Vegas, and I think he has set his sights on me. He knows what I do to people. He left another note after that, sent her roses. I…followed her to her Aunt's house. I just wanted…I wanted to see her one last time before I left."

"Left? You were going to leave?" Sarah asks me.

"I was going to go to NOLA until I was invited back. I was going to get away, see the swamp kitties, try to forget about Daphne, and figure out if Vegas was really right for me."

Sarah inhales and catches herself on a sob. "You'd leave?"

"Obviously not. I didn't say goodbye to Daphne. I watched her for a little bit. She woke up. We fucked. I knew I couldn't leave. She had flowers there from him. He left a note. He's left her three fucking notes to stay away from me. She should have stayed away from me," I whisper, staring up at the ceiling as I plop my head on the pillow. "Then Seer called—"

"We know. Seer called me too. Poor guy can't get away from us. Why didn't you say anything about the notes? We could have protected Daphne."

"You didn't even believe Daphne and I were together. You thought I was killing people, taunting her. You didn't trust me; why the hell would I trust you?" The anger can't be hidden because I've pushed it down for so long. "I thought I was on my own. I had Daphne. She was all I needed. I went to Maximo and asked if we could get married there, he had a condition. That I fight to kill and bring him in money, and I could have whatever I wanted. I wanted that for Daphne, so I didn't have a problem with it. Until Skirt showed up."

"I was there to make money too, Tongue," Skirt combs his fingers through his long red beard.

"You aren't ever alone, Tongue. You're our family. No matter how fucking mad I am or disappointed or want to fucking kill you for hurting Sarah, I know it was unintentional, you aren't alone. This is what we are here for. You've been worrying us, then the journals... We thought you were only obsessed with her, we didn't know—"

I hold up my hand and silence him. "I am obsessed with her. I stalked her. Don't think for one minute that my love for her isn't unhealthy and dangerous because it is. I will kill everyone who gets in the way, including my own family." I let the threat hang in the air, staring at all of them, daring them to stop me from finding her and bringing her into my arms once more. "He has her. What if she is buried? What if she can't breathe like I couldn't breathe? What if she's banging against the wood, calling out for me, and I can't hear her?" I twist my hands to-gether, feeling useless. I'm a horrible protector. A few seconds of the lights going out and her fingers...they were wrapped around mine. They were right there and then they weren't.

Then she was gone.

"I doubt it," Badge says, pushing his foot off the wall. "He seems to care, leaving her flowers, warning her about you, do-ing his best to protect her. I think she's fine. Well, as fine as she can be in the hands of a maniac." He purses his lips, "No offense, Tongue. I mean, a more obviously unstable maniac."

"No offense taken." I'm actually a little annoyed she's in the hands of another monster. I trust myself with her, she trusts me. There are a hundred different shades of crazy and the only one I know she has faith in, is mine.

Badge's phone beeps, and he pulls it out of his cut pocket and grimaces. "Well, we have a new problem."

"What?" Reaper snaps.

"There has been a missing person's report filed by her Aunt with a ten-thousand-dollar reward."

"So if we find her and return her, we get the cash? Sweet." Slingshot stuffs a taco in his mouth, and I try to lift my arm to slap him on the back of the head, but my arm won't lift because I can't feel it.

"If I had my knife, I'd kill you for saying that." I lean to the right and press my nose against his cheek. I hope he can smell the stench of my fucking breath, but I'm close to tearing into his skin with my teeth. "We will find her, and when we do, she stays with me. She isn't going back to her Aunt."

"She has to go back to her family, Tongue. That doesn't make any sense. You sound—"

"—Crazy?" I whip my head around and stare at Sarah.

"Maybe you've forgotten who I am. She isn't going back. I don't care what I have to do in order to make that happen. She stays by my side."

"We can at least let her Aunt know that—" Sarah starts to argue and sits up in the bed, grimacing as she holds her stomach. "That isn't fair, Tongue. You cannot be that selfish! She has family. You cannot be the only person in her life. That is toxic. Her Aunt loves her. You can't take that away from Daphne. She'll resent you for it. Maybe not now, maybe not tomorrow, but she will. You can't do it. I won't allow you to take that from her."

"And what are you going to do Sarah? What are you going to do to stop me?" I chuckle, knowing I'm being a complete asshole, but I can't focus on someone else loving Daphne when she isn't even near me right now.

"I'll burn you just like your fucking Uncle did! Just how he took from you, I will make sure you do not do that to Daphne."

I inhale a sharp breath from her cruel threat. A few guys look away from us, shocked by her statement. I have to admit, I am too. "You wouldn't," I say on a held breath.

"I'd have Reaper himself hold you down. I love you Tongue but taking someone else's love away from her because you want her all to yourself. That isn't fair."

"Love isn't fair," I say after a few seconds of silence.

"That isn't true. Love should be the fairest feeling you should ever experience. The only thing it should never be is selfish."

I disagree. I think it is the most selfish feeling on the planet and in existence. How is love not selfish when once you get a taste, it's all you ever want? It's powerful and all-consuming, then every word, every breath I get from her, every touch, it isn't enough. And every ounce of energy she uses on someone else, I want.

Selfish?

That's the least of my worries when it comes to Daphne.

"Save it, Sarah. Not everyone is perfect like you and Reaper. Me and Daphne are cut from the same fucked-up cloth. You don't know her. You don't know what she wants or likes. I know what she wants, and I know she'd never want to leave my side."

"Spoken like a true psychopath, Tongue."

"Spoken like a spoiled little brat," I spit at her, suddenly wondering how the fuck I'm friends with such a naïve little girl.

"Enough," Reaper warns, searing his brown, amber eyes at me. "You're on thin fucking ice. Don't talk to her like that, Tongue. Sarah, you know better because you know Tongue. Now, say you're sorry. The both of you."

"No," Sarah and I say at the same time and the stubbornness in each of us has me smiling. I lift my hand to rub away the tilt on my lips.

"I'm going to die young because of you two. No, everyone. I'm going to die young because of everyone here."

A ding chimes and Badge is taking his phone out, reading a message. "Okay, everyone put away your cocks, lady included," Badge gives Sarah a knowing look. Everyone knows Sarah has the most balls in the club. She glances away, folding her arms over her chest. "Mercy just messaged. He said he just received a package on his doorstep. He thinks it is from the Groundskeeper. He is on his way over."

"Is he still in the FBI?"

"I don't know. I haven't looked. I'm assuming, yeah. He closed down the Hellhounds. The FBI has to be promoting him or some shit."

They glance toward the ceiling when a loud pounding knocks on the front door. The dogs bark and Juliette's voice is muffled from the planks between the basement and the living room. I stare at Tool who is smiling just from hearing her and before I would have called him crazy, but now I get it.

I'd do anything to hear Daphne's voice one more time.

"I guess he is already here. I wish people would say that instead of saying, 'Hey, I'm on my way' when really they mean, 'Hey, I'm here." Badge stuffs his phone back in his pocket and stands there, still.

Reaper's head bobbles for a second, staring at Badge like what the hell is he doing and says, "Well, are you going to go answer the damn door?"

"It is answered."

"Badge, go get Mercy and see what he has."

"He can find his way down. It isn't hard."

Tool snorts and twists the screwdriver behind his ear. Reaper laughs, grabs my knife that's on the counter and throws it at Badge. It lands right in the material of his shirt above his shoulder, nailing him to the wall.

"I'm really sick of being tested. My patience is gone." Reaper stalks up to him and grips the handle of the knife, flicking the edge so it cuts the shirt. "I beg someone to argue with me again for the rest of the night and see what the fuck I do. Just see." Prez points the knife over Badge's chest and gives him a wicked snarl. "It's been too long since I've felt a heartbeat in my hand. Do you catch my fucking drift, Badge?"

Badge gulps and nods.

"Great. Now, go get Mercy. Let's get Daphne back so Tongue can get his fucking crazy on and we can all get back to normal. Okay?"

"Yes, Prez." Badge starts to walk away, and the basement door opens, heavy boots clonk, and I know it's Mercy finding his way down. Badge was right, but we aren't going to question Reaper when he is about to snap.

Sarah wipes her cheek and turns her back toward me, and a large part of me dies knowing she's mad at me. She's right. Everything she said about me was right, but I can't admit that.

Yet.

"Mercy, please tell me that the package is a snow globe your sister sent you," Reaper unlocks a small mini-fridge next to the staircase and takes out a small bottle of whiskey. He opens it, tosses the cap, and chugs the entire bottle down. He notices Sarah crying and grabs another bottle, shuts the fridge with his boot, and sits on the edge of her bed. "Here, Doll. Drink this and sleep." He tilts her chin up and lays a kiss on her lips. "Everything will be okay."

She chugs the bottle, then tosses it behind her, and the airplane bottle smacks me right in the face.

The guys snort and Skirt holds out his hand for a high-five and she slaps his palm.

That was just lucky.

Well-deserved, but lucky.

"Uh, no. I don't have a sister, sorry. So, there isn't an address on it, but it had a note that said to deliver it to Tongue. So, here, Tongue." Mercy hands me the box, placing it on my lap. My arm is strapped to my chest due to the wound.

I brush my hands over the ribbon, and I rub the silk, pinching my brows together. I stroke the fibers, playing them like a harp. They are soft, beautiful, and familiar. The rich brown tying the tan paper over the square is something I've seen and felt before. A sourness turns my stomach, and I untie the bow, watching the strands fall to the side. The breath that leaves me is broken and devastated as I bring the strands to my nose and inhale. "Oh god," I tighten my fist around the silk.

"What? What is it?" Slingshot wipes his mouth and sips a coke. The slurping noise breaks me, and I reach over, throw the cup across the room. The top falls off as it slaps against the wall, and ice scatters across the floor.

I shove the brown pieces in his face. "It's her goddamn hair!" I roar, then stare at every face in the room. "It's her fucking hair. No," my voice breaks as I bury my face along her beautiful shiny strands. I inhale, like I did that night she was asleep. The citrus hints has my mouth watering for tangerines. I'm hungry for Daphne. I'm starving for her.

I miss her.

"It's her hair," I whisper, feeling smaller. I am not a small man. My size is the one thing I use to intimidate people, but now I'm worthless. I've never felt like this before. I don't know how to handle it. What do people do in these situations? I've never loved before. I've never felt so lost and weak.

"Tongue," Sarah turns over and reaches out for me, pushing away her anger for me.

I don't hesitate. I grab my best friend's hand and try not to lose it. My chest rises and falls quickly, and pressure builds inside me. I can't breathe. This is why I've stayed in the shadows. This is why. I don't know how to deal with situations like this. I want to kill this Groundskeeper guy, once and for all.

He took what is mine.

I'm going to get her back, and I don't care if the attempt kills me.

"Tongue open the box," Reaper orders, reaching slowly for the strands of hair hanging from my fingers.

I rear back, holding them to my chest. "No. Don't take them from me," I say, not wanting to part with the only thing I have left of her.

"We can find her if we know what is in the box."

What if I open the box and it's a body part? Or worse, her heart?

I reach down, somewhere inside my barren fucking soul and find the last bit of strength I have, tear the paper off the box and peel the lids apart.

A fucking piece of goddamn paper.

In a box.

"You've got to be kidding me," I reach inside and throw the box off my lap. I stare at the words and grind my teeth together because it's a note for me, and I can't fucking read it. I know my name when I see it, but that's it.

I want to read it. I can't be less than anymore. I want to be the man Daphne deserves.

"Let me see it, Tongue. I'll read it," Sarah offers, and Reaper peels my fingers off the page, one by one.

"It's okay," he reassures, but he's just saying that. It isn't okay.

Nothing about this is okay.

It's not even embarrassing anymore, it's shameful.

Reaper hands the letter to Sarah and everyone sits back, waiting to see what it says.

"Tongue,

I couldn't bury you alive, but I can still bury you.

Ring around the rosy. Daphne's hair is cozy.

Ashes.

Ashes.

You will. Fall. Down.

-Groundskeeper"

Sarah stops reading and lays the letter on her lap and the silence is a high-pitched ring as the dizziness takes over.

The anger. The rage.

"Tongue. I need you to calm down. Your heart rate—"

I grab Reaper by the throat to shut him up. Like I give a fuck about my heart rate. I sling my legs out of bed and my fingers itch to crush his windpipe. The man that had no idea what to do a second ago is gone, I know what to do.

This is the man I've always been.

I'm the horrors people check their house for, I'm the reason people are afraid of the dark.

As they should be.

Because I'm the worst fucking thing this world could have ever created.

"Sorry, bud," Doc pierces my neck with a needle, and I growl when my hand falls from Reaper's throat.

"Daphne," her face flashes in front of me and the floor falls out from under me.

All I can think about is how the Groundskeeper was right.

I will. Fall. Down.

CHAPTER NINETEEN

Daphne

Holy Moly.

This place is going to crumble and fall on top of me. That's how I'm going to die.

"Aren't you going to eat? You have to eat. You have to keep your strength up. We have a lot to do. Lots. Lots. Lots. We will be here for along time. I have friends you know. Here. Coming. Here. This place is big enough for everyone. You know, it used to be an old insane asylum."

I push the canned green beans around on my plate. The metal fork squeaks against the plate, and I stab a string bean. The effort it takes for me to bring it to my lips is exhausting. My entire body is shaking. It's freezing in here. I can't wait for the sun to come up and for it to get warm. The desert nights are so cold and there isn't heat here. If this building doesn't crush me, I'll freeze to death.

I'll never see Tongue again, but maybe I'll see him in the shadows if I'm lucky.

I open my mouth to chew on the green bean, but it falls from my fork, and back onto the plate. I try again, but the trembling is too strong. I can't get the food to stick on the fork. I'm crying, not that it matters the man in front of me, he doesn't even seem to notice.

And he is still wearing that fucking mask.

I'm waiting for my mind to fail me to conjure up some sick, twisted, bent form of reality. Every time I see the old, tattered curtain hanging in the window blow from the wind coming inside the busted glass, I always think it's my brain playing tricks on me.

I'll be fine. I'm strong. I can do this. I can make it until someone finds me.

Someone will find me, right?

Tongue will look for me. He won't give up on me. He loves me. He's made for me. People who love each other don't give up on one another. No, I know he is searching for me. I feel it.

"You aren't eating!" he slams his fist on the old wooden table and I jump.

"I'm trying."

"You aren't trying hard enough. God," he runs his fingers through his air, tugging on the locks. The veins in his arms pop, and he rocks his jaw back and forth, either trying to calm down or figuring out if he wants to eat me.

Not in a good way.

I'm worried for my health.

"I tried so hard for you. I try. I try," he digs his fork into the wood and drags it, creating deep grooves. "I saved you from evil. He is pure fucking evil. And you are...." he gestures his hands out, like he wants to strangle me, and a rumble shakes the table. "You are special. You're innocent. You don't need a life with him. You need to be with people like you. Tongue doesn't care about you. He can't...he can't care about you. He isn't capable."

"He is. He is capable. I've seen it. He isn't the guy you think he is. I swear."

He slides back in the chair and swipes the plate off the table. It crashes against the floor and green beans fly everywhere along with their juice. Not that it ruins the place. The entire floor is ripped up and the only thing under us is a slab of stained concrete.

I think someone has died in here.

The brown on the floor is either rust or blood.

"I've watched him," he runs to my side and folds his elbows on the corner next to me.

I stare at my plate, blinking away the tears. I shiver from how close he is and I'm afraid. I'm so fucking afraid. This is the difference between Tongue and him. Not once have I ever felt like my life was in jeopardy. When he stares at me, when he swallows me in his presence, I'm blanketed in trust.

He'd never hurt me. He'd never scare me.

Tongue loves me. I have to keep that belief. I can't let this guy get in my head. I'm not an object to him. I'm more than that.

Right?

"You're so pliable, aren't you?" he sweeps my hair from out of my face, and I flinch away. I don't want him to touch me. He chuckles, then takes the fork from my hand and stabs a green bean. "Open."

I do as he says because if I don't, I have no idea what can

happen. "See?" He inserts the bean into my mouth and sighs. "Pliable. You'd do anything you're told and you have no idea that you'd do it. You think it's what you want, but really, you're just giving into the deep need others want from you. That's what happens when sweet girls like you get involved with men like Tongue." He stands causing a swift breeze as he maneuvers around me, laying his chin on my shoulder. The stubble on his face is sandpaper against my skin. "So naïve. So sweet. So innocent— Oh," he laughs again, dark and like he finds me ironic. "I bet you used to be innocent." He runs his nose over the shell of my ear.

I sit completely still, gripping the edges of the table and stare at the far end of the hall. I'm so tired, sluggish. I can feel the lack of the medication I need. The walls start to bend and morph, but then I close my eyes, telling myself that I'm fine.

"He took that, didn't he? I bet he doesn't even know you're gone."

His words echo in my head, and I sit straighter, watching a body pull itself out of the wall. The arm is grey, rotted, as if the body has been decaying for years. The hair is long, wet, and tangled. I squeeze my eyes shut and try to shake the warped reality in front of me.

It's not real. I'm fine.

"Oh, what do you see?"

"Nothing," I whisper, then stare down at my wrists. The zip-ties he put on me earlier were too tight, so he did me a favor and cut them off, so I could eat. My ankles are still bound, and the ties are digging into my skin so much that I can't feel my toes.

"Liar." He pounds his fist on the table, making me flinch and hunch over. The pieces f hair he cut off yesterday hang in my face, it's so short.

TONGUE

Will Tongue love me anymore? Will he find me imperfect? I don't care that all of it seems unhealthy to others, but to me it is. He's the nutrition my soul needs in order to thrive. I won't fall victim to the sickness in my head.

The woman lifts her head, and her hair parts to show her face. "Mom," I try not to cry when I see her for the first time in years. I've missed her so much.

She isn't real.

"You can always see her here, you know," he says, clapping his hands in excitement. "You won't ever have to go without seeing your mother again. Don't you want that? Don't you miss your mommy?"

"She's dead."

"She isn't dead here," he taps my temple. "She comes to life for you. Don't you know how fucking beautiful that is? How jealous I am that you can see someone you love? Imagine the conversations you could have, the happiness you could feel."

He's right.

I could be happy.

I have missed my mom.

A little girl shouldn't have to be without her mother. I think...now that I really think about it, I think she's why my mind broke. Losing her was by far the hardest thing I've ever had to go through.

A chunk of me died that day, fermenting a part of my brain for the rest of my life because of grief. I'm forever changed. I'll forever be sick. I'll always have this dread inside me that I'll hallucinate, but what if this is my new reality? What if I'm meant to be this way?

Paths of the future change, grow, and shrivel, but at the end of the journey, the same place waits for you no matter how many different ways you try and become better. One way or another, life is planned. There isn't a secret way out. There isn't a magical button to try and get away from who you are meant to be.

Who you are is who you will always be. People can't change, and if they do, they are lying too, because the need is inside them, gnawing, clawing, begging to give in to the person they used to be.

A murderer will always murder.

A rapist will always rape.

A thief will always steal.

And I will always have psychosis.

What I love about Tongue? He has never once tried to be anything other than who he is. He tried to stay away because he knew he couldn't be anything other than the stone-cold killer than he is. He isn't fake. He doesn't pray for forgiveness, if anything, he summons the damn devil because, holy moly, only something wicked could answer someone so dark.

Maybe I should give in.

Maybe I shouldn't pretend anymore.

"You're thinking about it, aren't you?"

I look away from my mother, who is filthy and looks like she just crawled out of the grave, and stare at my kidnapper. I blink, a tear catching on my lower lash line as I try to figure out what to say to him. "Who are you? What do you want with me? What did I do to you? What did Tongue do? Why did you bury him?"

"So many questions for a woman who is questioning if she is really here," he taunts.

"I know I'm here. You don't know much about my condition if you think that's the case. You won't be able to trick me into thinking otherwise."

"Power of persuasion is a beautiful thing and as for Tongue, did he not tell you about me? Did the club does not whisper in your ear about Halloween?".

I turn away and stare at my mom again. The gown we buried her in is disintegrating and I can't even see the color it used to be. It's been so long, I can't remember. How sad is that? How bad of a daughter does that make me? She was the prettiest woman I had ever met and now she's a warped sense of karma fucking with me.

He gasps, placing his hand on his chest, being overly dramatic in his baby mask. "You haven't met the club."

"I have," I defend myself, not wanting to say I've only met three of them. I've never been to the clubhouse. Besides Reaper and the other two, Tongue hasn't introduced me, but it isn't because he hasn't wanted to. He hasn't been allowed to go back to the clubhouse. Or what if he is embarrassed of me?

Ridiculous.

I can't fall for this man's scheme.

"You haven't. See, I have been there, unwanted, but I've been there. I've watched Tongue, seen how he lurks, how he..." his hand drops to my thigh and his finger runs along the shallow wound. "Cuts."

"I've seen it and I don't care." The wall morphs again and this time the person that comes out of it is my dad. A man I haven't talked to in months and he has a beer in his hand, yelling at my mom. I don't know what he is saying. I can only see his mouth moving. He lifts his arms and points a gun at the back of my mom's head.

I stand, stinging my palms on the table with how hard I hit it. "No! Mom!" I scream, trying to warn her, but it's too late. Dad pulls the trigger, and her body drops, blood splatters across the wall, and I scream again, cupping my hand over my mouth.

I hate watching my mom die.

I've always wondered if my mom really killed herself or if he did it. He was never happy with his life or with us, mostly me.

The bodies fade away and the walls morph back to normal. The drywall is cracked, and it decorates the floor like bread-crumbs. Apart of the roof is sagging, a chunk of missing, and the black sky is a canvas peeking through.

There are a few stars showing, and I'm reminded about how much beauty there is in this world, even when bad things happen, even when I'm in some abandoned building, beauty exists.

If I died, the beauty of the world would still be there.

It's depressing to think about.

"What did you see? You know what I think?" he stands be-hind me and gathers my hair in his hands, exposing my shoul-der. "I think whatever you say, Tongue would do." He dabs my cheek with a dirty napkin, drying tears. "There. There. Everything will be okay now. You're home now."

"God, go away! Leave me alone!" I struggle to get out of his hold, but he holds me down in the chair and the walls begin to melt, the window drips, and the curtains flow one last time before the image of Tongue appears. I sob, wanting him to be real.

Is he here for me? He has come to rescue me.

I smile when he walks forward, knife shimmering in his hand like a diamond since the ivory is so polished. "You came for me," I whisper to him.

I'll always come for you. I'm always watching you in the

shadows, remember? His voice reminds me of home, the comfort of walking through the door after a long day and feeling relieved and safe.

Tongue is my home.

We are surrounded by flames and doubt.

The foundation we have built is being threatened, but our house holds our hearts, and that is solid.

His head is jerked back, and his tongue is ripped out of his mouth, then tossed to me on a silver platter, bleeding, and twitching.

I scream at the top of my lungs.

"That's it. Scream for him," the Groundskeeper laughs. "Scream as loud as you can because guess what?"

The plate disappears and so does the disgusting appendage. I jerk my head up to see if Tongue is still there, but he is gone too.

"He isn't coming for you. No one knows where you are. Get comfortable, Kitty."

He yanks my arms behind me and zip-ties them again.

This isn't my home, Tongue is, and right now, I'm caught in the flames.

CHAPTER TWENTY

Tongue

Two days later.

I'M SHARPENING MY KNIFE AND HAVE ONE OF THE BOOKS I BOUGHT from Daphne at my side. The guys have asked about the novels because I can't read, but it's a symbol of her and me. I found her at the bookstore, placing a book on the shelf, and I knew I had to get a closer look.

It's hard to believe that the woman that caught my interest loves words and stories when I can't even read a sentence.

Love can really exist anywhere, between anything and anyone. I pause sharpening my knife and think back about the night she laid on my chest after we fucked, and she said something about a certain book in the bookstore that she wanted but wasn't permitted to touch.

Yeah, that's changing.

When I get her home, she's going to have all the damn books. I'm going to buy her that bookstore. Andrew is dead. She would want it. I should have killed him earlier and then maybe she could have gotten it sooner.

Sigh.

I can't change the past, but I can change the future.

"What did you say Seer said?" Reaper asks me for the thousandth time.

I reach in my back pocket and pull out one of my journals, flip to the first page, and see the drawing of her that I made while I watched her sleep.

I swear to god when I get her back, I'm always going to watch her. I don't need to sleep, but I need to make sure she's okay.

"Tongue! Focus," Reaper snaps his fingers in front of me, blocking my view of my drawing. He grips the journal and tries to take it out of my hand and a water droplet falls between the space of his finger and thumb. Damn it.

I need my punishment. Maybe then it will snap me out of my depression. I had no idea I could feel like this. I've been ice, stone fucking cold, but Daphne, her light, so warm and bright has melted me.

The man I'm becoming I don't know, but I'm better than what I used to be and that has to count for something, doesn't it?

"Hey, I've been there. All of have when it comes to our ol' ladies. The journey to get to happiness is a long one." Patrick slaps his hand on my shoulder and flips his sobriety chip in the air, catching it before it falls on the ground.

"I...don't understand why this is happening," I state confused. "But I feel like I need to. I feel..." I rub my and over my heart because it hurts. It physically fucking hurts. It's as if someone has reached inside me shredded me apart. "I feel..." I try to explain again, but I can't find the words. I stab the knife in the table and growl. I'm fucking angry. I'm angry she isn't here. I'm angry I can't move my damn arm from the fucking bullet. "I'm so pissed off."

"Good. We need that," Knives says, throwing his ninja star into the air. "Use it because wherever she is, she's going to need you to fight for her."

"Till my death," I say with obvious undertones.

Reaper gently tugs the journal out of my hand and closes it. "I know it's a tough time, but I need you to focus. What did—" Reaper's ringtone goes off and Poodle snickers when the Hocus Pocus theme song blares as the cellphone chimes. "—Who did this? I'll find out," he seethes. "And when I do…you'll be fucking sorry."

"It was me," Slingshot whispers in my ear. "It was me, I changed it. Good, right? I set it for the NOLA group. It's fitting."

"I don't care," I grumble, sliding the journal back in front of me.

"Seer, we were just talk—of course you know that" Reaper drops his head in his hand and exhales, stressed. "No, we haven't found her. Yes, I know we exhaust you. I didn't ask for you to have visions of us. Seer, I am very thankful. Why are you being a prissy fucking bitch about this? Jesus, you blame us for your gift, if you don't want to fucking help, don't, but the last thing I need is for you to continue bitching about it. The next time you have one of your visions, just ignore it if you hate it so much." Reaper hangs up the phone just as it rings again and he throws it across the room, smashing it against the wall. It crumbles to pieces and the Hocus Pocus movie ringtone droops to a stop. "Damn it."

"You need to stop doing that. It's getting expensive," Tool states.

Reaper narrows his eyes at Tool, daring him to say one more thing that Reaper already knows.

Another phone rings, and it's the Adam's family ringtone. "What the…" Bullseye pats his pockets and hangs his phone to Reaper. "It's Seer."

"I did that one too," Slingshot snorts. "God, I'm so good."

I stare at the map on the table, knowing I'm not going to be much good. Jesus, not being able to read anything is making me feel worthless. When we get Daphne back, I'll have her teach me. It's something to look forward to.

"What, Seer?" Reaper snaps and starts to pace the area next to the sink, prowling like a caged animal. "I'm in the middle of a rescue mission here for my most vicious member who is barely hanging on to his sanity and only has one working arm while my fucking ol' lady is healing from a stab wound. I have a mafia boss missing, his brother is a raging pain in my ass, and two of my members were pinned against each other and killed ten cops. So, stop yanking my fucking dick and tell me the news you have because I—" he holds out the phone and yells into it. "—Am about to lose my shit!" He places the phone against his ear, nodding until he freezes. "Is that so? Are you serious? Okay, yes, thank you. He's expecting a gift. From you? He'll know when he sees it. Yeah, I'll tell him. Thank you, Seer. Again. I'm sorry for the trouble." Reaper hangs up the phone and hands it back to Bullseye. "That was our favorite wizard. Tongue, you said it was a run-down brick building, right?"

"Yeah, Prez."

"Seer just told me there is one close to here about five miles that way." Reaper points to the map and then glides his finger across along the red line. "And guess what? It's an old fucking looney bin and it's up for sale. It's been up for sale for a while and no one has wanted to buy it because apparently it's haunted."

"Yeah, don't tell the NOLA guys that. They will come up here with sage and fucking voodoo bones or some shit," Tool shivers in discomfort. "Freaks me out."

"Anyway, Seer said he saw another glimpse of the place. You guys have to remember this building. It's right off the side of the Loneliest Road. Kids go there all the time, dare each other to go in and all that shit. The Groundskeeper has her there. It's the only rundown brick building close to us."

"I know the place. It's old. It's falling apart. Who the hell would go there?" Poodle asks, scratching the top of Lady's head as she lays her chin on his lap. She hasn't been feeling too well lately and Poodle has been pretty sensitive about it, so we have let it go, but she's old.

I'll make sure to cut her tongue out for him when she dies. He'd like that.

"I'm about to make a call to the bank and buy the place. Cash. Because then not only can we get that asshole for kidnapping, but we can get him for trespassing and breaking and entering and whatever else we can conjure up. Plus, I think it would be a good place to have. Maybe we can fix it up and rent it out."

"Isn't a good reason to buy it," Bullseye says, eating a banana to help bring up his sugar.

"It is if it stops the Groundskeeper from staying there. Give me your phone. I'm making the call to the bank. It's up for auction, and I'm going to place a bid they can't refuse, and I swear to fucking god, the next mother fucker to get buried will be the Groundskeeper. I'll stake my damn life on it."

Reaper snatches the phone from Bullseye's hand and stomps down the hallway, then slams his office door, shaking the floorboards.

"Does anyone know where this place is at?" I ask. "I don't remember seeing it, but I don't want to wait for Reaper. She's been gone too long. She's only been five miles away. I'm so stupid. I'm so goddamn stupid. I'm an idiot! A brick building. It's old! It wasn't hard to look for. I'm so stupid. Stupid, stupid, stupid," I bang my hand against my head, berating myself for being the person my Uncle said I would always be.

"Stop it, Tongue! You aren't. We were all looking. We thought downtown, not remote. We will find her."

I shake my head. I don't want to hear anything he has to say. I deserve punishment. I run over to the fireplace that Reaper just had installed in the main room. It's in the corner, wood-burning, and there are a few fire pokers leaning against the mantle.

"What are you doing? Tongue. Don't do anything crazy," Tool says.

"Do you know who you are talking to?" Bullseye asks him.

I grab a few logs from the box and throw them in the fireplace, grab a match from the shell of a grenade that is a makeshift vase and strike it. Soaking the logs with lighter fluid, I toss the match and watch the flames whoosh and heat, nearly burning my skin. I grab the fire poker and shove it in the fire, letting the iron turn from black to scorching red.

"Put down the poker," Skirt and Poodle corral me with Tool and Bullseye flanking their sides. "Don't do anything crazy. We will find her. We will bring her home."

"I deserve this." It takes some maneuvering, but I dip my

head under the strap of the sling and take it off, my arm falling limp to my side. Next, I rip my shirt off and throw it in the fire.

"No, you don't. You're human, Tongue. You're human," Braveheart says from the doorway, coming in from watching the gate. "Look at me," he says gently. "Tongue, you're human. I think you need to hear that. Look at me."

I rip my eyes away from the bright glowing orange at the tip of the fire poker, smelling the smoke taunting me for my punishment, and give Braveheart my undivided attention. Nothing he says will change my mind. I deserve the pain. I always have. It's why my Uncle burned me. Reaper cuts to inflict pain, but that won't do anything to me. I'll only enjoy it.

Fire, heat, getting burnt.

That's where my fear and pain lives.

He holds out his hands, something people do when they are talking someone down from the ledge. Nothing can be done for me. What does Daphne see in me?

I'm not someone a kind person bets on for the future. I wreck them.

"Tongue, you're human."

"You keep saying that—"

"Because I don't think anyone has ever told you," Braveheart, the skinny new member says. "I think," he licks his lips, staring at the poker. "I think you were raised to be an animal. You were abused. You are trained to be a certain way. It's how you're programmed but guess what, man? You aren't a killing machine. You. Are. Human. You're allowed to feel what you're feeling. You're allowed and it's okay."

"It isn't okay. She's in danger. I should have been more for her."

"How can you be more? You're obviously everything you need to be for her, or she wouldn't love you. She loves the human, Tongue." He pounds his chest with his fist, right above his heart. "That part of you that you keep hidden from us or the part that maybe you didn't know existed because of her. We are human at the end of the day, and I think you've felt a lot of those things that make us vulnerable, that makes us…"

"Human," Poodle finishes.

"Right," Braveheart says.

"Human," I mutter, a concept I haven't thought of before. I know I still need punishment, if not for what has happened to Daphne, for what has happened to Sarah. I fall to my knees and turn around, giving them my back. "Punish me, anyway."

"Tongue."

"Please, Tool. Someone do it." I slide the poker across the floor and Bullseye picks it up before it can burn the wooden slabs.

"No," Bullseye says. "Daphne needs you at your best. If after you want punishment, I'll be the one to do it. I promise," Bullseye states.

"You swear?" I ask him, but he has no time to answer because Reaper is pounding down the hallway.

"Alright. Let's ride. We have Tongue's special lady to rescue, then I think I remember something about a wedding?" When he comes into the main room, he sees me on the floor, kneeling and then eyes the poker in Bullseye's hand. "I'm not going to ask. No time. We need to go. Seer has saved the day again. Also, Tongue, he says to look out for a gift and that you'd know what it is when you see it."

"Daphne," I get to my feet and dig into my pocket for the keys to my bike, but Braveheart takes them from me.

"You aren't driving with your arm like that. We will take my Ford Raptor."

"Come on, his little lady might not be able to save herself."

I bet she could, but if she can't, I'm going to get her out of there.

And then I'm going to show her how she can kill with a swipe of a knife.

Then she'll be able to save herself.

It's important to me that she can because I'm starting to realize, there might be times when I can't.

CHAPTER TWENTY-ONE

Daphne

I'M SO TIRED.

I have to keep my eyes closed because the moment I open them, I see things I do not want to see. I've cried. I've begged. I've screamed.

But the Groundskeeper keeps me here thinking he is doing what is right.

I'm on a cot in a room that only has half a roof. Opening my eyes, I notice the wall is black with mold and there is a stench coming from somewhere that I really can't think about because I'll throw up.

The Groundskeeper zip-tied me to an old, rusted iron bed frame, and then disappeared. He said, "He had errands to run."

Whatever that means.

It's surprising that someone so sick in the head has to go out and do actual things in life. I bet he is going to go buy groceries or real food would be nice. Something other than green beans because I am starving. If I have to live here with a crazy person, I want some fattening food.

My eyes are raw from crying, and my entire body is sore. I've never felt so beaten and defeated. I want to go home. I want this all to be over. My shoulders hurt, my skin is killing me from the zip-ties, and I'm fucking scared out of my mind of this guy. If he can get the best of Tongue and bury him, what am I going to do against him?

The cot moans when I attempt to turn to my side, but I can't because of the way my arms are lifted over my head. Closing my eyes, I wish for sleep and dreams that lead me anywhere other than here.

I hear a door open somewhere in the distance and the hairs on the back of my neck stand up. It's the Groundskeeper.

"I have a treat for you!" he singsongs from a distance.

I yank and pull against the iron bed frame, then feel it bend. Holy Moly. It worked. Of course it worked because it's old and rusted. I need to use this to my advantage. I hold my breath and tug again. Every second that passes by, the metal gets weaker and bends.

He enters the room, still wearing that damn mask I hate so much. "I have a challenge for you."

"I don't care," I hiss just as the metal gives.

He lunges to me, pinning me down with his weight, but I don't go down without a fight. I refuse to give up. The walls start to move again, and the people that live in my alternative versions of reality come forward, watching me struggle against the Groundskeeper. Tongue is in the corner, staying in the dark, watching me.

I get the same feeling I got when he was real. Power surges

through me and I lift the bar over my head and slam it against the Groundskeeper's back. The force has him rolling off the cot and slamming against the floor. My hands and feet are still tied together, but at least I have a chance at getting away from him. I scoot toward the edge of the bed and hop to my feet. The concrete is cold, turning my nerves to stone.

The rusted bedframe is still in my hand and I bring it down on his head again, swinging it like a golf club. The mask flies off his face and rolls across the floor. It stops, creepy baby face up. This is my chance to see the face of the man that kidnapped me, but every second I wait to run is a second wasted.

I hop toward the door and keep hopping my bunny ass out of here. I look left and right to see which way to go. This place really was an old Asylum. There are old wheelchairs in the hall that had been stranded and a few gurney's, which isn't what creeps me out. It's the long hallway that never seems to end, tunneling into oblivion. Then there is the number of doors.

So many rooms.

So many painful memories are trapped within these four walls.

I want out of here.

Now.

I hop along again, passing the table we ate at. The green beans are still on the floor, and rats are nibbling on the leftover food. They are huge with long pink tails, staring at me like they haven't had human flesh in a while.

That's not true. I'm being dramatic. I'm hungry, tired, sore, and I miss Tongue. My head is killing me. I want my medication. I never want to see what I've been seeing again.

Taking a quick break, I lean against one of the old beams and take a deep breath. I'm sweating and cold. I wheeze, holding my side when a pinch starts to form. The floor sways, moving like slow lava, and I grab onto the beam to stop myself from falling when the cement disappears and there is nothing but sky.

"It isn't real. It isn't real. It isn't real," I chant, but the only way to really know is if I try to walk—hop—across it.

My sanity is gone; what else do I have to lose?

With shaky arms and closed eyes, I let go of the beam and jump, waiting for a freefall experience and a rush of air blowing over me.

My feet land on solid ground, and I snap my eyelids open, staring at the wobbly floor in awe. The endless blue sky is still there and with every hop, I get closer to the door.

Until I land on broken glass. It crunches under my bare feet, cutting and digging into my skin like the unforgiving knife Tongue uses against his enemies. I slip and my arms land against the shards. The cuts sting and the glass penetrates my skin. Blood decorates the different varieties of colors. The hallway of glass puzzle pieces is almost pretty. There are clear, green, dark green, brown, black, red, blue, all different colors.

I guess I know what the Groundskeeper was doing on his errand. He was going to challenge me to escape thinking this would hurt me.

Well, the joke is on him.

I like to be cut.

My feet are too sore to try and stand up, so I begin to army crawl toward the door that's about twenty yards away. I move one elbow up, drag down the glass, then the other, and drag down more sharp pieces. It hurts. I'm holding back tears, knowing this isn't the same as Tongue cutting me because when he does it, it's with a tender touch.

Right now, the glass is cutting my chest, my legs, my hands, every part of me that is showing is bleeding. I'm not going to give up.

"You're doing so good. Don't stop," my mom's voice has me lifting my head up and this time when I see her, she's clean, dressed in a pretty blue dress, and smiling. *"Don't ever stop."* I know she isn't real but seeing and hearing her say those words to me is exactly what I need to move my elbows again and crawl.

When I come to the door, my arm shakes as I reach for the door handle. Glass is embedded in my forearm, hundreds of pieces. Thick medallions of blood drip down my arm and onto the floor. Everywhere hurts, but it won't hurt nearly as bad when I get to Tongue.

Before I can open the door, someone else does, and shiny black boots enter my vision.

I didn't make it.

His friends came.

I collapse with exhaustion, laying my cheek against the broken bottles, giving in, and giving up. I'm so tired.

"Tongue! Tongue, she's here, man. She's right here. Hey, Daphne," a kind, warm voice has me attempting to see who my visitor is. They know Tongue. Am I seeing things? How do I know if this is real? "Hey, you're safe. It's me, it's Slingshot, blue-eyes. Jesus Christ, what did he do to you?"

"Slingshot?" my voice is pitchy as it breaks from a high note of relief.

"Hey, let's see those blue-eyes, come on. Tongue is right behind me."

"Really?" I lift my head and give him my eyes like he wants.

Slingshot is about to answer me when he is picked up and thrown to the left, discarded without a second glance.

"Comet." Tongue's nickname for me has the dam breaking,

and I sob as he scoops me into his arms, not caring about the glass that cuts him along the way and cradles me to his chest. "Daphne. My Daphne." He brings me outside and sits on the steps, holding me gently as he lays me against his thighs and peers down at me. "You saved yourself," Tongue says, plucking the pieces of glass out of my arms.

I don't moan in pleasure this time because how the glass got there is different than last time. The situations, emotions, atmosphere, and person were different.

"I wanted to get back to you," I say, then grin like a drunken fool, but instead of having too much beer, I've had too much pain. "You found me. You came for me. He said you wouldn't."

Tongue presses his lips against mine, cupping the back of my head with his hand as he owns my mouth. "Comet, not even death would keep me from you. I'd haunt you."

"You'd watch me from the shadows?"

"Every single shadow, every time night falls, in every corner."

I lean my head against his shoulder, finding comfort in his insanity.

Love is madness.

Tongue

One day later

"I swear he was there," Daphne says as she lays down in bed, nearly every bit of her wrapped with gauze. I'm about to call her my Mummy instead of my Comet, but that might not go over well, so I'm going to keep my mouth shut.

"I believe you."

"You do?"

I hand her the pills she has not been taking, the correct ones. Doc replaced the ones the Groundskeeper switched out and gave her the ones she needs to have her psychosis bearable.

"Of course, I believe you."

"You don't think my mind played tricks on me?"

She told me about how she saw me, her mom, and dad, and not once did it make me think she was unstable. If anything, I only loved her more. "No, I don't," I state without a doubt and watch as she tosses the pills back along with a swig of water. I take the cup from her hand and place it on the nightstand. The light from the lamp shines against her brown hair and I can see the hues of caramel and red. "You're beautiful," I say, bending down and placing another kiss on her lips. I've missed them.

"So are you," she replies, placing her palm against the only spot of my chest that doesn't have a tattoo.

I'm about to give her a knife and ask her to carve her name into my skin when someone knocks on the door. I want to be left alone with Daphne. I've been apart from her for far too long. "What?" I growl and never stop staring at her intense blue eyes.

"Uh, Seer's package arrived," Reaper says. "And it's hissing."

Now that has my attention. I roll off the bed and open the door to see the Prez pointing down at a wooden box. "You better fucking hope it isn't what I think it is." Reaper stomps away and I bend over to pick up the box, it's light, but I do hear hissing.

"What is it?" Daphne asks, pushing her glasses up her nose. I love it when she does that.

"I don't know. It's from Seer." I sit down on the bed and

rip the card from the staple against the box. "Can you read it to me, Comet?"

"With pleasure," she smiles.

She still finds a way to smile at me after everything she has been through. She takes another sip of water and clears her throat.

Tongue,

I saw something that told me your ol' lady wanted a swamp kitty. Glad you're safe. I'll be in touch.

-Seer

"Fuck. Him being in touch is never a fucking good thing. He said he wasn't going to get involved with us for a while," I sigh, wondering why he won't leave us alone like he wants.

"Oh my god, did you get me a kitten?" She tosses the card away and bounces her butt on the bed.

"Uh, I think your version and my version of kittens are different, Comet." I pry the box open and find a baby gator with a red bow on his head. His tiny mouth is open, probably hungry no doubt, and he is hissing. I pick him up and cradle him to my chest. "Oh, he knows who his momma is. He isn't hissing." I stroke his back and look up from his big forest green eyes to see Daphne staring at me, open-mouthed and a bit pale in the face. "This is a swamp kitty," I tell her. "Ain't he cute?"

"A swamp..." she doesn't finish her sentence. "It all makes so much sense now."

"You don't like him?" I panic, holding him closer to my chest. "We can build a home for him, you know. Out here. We can build him swamp."

"What are we going to do with him until then?" Daphne leans forward and drags a finger under our new pet's chin. "Aw, I think he likes that."

I stroll to the bathroom, put the stopper in the tub, and fill it with a little water. Next, I take the bow off and set him in the tub. "Aw, you're a happy camper. That's what I'll call you—Happy. I have some good food for you later. I keep a few tongues on ice. You'll be pleased. Night, Happy."

The gator hisses at me, and I know it has to be with love, and I turn around, turn off the light, and shut the door. I stand in the corner, not in darkness since the lamp is on, but I just watch Daphne, thankful that she exists and is safe.

"I feel your eyes on me," she singsongs. "And tomorrow, when I'm not exhausted, I want to play with Happy."

"Which happy?" I lower my voice, rumbling when I think about her touching my cock.

"Anyone one you want," she quips.

I stalked, watched, and obsessed over Daphne when I shouldn't have. I won't ever regret finding her in darkness because she's the light.

I'm an endless abyss of black space and she's a comet, soaring through my skies.

She's a rarity.

And she's *mine*.

Happy For…

The Groundskeeper

They think they won.

I have news for them—as long as I am breathing, they will never know peace.

Tongue is the bane of my existence. I didn't only choose him because he is everyone's favorite and was the freak of the fucking pack.

I hate MCs.

But most of all, I hate Tongue.

He'll never be rid of me.

After all, we share the same bad blood.

Like mother, like *sons*.

TONGUE PLAYLIST

STONE COLD BY DEMI LOVATO

HELL OF A VIEW BY ERIC CHURCH

SHAMELESS BY CAMILA CABELLO

USED TO THIS BY CAMILA CABELLO

BLACK SHEEP BY MILCK

DEVIL DEVIL BY MILCK

WHERE THE DEVIL DON'T GO BY ELLE KING

HURTS LIKE HELL BY FLEURIE

CRAZY BY ADONA

IN THE SHADOWS BY AMY STROUP

ACKNOWLEDGEMENTS

To our greedy Ruthless Readers thanks for loving our most Ruthless King to the point of insanity.

Give Me Books that's for working so hard on our releases.

Wander and Andrey thanks for always being there.

Donna thanks for all you do. #BOOMERISDONNAS.

Special thanks to Stacy at Champagne Book Designs for the amazing job on formatting.

Lynn as always thanks for being my rock.

To my Instigator 2 Foots Down, glad you finally understand why you're my instigator.

Harloe thanks for being there, you're amazing. Congratulations.

Silla you deserve all the Reese's.

Austin so glad we're doing this ride together.

Mom thanks for always having my back.

Jeff thanks for the countless hours you put in.

ALSO BY K.L. SAVAGE

PREQUEL - REAPER'S RISE
BOOK ONE - REAPER
BOOK TWO - BOOMER
BOOK THREE - TOOL
BOOK FOUR - POODLE
BOOK FIVE - SKIRT
BOOK SIX - PIRATE
BOOK SEVEN - DOC
BOOK EIGHT - TONGUE

OTHER BOOKS IN THE RUTHLESS KINGS SERIES
A RUTHLESS HALLOWEEN

RUTHLESS KINGS MC IS NOW ON AUDIBLE.

CLICK HERE TO JOIN RUTHLESS READERS AND GET
THE LATEST UPDATES BEFORE ANYONE ELSE. OR
VISIT AUTHORKLSAVAGE.COM OR STALK THEM AT
THE SITES BELOW.

FACEBOOK | INSTAGRAM |RUTHLESS READERS
AMAZON | TWITTER | BOOKBUB | GOODREADS |
PINTEREST | WEBSITE

Printed in Great Britain
by Amazon